Mad Love

A Nolan Brothers Novel ~ Book Four

AMY OLLE

Ebook ISBN: 978-1-944180-06-5
Print ISBN: 978-1-944180-07-2

DEDICATION

To Jimmy, with all of my heart.

Chapter One

Fear.

It was the first thing Leo Nolan remembered.

Since those earliest fractured memories of his mom's illness and death when he was five years old, fear had gnawed and festered inside him until it was all he knew. All that made sense. All that mattered.

He longed to destroy The Fear, and had spent most of his life trying to do just that. But of course, The Fear could not be destroyed. So the day he turned eighteen, he decided he'd had enough of being afraid and chose to become the feared instead.

He became a US Marine.

The fire of combat taught him that, although The Fear could not be conquered, it could be tricked into usefulness—for a time. He became the best there was at fooling it. Deception became his game, madness his playing field. There were no rules, only the desperate, reckless will to survive.

Now, four years removed from a decade of service in combat zones around the world, he hadn't just been to hell and back, he was a permanent resident. The Fear was real. It lived inside him. Every time he thought of them. Every time he tried, but failed, to make the next drink his last. Every time he recalled the reason she'd died was because of him.

Every. Fucking. Time.

Which was every minute of every day.

He *was* The Fear.

So it shouldn't have unnerved him as much as it did to receive the phone call from his good buddy and former comrade Owen.

"You want me to do what?"

"I need you to check up on my sister," Owen said. "I think she's in trouble."

"What kind of trouble?"

Immediately, Leo wished he could take back the question. He didn't care what kind of trouble Owen's sister was in. All that mattered was that he not be responsible for her—or anyone else's—well-being in any way, at all, ever. Not ever again. Never.

The weight of Owen's heavy sigh through the phone only intensified Leo's resistance to the cause. "Nothing too serious, I hope. She pissed off some internet trolls and they've been harassing her online. Gideon's looking into them, but I want to make certain nothing has carried over into real life."

Leo dragged a suddenly trembling hand through his hair. "Why don't you just ask her?"

"I have. She swears she's fine, but I fully expect her to lie to me."

Leo yanked on the ends of his hair. "What makes you think she won't lie to me?"

"Oh, she will." A hint of laughter infected Owen's tone.

"That's why I picked you. Well, that and you live in the same city."

Leo had no idea what city Owen thought he lived in anymore. For the past four years, he hadn't lived in any one place longer than a few months, preferring to bounce around instead.

"I'm not asking you to babysit her," Owen said. "Just do some recon, make sure things stay quiet for a few days. I'll be home at the end of the month and will take it from there."

Denials screamed inside Leo's skull. "I don't know...." Desperation clawing at him, he paced the living room floor at his brother's house where he'd been staying. "Maybe Claymore can help you out."

"I don't want Claymore's help. I want yours."

"But why?" The words rasped from him.

After a beat, Owen responded, "I trust you."

Leo drew up. "Don't you trust your sister?"

"It's not that." Owen seemed to pick his words carefully. "She's a bit naïve sometimes, that's all."

Except that wasn't all.

"And... soft-hearted. You could say a little... fragile even."

Fragile?

Oh, for fuck's sake.

"It's not as bad as it sounds," Owen was quick to add. "She's the baby of the family, and well, you know how girls can be...."

The only thing Leo knew was that if Owen's kid sister wanted to play damsel in distress, she'd have to find some other poor sap to act the hero. He opened his mouth to say exactly that, but Owen beat him to the punch.

"I need your help, man." Through the phone, Owen's voice deepened with a shadow of fear. "I promise, I won't ask anything of you ever again."

The weight of inevitability settled around Leo's shoulders, cementing his feet to the floorboards. Owen had been there for him more times than Leo cared to count. He didn't want to turn his back on his friend, but The Fear rose up to choke and silence him.

Then, while he stood there, powerless and mute, his sister-in-law, Emily, waddled into the room, her large, heavily pregnant belly leading the way, and the despair he'd wasted the last four years trying to move past ripped through him. All he could do was stare while the agony rolled over him in sickening waves.

Finally, with a vicious wrench, he twisted away from the sight of her.

"Fine, I'll do it." He despised the telltale quiver in his voice. "Where do I find her?"

☪

432, 433…

Prudence Lockhart leaned to the side, causing her desk chair to groan.

434, 435…

She stretched a tad more, peering into the far corner of the room. "Four hundred and thirty-six."

Collapsing back in the chair, her satisfaction was short-lived. After all, she'd known before she'd begun counting that there were 436 carpet squares covering the floor of the Cambridge Science Institute's reception area.

It wasn't the first time she'd counted them.

A glance at the wall clock pulled a groan from her. An hour remained in the workday.

On a typical day at the Institute, Prue answered the phones, scheduled meetings for the staff of scientists, and kept the coffee brewed. She always completed her duties with time left in the workday. Hours, usually. To fend off boredom, she often helped Amanda with her work in payroll, or cleaned the staff break room, but this Friday afternoon, in the middle of summer, she'd finished all such tasks and was one of only a few people who remained in the building.

Hence she counted the carpet tiles.

But the thrill of the count was long gone. She feared she was going to have to start naming the squares.

A scowl pulled at her features as she eyed the floor. So what if her job didn't challenge her? Or that the most interesting part of her day involved picking out a color to paint her toenails, or a new screensaver image for her monitor? Boredom sure beat the sharp bite of failure.

She sighed heavily in the empty room.

Sally, Louise, Natasha–

The soft jingle of her cell phone saved her from her fate. She dove for the desk drawer where she had stashed her purse and retrieved the device from a side pocket. Anticipation bubbled up when she opened the private message sent to her social media account. Maybe Paul had something new to share.

You stupid bitch, you need to stop with your insane attacks. You're going to regret–

She closed the app without reading the rest.

It wasn't the first time she'd been a target of harassment online, though she didn't recognize the username behind this particular note. The threats, which began about a month ago, now came in droves. At first they'd disturbed and frightened her, but then a pattern emerged and she started tracking which of her posts generated the strongest attacks. Now the menacing messages only served as proof that she was getting closer to the truth.

She slid the wire-bound notebook from her purse and laid it on her desk. A thrill chased through her as she flipped to the last pages containing her scribbled handwriting. For the first time in years, she'd taken up work of her own. It was the only project she'd cared to undertake since Aron King ripped her world out from under her feet, but before then, she'd spent hours filling notebooks with her studies. Everything from chemistry and physics to quantum theory and nanotechnology. But these days, she was focused on only one thing.

One man, actually.

Aron King.

Her mind churning over the seemingly disparate notes she'd scrawled, she turned to her desktop and logged in to her social media account. While she posted the latest nuggets of information from her notebook, she frowned at the monitor, puzzling over the pieces that refused to fit together.

Absorbed as she was in her project, the last hour of her workday melted off the clock, and, with a jolt of surprise, she realized she'd remained at her desk more than an hour past the close of business. Now she was late for dinner.

She shut down her computer and snatched up her purse and notebook on her way to the building's back door exit. Outside, heat from the summer sun radiated off the asphalt as she crossed the nearly empty employee parking lot. Drawing in a lungful of fresh air, she lifted her face to the sky and relished the sun's warmth on her skin.

Not so long ago, she'd only been able to observe the sunshine and gentle summer winds from within hospital walls. One of her sharpest memories from that time was wanting to be outdoors again, enjoying something as simple as a beautiful summer day. The wish had marked the moment her recovery veered away from illness and back toward health.

But as she approached her car, her peace was shattered.

The driver side door stood slightly ajar, and she pulled up abruptly. Through the windows she saw the interior of the vehicle had been trashed. Her dirty laundry had been ripped from its bag and strewn throughout the car. The contents of her glove compartment and center console were scattered among the mess, and her coin tray, filled with quarters for the laundromat, was empty.

Someone had broken into her car.

Chapter Two

Panic squeezed Leo's chest with painful spasms while sounds from the hotel tavern swirled around him. Propped on a barstool at the end of the bar, he clutched a tumbler in his white-knuckled fist and stared down into the amber liquid.

He hadn't had a drink in more than two months, mainly to test whether he could do it. It'd ended up being one of the hardest things he'd ever done, and now his tenuous resolve for sobriety had snapped. All because he'd agreed to play bodyguard to Owen's kid sister.

What the hell had he been thinking? Lord knew he couldn't be trusted to keep anyone safe from harm.

He snagged the glass and swallowed several large gulps of the smooth whiskey.

Alcohol was like an old lover he kept coming back to. Though he'd later regret the lapse in judgment, she gave him what he needed to get through the dark, lonely moments. Beer for those times when he couldn't afford to get drunk but couldn't bear to stay sober. Wine to curb the sadness. Vodka to cool the rage. Whiskey to dilute The Fear. None, however, no matter the quantity, managed to truly black out the memories, and his search for The One continued.

The bartender stopped in front of Leo. "How we doing tonight, sir?"

"Good."

It was a lie, of course. Just one of many Leo told these days.

"What brings you to Boston?"

"Visiting some friends," he mumbled.

The lies were the only thing that gave him comfort. They were soft and soothing, and he unashamedly wrapped himself with their fuzzy warmth. Alcohol made the lies believable, and for that, he'd love her forever.

"You need another?"

Leo nodded and downed the last drops of liquor before sliding the empty tumbler across the bar.

While he waited for his drink, he checked his cell phone again. Relief rattled through him that no new messages had come in, including none from Owen, who was supposed to text Leo the sister's address.

A freshly poured whiskey appeared on the bar before him and he wrapped his hand possessively around the stout glass. It seemed he'd been given a night's reprieve from his unpleasant task.

Tomorrow, when Owen sent the information, Leo would stop by the sister's house, make sure she wasn't dead, and do not one single thing more. If she *was* in trouble, or needed help, Owen was going to have to find someone else to deal with it.

Leo was too busy tending to the one and only item on his to-do list. He signaled the bartender.

Drink and stay drunk.

CB

By the time the police finished their report, the sun barreled toward the horizon and Prue's stomach grumbled with hunger. Rather than return to her apartment to change out of the peasant top and fitted capri pants she'd dressed in for work that morning, she drove straight to the hotel where her sister, Faith, was staying while in town for a professional conference.

She parked near the restaurant's front entrance and scurried inside. In the soft lighting, she scanned the crowded room until she caught sight of Faith waving at her from the far side of the bar.

Prue picked her way through the crush of bodies, then collapsed on the barstool next to Faith.

She expelled a sharp puff of air. "Sorry I'm late."

Older by two years, Faith had inherited their dad's light hair and their mom's ample curves, while Prue got her mom's darker coloring but missed out on the curves.

Faith pushed a red daiquiri at her. "What is going on?"

"Someone broke into my car." Prue reached for the daiquiri.

Faith gasped. "*What?* Are you okay?"

Sucking on her straw, Prue nodded.

"Do the police have any idea who did it?" Faith asked as she scooped a slice of cheese pizza onto a plate and slid it in front of Prue.

"Not yet, no." Prue used the straw to stab at the icy concoction in her glass.

Faith's large round eyes narrowed to slits. "But you do."

"I do not."

Faith rolled her eyes. "You're a terrible liar."

As a trained journalist, Faith sniffed a story in

everything. For the longest time, Prue assumed her sister's ability to ferret out all her secrets was due to the strength of their sibling bond. Now she knew otherwise.

"C'mon, spill it," Faith urged.

Prue pulled her bottom lip between her teeth. At one time, she'd have jumped at the chance to talk to someone, anyone who would listen, about her latest research project, but those days were far behind her. Now she didn't like to share. Not anything. Not with anyone.

Faith nudged Prue with her elbow. "I'm just going to keep asking."

"All I have so far are suspicions," Prue admitted.

"Suspicions are good." Faith lifted her daiquiri off the bar and settled back in her chair. "Tell me more."

But Prue hesitated. She sipped her drink while she sorted through what information she would disclose, and what she preferred to withhold from her sister.

"Do you remember that coup attempt in Montenegro last year?"

Faith sucked on her daiquiri straw. "Not at all."

"Well, according to some news reports I read, the coup was led by one of the losing candidates in their national election, and he had help from a whole host of bad guys. Mobsters and drug dealers from all around the world kicked in the cash, and a group of American mercenaries provided the military support for the attempted overthrow."

Faith's gaze sharpened.

Prue shifted in her seat. "So anyway, I started tracking some of these bad guys, their business ties and dealings, and the same names kept popping up."

"Okay." A frown tugged at Faith's features. "But what does this have to do with your car being broken into?"

"I'm getting to that. Do you remember Blackstone?"

Faith's conspiratorial zeal turned to pity. "Oh, Prue."

"What?"

"This is about Aron King?"

"No. Yes, but it's not like that."

Doubt tainted Faith's expression.

"It's about what he's done—what he's *doing*," Prue said. "Right now."

"So this isn't about what happened between you two?"

"Absolutely not."

Faith appeared unconvinced. She leaned forward and captured Prue's gaze with hers. "Look me in the eye and swear to me that you are not still hung up on that jerk." She cringed. "You aren't, are you?"

Bitter bile rose in Prue's throat. Faith thought Aron had broken Prue's heart, and in all honesty, he had. Just not in the way her sister believed.

"I most certainly am not still hung up on that jerk," Prue said. "That was years ago, and it has nothing to do with any of this."

"What is it you think he's doing, exactly?"

Prue tucked a strand of hair behind her ear. "I don't know, *exactly*. Not yet. But since he left Blackstone, he's been running around the globe causing all kinds of trouble. Already he's worked for at least one wannabe, two-bit dictator, and he's about to marry into one of the most notorious mob families in Europe."

Faith's eyes grew huge. "He is? Wow, he's a real social climber, isn't he?"

"For sure. But what if there's more to it than that?"

Skepticism clouded Faith's features. "What more?"

"He's started a new private military company, and he seems hell-bent on causing instability and corruption everywhere he goes. There's big money in armed conflict. Lots of opportunity for power grabs. If Aron King is capable of love, it's going to be for things like money and power."

Faith's gaze slid away. "I have to say, it all sounds

remarkable. A little... unbelievable even."

"Aron's goons broke into my car."

Faith's head came up. "Seriously?"

"They're trying to intimidate me so I stop investigating what they're doing," Prue said.

"Then you should stop."

Prue gaped at her sister. "Are you kidding me? You're a journalist. Would you stop reporting because your subject didn't like you asking questions?"

"If I were being stalked and harassed? Yes, I probably would. No story is worth my life. Or yours."

Prue wanted to argue but she suspected she'd never be able to convince her sister otherwise.

"Let's just say, for the sake of argument, that you do uncover some plot for world domination or whatever," Faith said. "What are you going to do about it?"

"I'm going to expose him."

"To who?"

"To everyone. To anyone who can stop him. It depends what I find, of course, but I'll go to the police, or maybe the FBI."

Faith tipped her head to one side. "Do you really think anyone is going to believe you?"

Prue reared back with the stab of pain Faith's words caused.

"I don't mean that like it sounds," Faith rushed to add. "But when people find out what happened between you two, they're going to think you're just bitter or vengeful. That it's all just a conspiracy theory you cooked up to get back at him."

"Well, none of those things are true, so it doesn't matter what those people think."

"It does matter. Aron King is a powerful man. He knows powerful people. Mob-connected people, apparently. This isn't science, just facts laid out in a logical sequence to be observed. Public opinion, legal interpretation, optics—it all matters."

"All that stuff will work itself out. If it's the truth—"

Faith was shaking her head. "You need to let this go."

"Why?"

"C'mon, even you have to admit it sounds crazy. People are going to think—"

At Prue's sharp intake of breath, Faith bit off her next words.

"What are people going to think?" Prue hated the tremor in her voice. "That I'm crazy?"

Faith's silence hurt worse than any words could have and Prue's throat constricted with the aching. "Is that what you think?"

"Of course not. I think he's a bastard, and if I were you, I'd want revenge, too."

"God, Faith, I don't want revenge. I want the truth."

Faith eyed her. "That's all you want?"

"Yes," Prue said, and then, considering, added, "All right, a little justice would be nice, too. Not revenge. Justice."

"Justice, huh?" The corner of Faith's mouth quirked. "How noble of you."

Her appetite ruined, Prue nonetheless picked up her slice of cold pizza and bit off a mouthful.

"So, if you're not still hung up on him, why haven't you dated anyone since you two broke up?"

Prue frowned. "I've dated."

Faith shot her a look. "More than three dates."

"I haven't met anyone." At least no one she trusted. And after Aron's betrayal, she wasn't sure she'd ever trust anyone again. At least not a man she wasn't related to.

She ripped off another bite of the pizza.

"Not one guy?" Faith demanded. "It's been years. How many? Four? Five?"

Prue lifted one shoulder. "I'm picky."

"Let me set you up with someone. I know this great

guy...."

But Prue was no longer listening to her sister. Struck dumb by the sight of the man at the opposite end of the bar, she stared while prickles of awareness lifted the hairs on her arms. She blinked several times, trying to clear the webs of deception from her eyes.

The vision before her remained. It was really him.

Prue had first met Leo Nolan a lifetime ago. As an awkward fourteen-year-old girl, she'd spoken to the handsome eighteen-year-old briefly, on exactly three separate occasions. But for years afterward, she'd fancied herself in love him. That was back when she was young and naïve and prone to silly dreams about things like falling in love.

She was no longer that girl, and while he resembled the memory of the boy she'd held in her heart all those years, everything about him had changed.

"Hello? Earth to Prue. What are you looking at?" Faith craned her neck, then turned back with a wide grin. "Oooh. Do we know him, or are we just appreciating the hotness?"

"He was one of Owen's friends."

Faith peered across the bar. "He doesn't look military. Did they go to high school together?"

"He's military, all right. Marine."

"Really? He looks kind of... scruffy."

Rather than the buzz cut Prue remembered, Leo wore his dark hair longer, so that the curling ends brushed the tops of his ears and nape. The dark shadow on his jaw marked the hour well beyond five o'clock. His faded T-shirt had a tiny hole in the shoulder, and his board shorts hit well below his knee. And... were those flip-flops? Prue agreed, he looked less like a trained warrior and more like a California beach bum.

"You should go say hi," Faith said.

Prue shook her head. "I haven't seen him in years."

Last she'd heard, he had retired from the military and gone to work with a private security company—

Her spine snapped straight.

He'd worked at Blackstone, hadn't he?

Her mind scrambled to pin down the details, but her memories were too clouded. She bit down hard on her bottom lip.

Leo knew Aron King. Had they worked closely together? Were they friends? She discarded the notion at once. Aron King wouldn't have bothered with such things as friendships. But at the very least, Leo knew of him. What kinds of things did he know? Certainly things she didn't. Would he tell her those things if she asked? Could he be… persuaded to tell her?

But even as her mind calculated, her heart constricted to see his troubled expression, visible even with the distance between them. The urge to go to him overwhelmed. She wanted to pull him into her arms and brush her fingers through his thick hair. She longed to smooth the lines of worry from his forehead.

"You know what?" she heard herself say. "I think I will go say hi."

"Really?" Faith's smile blinded, and then she plucked her purse off the bar. "Okay, well, I've got a networking thing I've got to be at in, like, seven hours." She waggled her eyebrows. "Call me if anything good happens."

Prue rolled her eyes, mainly to distract from the heat warming her cheeks. "Stop it."

"See you Sunday?" Faith slid off her barstool.

"Yep."

"And Prue, think about this Aron King thing, okay?" Concern stamped her features. "I don't like it."

Prue's heart dropped. "I'll think about it."

As Faith strode toward the exit, Prue fought off the morass of misery her sister's reaction threatened to engulf her in. She chucked the straw from her drink and gulped down the last of the daiquiri.

With the tip of one finger, she wiped a sticky droplet from the corner of her mouth. Then she slipped off her barstool, squared her shoulders, and aimed directly for Leo.

Chapter Three

The after-dinner crowd flocked to the bar, and she squeezed between a few big bodies to reach him. When she slipped into the space beside him, her elbow brushed against his forearm, and he turned his head to look at her.

Even her adoring memories hadn't done him justice and her breath caught in her throat. The last traces of boyhood had melted away, and a man stood before her. He possessed the same dark coloring, though he somehow seemed brighter, more vivid, and the sharp contours of his straight nose and high cheekbones were more pronounced than she remembered. When her gaze dropped to his soft, supple mouth, a sigh rattled through her.

"Hi," she breathed, still struggling to reconcile her memory with the man.

A light flashed in his heavily lashed green eyes, but he

didn't speak. Instead, he shifted on his barstool, and suddenly, she stood between his thighs.

His gaze wouldn't let her go, and she shivered in response, even as uncertainty flooded her. What should she say after so many years?

"How are you?"

With a shudder, her question seemed to set off a battle in him. "Better, now that you're here."

Clearly he was not sober, and yet a warm pleasure bloomed in her chest.

He reached out, and one of his fingertips traced the outline of her cheek. "Wow."

"Wow, what?"

"Your smile." He pulled his hand away, rolling it into a tight fist. "I like it."

Her cheeks heated. "I didn't know you were so charming."

"It's the alcohol. Makes me tell the truth." He lifted his glass to his lips and drank. "Don't think I've ever been accused of being charming though. Most conclude I'm an asshole."

Behind her, a broad man in pursuit of the bartender's attention pushed into her space. Leo's hand slipped to her waist and he angled his bigger body protectively around her.

"I don't think you're an asshole." At his touch, a delicious tension pulsated through her.

The faintest hint of a playful light came into his eyes. "You're naïve."

She tried to laugh, but the sound she made rang hollow. "I'm hardly that."

His gaze dropped to her mouth, and her smile fell away when his dark pupils dilated, swallowing the gold flecks that glinted around the black centers.

Her breaths came quick, so she sounded oddly breathless when she said, "What are you doing here?"

"Drinking."

"No, I mean in Boston. Are you visiting, or do you live here?"

A body bumped into her from behind and she pitched forward. Her palms landed on his chest when she tried to steady herself. Beneath the fabric of his faded blue T-shirt, hard muscles bunched.

"Just visiting." His mouth near her ear, his breath stirred her hair when he spoke. "You?"

"I live here."

She pulled back to see his face. With only inches between them, she got an intimate glimpse of the dark sadness hanging at the edge of his features. Her heart constricted as she remembered a different Leo. Playful, with a quick smile and a sneaky sense of humor. Or maybe she'd only built him to be that way in her mind? Because there was no humor in this man. At least not tonight.

Tonight, he was lost and hopeless. Broken.

Her hammering heart lurched. What had happened to the guy she'd crushed on half her life?

He's been to war, you idiot.

He would've witnessed up close the distant horrors that haunted her.

More patrons packed into the area surrounding them, and his gaze darted around the circle closing in on them. An agitated scowl disturbed his smooth features.

Her fingers brushed against his hand. "You wanna get out of here?"

With his curt nod, she stepped out from the safety of his warm body. He dropped a few bills on the bar and let her lead him through the crowded room toward the exit.

Outside, darkness had settled over the city, though the day's heat remained, hanging in the muggy air. The bar noises quickly faded away as Leo dragged in a deep breath, and another. His hand still nestled in hers, she reached up with her other hand to touch the side of his face.

He flinched, but then his gaze latched on to her face with the desperation of a drowning victim clinging to a life raft. She pushed a dark lock of hair off his forehead. Some force seemed to draw him to her and he leaned close.

Her hand moved to the back of his neck. "Do you want to go someplace quiet where we can talk?"

"I'm not all that interested in talking tonight." His voice grew thick, husky.

A delicious shiver ran through her with the slow lick of arousal sloping in her veins. Gently, she applied pressure to his nape, pulling him closer. His palms came up to smack the brick building on either side of her head, as if he needed the support to remain standing.

His head bent low, but he stopped when his mouth hovered above hers.

"There are a thousand reasons why I shouldn't do this." His puffy lips parted. "But I can't recall even one of them right now."

His hands shook when he cupped her face, as though he was terrified he'd break her, or that he'd screw it up.

He didn't screw it up.

His lips touched hers with the faintest hint of a kiss. "My God," he murmured while he toyed with the hair at her temples. "It's been so long, and now you're here."

Her heart cracked open. Could it really be true? That all these years, he had thought about her, too? She ached for his kiss, and his name dropped from her lips as a plea.

His mouth caught hers, and he pressed her against the building, his hard body steadying her while the lush pressure of his mouth sent dizzying sensations spiraling through her. The delicious smell and feel of him scalded her senses. Clean skin and whiskey mingled with the prickly delight of his day's beard growth.

Unsure how to please him, she mimicked his slow licks and soft bites. With one hand, she stroked the hair at his nape, while with the other, her fingers captured his earlobe and she rubbed the soft flesh, because honestly, even the man's earlobes were sexy.

She'd meant only to talk to him. To poke at his life a little, maybe find out some information, any information, about Aron King. But when his mouth grazed the sensitive skin on her neck, every thought except one scattered from her mind.

It wasn't even a thought, really. It was a feeling. A sensation. Her eyes fell shut and a low moan vibrated in her throat. She wanted to chase the feeling, explore it. Revel in it. For once in her life, she wanted to spurn facts, shun rationality, and let her heart take over. She wanted to let her desires rule her and find out where they might lead.

For as long as she could remember, she'd wanted Leo Nolan to be hers. And by the way he kissed her, he wanted her, too. Later, she'd figure out a way to get some information out of him. After she knew the feel of his body on top of hers and the sounds of his pleasure.

His hot mouth found the throbbing pulse point on her neck.

She whimpered. "Are you staying at the hotel?"

"I'm staying wherever you are tonight." Desperation overrode the hint of playfulness in his tone.

"Wait."

He pulled back instantly, concern puckering his brow.

She peered into his face. "What do you want from me? I mean, other than the obvious."

All traces of humor vanished and he dropped his head. "I just... I need some peace."

Pain rolled off him in terrible waves. Unable to bear it, she reached for him. Taking his face in her hands, she pressed a kiss to his forehead. He sighed and closed his eyes, so she dropped kisses on his cheeks and his temples, too.

"Okay, Leo."

His head came up, and surprise shaded his features a moment before a look of ravenous hunger eclipsed all else. "Are you sure?"

She hadn't been so sure of anything in as long as she could remember, but her heart had wedged in her throat and she couldn't speak. Her pulse pounding in her ears, she led him to her car. When he appeared slightly unsteady on his feet, she slipped her hand inside his. Her mouth still tingled from the heat of his kiss, and if not for the crunch of gravel beneath her feet, she might've believed she floated across the parking lot on a poufy, wanton cloud of carnal lust.

Leo climbed into the passenger seat as she slipped behind the steering wheel. At the sound of crinkling paper, she glanced over to see the police report balanced on his fingertips. He frowned down at the paper in the dark.

She snatched the white sheet from his grip and sent it sailing into the back seat.

As she steered the car through the city streets, she was hyperaware of him in the seat next to her. He flooded her senses. His heat and his size, his clean, masculine scent and his dark beauty. Her nerves grew taut. She could do this, couldn't she? She'd never picked a guy up in a bar. Had never taken one home, from anywhere. As Faith so helpfully pointed out, Prue hadn't even dated a guy in years. Was she really prepared to jump into bed with one now?

She gave herself a small shake. This wasn't some random guy she'd met at the bar. It was Leo. Her brother's friend. A soldier willing to risk his life in the protection of others. The first boy to capture her notice, and, moments later, her heart. To her, Leo Nolan was as improbable as Bigfoot or a fluffy unicorn. He was a man she trusted.

But how could that be? She barely knew him. Other than the fact that he'd served in the military and was friends with her brother, she knew very little about him. Next to nothing, actually.

Yet there she was, ready, eager to let him into her bed and her heart, as though he belonged there. Maybe she was crazy, and Faith was right about that, too.

Prue frowned at the road in front of her. It was a cruel thought and she inwardly scolded herself for entertaining it. After years of building Leo up in her mind, she was just a little nervous. Which was completely reasonable. Logical. Once she knew the man better than the memory, her anxieties would recede.

Her hands clutched the steering wheel too tightly and she loosened her grip. "Uh, so, where did you grow up?"

He turned his head and looked out the passenger side window. "A lot of places."

"How about your parents? Where do they live?"

"My parents are dead."

A slash of grief sliced her heart. "Leo, I'm so sorry. I didn't know." She smoothed a clammy palm down her thigh. "Do you have any brothers or sisters?"

"No."

Another pang struck the center of her chest. He was alone in the world? That made her incredibly sad, and she abandoned the small talk.

She wasn't sure why she'd bothered to try it in the first place. She'd always sucked at it. In school, she'd been consumed by her studies and never really connected with the other kids. It didn't help that her parents had enrolled her a year early, and then when she skipped first grade, her awkwardness among her peers had only deepened. Two years younger than everyone else, she'd lacked their emotional maturity and didn't develop physically along with the other girls. At sixteen, she left high school to enroll at MIT, which only replaced her high school ills for college ones.

Until five years later, when she was twenty-one and halfway to earning her PhD, and a handsome classmate took a sudden interest in her. She should've realized something was up when Aron King asked her out on a date, but she'd been so elated by the male attention, she'd thrown all her common sense and sound judgment away for a chance to be with him.

Six years later, her foolishness still mortified her. Doubt brewed inside her as an impending storm of insecurity she was helpless to protect herself against.

Until Leo's hand brushed hers. "You okay?"

She risked a glance at him. "I'm sorry if I was rude, asking you all those questions."

For a moment, his expression turned agonized. She cut a quick look to the road and then back, hoping to make a study of that expression. But he'd turned his face to the window once more.

"It's not rude." A surprising softness filled his voice. "I like that you want to know more about me."

Her insecurities melted like butter on a hot sidewalk. From the passenger seat, he watched her with a concentrated stare that made her pulse skid. By the time she turned onto her street, the tension between them pulled unbearably high and tight.

She parked on the street a block from the old Victorian house, which had been converted into apartments years before and where she now rented one of the units. As they walked, the warm summer night air aroused a smattering of goose bumps across her skin, or maybe it was the way Leo's eyes roamed over her body, like hot, questing hands.

In the dark, his heat and hunger teased her, stoking her desire as they ascended the brick walkway to the home's front entrance and climbed the stairs to her second-floor apartment.

At her door, his hands moved to her hips while she fumbled to insert the key in the lock. When he bent his head to nuzzle the spot below her ear, the slow burn of her passion ignited.

She threw open the door and dragged him inside her apartment. He buried his hands in her hair and as he backed her into the room, his mouth seared a scorching path down the side of her neck, to the swells of her breasts. She yanked up the edge of his T-shirt, and he reached behind him to haul it over his head.

In the darkened room, she glimpsed a tapestry of tattoos spanning one pec and shoulder before his hard body pinned her against the wall and his mouth recaptured hers.

God, he gave good kisses. Soft but not sloppy, fiery but not domineering. While he tasted and explored her mouth shamelessly, he yielded often, then rewarded her each time she took her pleasure in him.

She kicked off her black flats, and they separated long enough to rid her of her top and capri pants. His hands spanned her rib cage. One thumb brushed the underside of her breast while the fingers on his other hand danced along the waistband of her underwear. Then they trailed lower.

When he stroked her through her panties, a vicious moan vibrated in her throat. She placed her hands on his shoulders and shifted, giving him better access. With each soft glide of his fingers, the coil of sensation in her belly wound tighter.

Reaching between their bodies, she fumbled with the fastening of his shorts. His hard erection pressing against the fabric of his briefs filled her hand, and he groaned. At the sound, her hunger swelled. She was hurtling toward the cliff, but she wanted him to go there with her.

She dragged her mouth away from his. "Wait."

He drew back immediately. His chest heaving with his heavy breathing, he pressed his palm to the wall and squeezed his eyes shut, as though he were in pain.

She ducked under his arm, slipping out from between his body and the wall. He turned with her and she took his hand in both of hers to guide him down the hallway. In her bedroom, she led him to the bed.

He sat heavily, but even before he landed, he wrapped his arm around her waist and hauled her to him. With a swiftness she found mildly alarming, he freed one of her breasts from its bra cup and lightly brushed the pad of his thumb over her nipple. When his hot mouth covered the pebbled peak, her head fell back.

The fog of arousal closed around her once more, until, with a pang of regret, she extracted herself from his arms. "I... I... just need a minute."

At the bathroom door, she glanced back over her shoulder. When her gaze tangled with his, he straightened, suddenly alert, and an odd expression chased across his features. He appeared startled, stunned even.

And worried. Definitely worried.

He must've felt it, too, the pain of their bodily separation. It was more than delayed gratification. It physically hurt not to touch him.

She offered him a reassuring smile.

In the bathroom, she flipped on the light and fumbled through the cabinet drawers, searching for the box of condoms she'd bought last year but never used. She'd been entirely too optimistic about the new guy in IT.

Though she'd been on the pill been for years, ever since she was diagnosed with mild endometriosis as a teen and her doctor prescribed the hormones to help regulate her periods, striking up a conversation with Leo just then about past partners and STD screenings didn't hold much appeal. Besides, he'd already made it clear he didn't want to talk tonight.

Neither did she.

Snatching up the box, she ripped into it. Optimism won out once again and she removed three of the foil packets before turning toward the door.

Then she caught a glimpse of herself in the mirror. Her hair was disheveled, so she shoved her fingers through it. The effort didn't improve the mess, so she snagged the hairbrush off the vanity and yanked it through her dark tresses. Once done, she wiped a dark smudge of makeup from under one eye.

Her critical gaze dropped to the mismatched bra and panties she wore, and for the first time in her life, she wished she owned a sexy negligée or lingerie. Or at the very least had coordinated her underwear that morning. Before she started cataloging all the other imperfections visible in that mirror, she flipped off the bathroom light and returned to her bedroom.

Her eyes took a moment to adjust in the dark. Leo lay on the bed, exactly where she'd left him, with his feet hanging off the end. With every step she took back to him, her heart tripped.

He didn't sit, or stir, and at the bed's edge, she stopped.

"Leo?" she whispered.

Nothing except the deep, rhythmic sound of his breathing.

She went to the night table and switched on the lamp. Soft light flooded the room.

His eyes remained closed and his mouth hung slightly ajar while his chest rose and fell in a steady pattern. She gaped, too stunned to know what to do.

"Leo?" She didn't whisper that time, and instead injected her voice with strength.

He didn't stir.

Disappointment tore at her heart. The first time she picked up a guy at the bar and he passed out drunk before they did it? She moved to his side, intending to nudge his shoulder to try to wake him, but when she gazed down at his sleeping form, a soft gasp slipped through her lips.

His broad shoulders and lean, well-muscled torso didn't surprise her, but the angry scar that zigzagged through his smooth, tanned skin did. It was an old wound, jagged and severe, running along his side to his hip bone before disappearing beneath the waistband of his shorts. Emotion clogged in her throat as she tried to imagine the scenario that'd brought about its mark on his body.

As she watched him sleep, her disappointment morphed into something else entirely. Sadness? Longing? Regret?

All of it.

The troubled frown had released its hold on his features, and while she enjoyed her first glimpse of the well-defined muscles on his chest and stomach, she realized now that he was actually quite thin. Too thin.

Unable to resist him, she dropped a kiss on his forehead. Then she retrieved a nightshirt from her dresser, pulled it on, and climbed onto the bed to lie beside him. Lying in the dark, she listened to the sound of his breathing until her eyelids grew heavy. When a deep sigh eased from him and he settled deeper into sleep, her heavy heart lifted a little.

At least he'd found his peace.

Sometime later in the night, a noise woke her. It took her a moment to recall where she was, and that Leo was in her bed.

He groaned as though he were in pain and she sat up in the bed, a bubble of fear ballooning in her chest. Was he sick? Or hurt?

He mumbled something she couldn't understand. Was he dreaming?

She gave him a shake. "Leo, it's time to wake up." She spoke in a soft voice, not wanting to startle him but very much wishing to rescue him from the pain of his dreams.

But he didn't wake up.

His body rigid, he rolled toward her, and she realized he was crying. Crying so hard he wasn't making any sounds at all.

Her heart hammered beneath her breastbone.

"Leo, wake up. Please wake up." She brushed back a lock of hair that'd fallen across his forehead.

With a flash of movement, his arm shot out to snatch her wrist and he bolted upright in the bed. Air wheezed through his lungs and fire blazed in his eyes, burning into her, as he glared at her. Her heart in her throat, she stared back, and bore witness to a million heartbreaks.

Then he collapsed back on the bed.

"Don't go." He fumbled through the sheets until he found her hand. Clutching it tightly, he pulled it to his chest. "Please, Rose, don't leave me."

His plea was fierce and desperate, and hearing it, a little piece of her heart broke off and crumbled to dust.

With her free hand, she rubbed his damp forehead. "I won't leave you, Leo. I promise."

Chapter Four

For Leo, sleep was another battlefield. Littered with the landmines of his memories, he preferred the nightmares to the dreams, because at least when he woke from a night terror, he experienced a moment of relief.

Not so with his dreams. Soft and hope-filled, they appeared either as memories of what he'd lost or longings for a future that would never come, and when he awoke, all he was left with was the sharp ache of grief, and more regret than all the liquor in the world could obliterate.

Every time he awoke and remembered, he relived the sickening realization that they were gone, and they were never coming back. And every time, he reached for the bottle he always left beside the bed. As he did now.

But when he rolled to his side, the pain between his temples shifted and a wave of nausea knocked into him. He groaned as his head started to throb. When he tried to recall the previous night, a black hole of nothingness formed where his memories should have been.

He pressed the heel of his palm to his forehead and rubbed. Obviously, he'd been drinking. A lot. Enough to black out.

With his self-disgust, a curse fell from his lips. He'd never drunk so much he'd blacked out, and not for lack of trying either. How the hell had it happened? He remembered checking in at the hotel, the repulsiveness of Owen's task, the overwhelming compulsion to drink, and that moment of weakness when he succumbed.

Last winter when he crashed his car into a tree, he'd thought he'd hit rock bottom. But this was a new low for him.

Movement at his side startled him, and he stilled. Slowly, he turned his head to find a small, scantily clad feminine form at his side.

Oh fuck.

His gaze darted around the room, taking in the soft blue comforter draped over their bodies, which matched the lampshade on the bedside table, a table with delicate woodworking identical to that of the dresser and headboard, all of which were painted the same creamy-white color. A girl's bedroom.

His head landed with a thud against the headboard. Apparently rock bottom had a basement.

The form beside him stirred and his head snapped back to her. Long dark hair fanned out across her pillow, a tangle of deep brown and golden chestnut. She was turned away from him, so he couldn't see her face, but his gaze followed the trail of smooth, bronzed skin from her slender neck and shoulder farther down, to the shapely leg and bare foot sticking out from under the covers.

A punch of lust struck him so hard it would've knocked him on his ass if he weren't already lying down.

The yearning was potent, palpable. After all, it'd been four years since he'd been with a woman.

Four fucking years.

Until last night.

And he'd been too fucking drunk to remember it? What the hell was wrong with him?

He didn't remember anything. Not how he met her, or when or where. Not how he got to her bedroom. Not the sensation of being buried deep inside her.

Self-loathing took on a new potency as his gaze strayed back to her exposed leg. The smooth, well-toned thigh and the gentle curve of her calf. Her small, narrow foot with the toenails painted pink.

Lust and want and need warred inside him.

Fuck, fuck, fuck.

He threw off the girly blanket and launched himself from her bed. Panic mounting, he searched the room for his cell phone. Tracking it to her nightstand, he lunged, seizing the device with shaking hands. He tapped the screen to open the GPS program. While the app traced his location, he dragged a hand through his hair and tugged at the ends.

Then something brushed his leg and he wrenched away with a yelp. Hand over his racing heart, he looked down to find a fuzzy gray kitten twining between his ankles, purring with the steady rumble of a fine-tuned motor.

On his phone, the address had popped up on the map: 44 Harpers Way. With a few flicks of his finger, he panned out to pinpoint the dwelling on the city's north side, minutes from his hotel downtown.

When the hairs suddenly lifted on the back of his neck, he looked up to find her watching him with big, solemn eyes. She had a small, square-tipped nose and a plump, kissable mouth, which turned up at the corners with her hesitant smile.

A memory struck him with the force of a concussion blast, of her looking back at him over her shoulder while that same soft smile played on her lips, and in that moment he knew, absent of even the tiniest shred of doubt, that she was going to be the end of him. One way or another, when it was all said and done, she'd either usher him to his death, or she'd be the one to bring him back to life.

In his hand, his phone buzzed, and he looked down at the display to see Owen's name flashing on the screen.

∞

Prue stared at the man standing in her bedroom, wondering where the guy she'd brought home last night had gone.

Sober now, and alert, a hardness clung to him as a cold, inscrutable mask. The sharp intelligence still gleamed in his arresting eyes, but no passion simmered amidst their green and gold flecks.

The cell phone in his hand whined with a soft buzzing sound.

He bent his head to check the device, and when he looked up again, a tremor of panic chased across his face. "I'm sorry. I need to take this."

She nodded because he seemed to want her permission.

He pressed the phone to his ear. "Hey, what's up? You got that address?"

Turning at the waist, he scanned the room, then crossed to her writing desk in the corner. He plucked a pen from the desktop and raised the tip to his palm.

"Yeah, I'm ready."

The pen moved with his writing before it stopped suddenly. His panicked gaze latched on to her face. As she watched, a storm cloud gathered around him, sucking all the air in the room into his sphere.

Her heart started to pound. Why was he looking at her like that?

"Yeah, I'm here," he said. "I will. Today. Right now. I'll update you as soon as I... know something." He listened to the caller, then said, "You didn't tell me. What's your sister's name?"

His hand dropped to his side and his thumb slid over the phone's screen. The display went dark.

She licked her dry lips. "Is everything okay?"

"What's your name?"

She wanted to lie, but she didn't know why. "You know my name."

"I want to hear you say it." He bit out the words.

"It's Prue."

His shock gave way to something else, something darker. The hairs lifted on her arms.

"Prue what?" A muscle ticked along his jawline.

"Why are you—"

"Your last name," he snapped. "What. Is. It?"

"L-Lockhart."

A nasty curse shot from him.

Alarm drove her to her feet. "Leo, what is going on?"

The words died in her throat when his gaze raked boldly over her body, zeroing in on all the places her flimsy sleepshirt didn't provide cover. Her heart performed a series of perilous flips.

Then his eyes returned to her face with enough force to knock her back a step. "You're Owen's kid sister?"

She blinked at him. "You know I am."

"What are you talking about? I never met you before."

"Of course you did." She spoke around the sand filling her mouth. "Several times."

"When?"

"When you came home with Owen on your first leave,

and at your graduation–"

"That was ten years ago." His voice filled with fury and made the statement sound like an accusation.

"It was eight."

"How in the hell am I supposed to remember something that happened eight years ago? Hell, I don't even remember what happened last night."

She sucked in a sharp breath.

A flicker of regret touched his features. Hands on his hips, he dropped his head and stared at the floor.

He didn't remember her? But... he'd talked about how long it had been, and the way he'd kissed her, and touched her, and stripped off her clothing.... Humiliation burned her cheeks.

What had she been thinking? Letting another man, any man, get so close? She knew better. Men could not be trusted.

But he wasn't just any man, the teenager inside her argued. He was Leo, her first crush. He was different. Wasn't he?

Her sinking heart supplied the answer. No, he wasn't. He was exactly like all the others. She was wrong about him.

"Look, Prue, what happened last night... if Owen found out, he'd cut off my–"

"Owen? What does he have to do with this?"

Leo ran a hand through his hair, standing the dark strands on end. "He asked me to check up on you."

"He *what?*"

"He thought you might be in trouble."

"Wh-why did he think that?"

"He said you're being harassed online."

Shit. Owen followed her online? Did he know she was investigating Aron King? If so, did he, like Faith, assume the worst about her motives?

To her family, the dark spiral Prue had fallen into after

she and Aron broke up must've looked like heartbreak. But she wasn't so delicate as to let a heartless man devastate her so completely, even back then. Aron's betrayal went far beyond him being a jerk.

She became acutely aware of Leo's sharp gaze on her, observing. Assessing.

"It's nothing." Somehow, she managed to keep her tone casual. "I got caught up in a bot attack, but it's over now. Too bad, but you went through all this for nothing."

A frown pressed between his brows. "What the hell does that mean?"

"A bot attack? It's when–"

"Not that. When you said I 'went through all this for nothing'?"

Her pride demanded she lift one shoulder and slice him with a haughty look. "You did your job admirably, even sacrificing your body for it."

She watched her words hit their mark.

"That's not what happened."

"How do you know?" The tremor in her voice threatened to expose her ruse. "I thought you couldn't remember."

Intense green-gold eyes held her captive. "I didn't start the night drunk, and I remember it was you who approached me."

She folded her arms across her abdomen. "Well, consider your duty fulfilled. You can report back to Owen that I'm fine. Though I'd appreciate it if you left out the, uh, dirty details."

Except for the color heightening his cheeks, he appeared unaffected by her words.

Which was why she didn't tell him the truth. She knew she should have. He deserved to know that they hadn't had sex. That he'd passed out instead.

And that she'd held his hand most of the night.

But her face was on fire and once she got him out of

her apartment, she fully intended never to see him again.

The moment stretched out while he studied her. "Are you in trouble?"

She didn't want to tell him about the break-in or the online attacks, and she most certainly didn't want to tell him about Aron King.

"Nope." She managed to infuse some strength into the lie, though she couldn't quite hold his gaze.

"Let me give you my number–"

"I don't want your number, Leo."

He was silent a moment. "I'm in town for a few days. If anything changes, you can give me a call. Anytime. Day or night."

"I'm not going to call you."

"Okay." He crept closer. "Then give me your number."

"I don't want to."

He continued moving toward her, so she backed away, a step for each one he took, until she bumped against the wall.

Pressing into her space, he filled her senses. "What's your number?"

"I don't want you to call me."

"I'm sorry." His voice was thick, heavy with some emotion, and she didn't think he was talking about making phone calls anymore.

She tilted her chin up so she could see his face. "Sorry about what?"

The gold flecks in his eyes, dancing like flames, gripped her insides. Then his gaze dropped to her mouth, and his head dipped lower.

He brought his mouth within a whisper of hers before he abruptly stopped himself.

The slash of her disappointment rankled.

"It was never my intention to hurt you. Prue." He hooked her name at the end of his sentence.

She wanted to deny the hurt, to tell him he was

delusional and arrogant and not to flatter himself, but she couldn't bring herself to tell even one more lie.

His gaze never left her face when he reached over and filched her cell phone off the nightstand. With a few taps on the screen, he added his number to her contact list.

She scowled. "I'm not going to call you."

He returned her phone to the bedside table. "If you need me, I'll come."

"I won't need you."

But by the time she forced the denial past the lump lodged in her throat, she spoke to an empty room.

Chapter Five

Leo returned to his hotel room and walked directly to the desk where he'd left his laptop. He switched it on and settled in front of it with two aspirin and a bottle of water. Within minutes, he'd navigated to each of her social media accounts.

Only to discover she'd deleted them all.

Placing his hands behind his head, he eased back in his chair and gaped at the bold lettering on the screen. He'd left her place less than an hour ago, and already she'd wiped out her online existence?

Now why would she go and do a thing like that?

He played out a few scenarios in his mind, and no matter the motivation he assigned to her actions, they all circled back to one central cause: she was hiding something. What, and from whom, he didn't know.

A determined smile tugged at the corner of his mouth. He was going to find out.

"All right, Prue." He sat forward in the chair and cracked the knuckles on both of his hands. "Game on."

It took him several hours, but he managed to dig up her accounts at an online digital archive. He downloaded everything. Years' worth of posts from three separate platforms. When he'd captured it all and saved it to his device, he started to read.

Mostly she posted articles about plants and outer space. A few posts mentioned family and friends, but all her recent interactions were with some guy named Paul Cook. Leo clicked over to Cook's bio, and when he read the words "foreign correspondent," his uneasy stomach wrenched with nausea.

In a fit of dismay, he closed his laptop and paced to the opposite side of the hotel room, as though he might be able to outrun the memories haunting him.

Of course, he knew better.

After a long hot shower, he dressed in a clean pair of shorts and a T-shirt. His cell phone sat on the dresser and he eyed it warily. By now, it'd been hours since he'd talked to Owen, and Leo knew his friend was waiting to hear back from him. Probably worrying while he waited.

But at the moment, Leo would rather eat rations for a month than talk to Prue's brother.

What was he going to say? "Hey, man, guess what? I got drunk, fucked your sister, and I can't remember any of it. That's funny, right? Oh, but she's fine though. What's up with you?"

He cursed, and instinct had him reaching for a drink, so he cursed again. The longing was sharp and visceral, and cold terror slithered through him. What if he couldn't stop drinking this time?

Rather than face the alcohol-free mini-fridge, or devise a plan to fill it, he grabbed the car keys off the console and headed for the door. Before he called Owen, he really should gather some more information. It was the responsible thing to do.

The late afternoon sun slipped behind the highest treetops as he drove up the street toward the Victorian-style house. A few doors down, he sidled up to the curb, parking in the shadow of a massive oak tree. The minutes ticked by, and he expected the tedium of surveillance would take hold before long, but the boredom never came.

Instead, anticipation kept him alert to the activities surrounding her second-floor dwelling. Hope that he might catch a glimpse of her.

Hope.

Hope? When was the last time he'd felt hopeful?

Sometime later, his patience was rewarded when he caught sight of her on the small balcony. She wore short shorts, and her loose-fitting top slanted off one shoulder, exposing a lovely span of her smooth, golden skin. A metal watering can in one hand, she poured water over the throng of flowering plants crowding the terrace. With meticulous care, she tended to each plant, picking off the dead leaves and flowers and inspecting their large blooms.

When finally she retreated indoors, he deflated a little in the seat.

Darkness filled the sky, and still he maintained his lookout. The light in her bedroom came on and her shadow passed before the sheer curtains as she moved around the room. When eventually the lights went out, he climbed from the vehicle and set off on foot through the quiet neighborhood.

On this Saturday night at the height of summer, people gathered in their yards and on their front porches, enjoying the warm evening. Satisfied with his recon, he circled around to his car and made the short drive back to the hotel.

But the next morning, he returned to his curbside

hideout, and less than an hour later, she appeared through the old home's front entrance. Oversized sunglasses concealed much of her face, but the flowing tank top she wore had a plunging neckline, and skintight leggings molded to her tight ass and shapely legs.

The tug at his groin was more surprising than inconvenient, and it was damned inconvenient. She was a beautiful woman, with graceful curves and ample other assets, like long legs, smooth skin, and a full, perfectly round ass. The hours spent in her bed had to have been glorious. Had he really seen her naked? How could it be that he had no memory of her? His mind tried to conjure the images, any images, but nothing came to him.

It was quickly becoming the stupidest night of his life. He'd finally taken the chance on hooking up with a woman after so long, only to forget being with her? To forget the feel of being nestled between her thighs? Being buried deep inside her?

With a visible jolt, he slammed a blockade in the path his mind had traveled.

Seriously though, did she have to be Owen's sister?

She climbed behind the wheel of the car, and a few moments later pulled out into traffic. At a discreet distance, he pursued her to the grocery store.

After spending fifty-seven minutes inside the store, she reemerged with a full shopping cart. While she wrestled with the bags, stuffing them into the trunk of her car, the heat in his veins started to rise all over again at the interesting ways her body moved and wiggled.

Leo tracked her route back home, then watched as she loaded the horde of canvas bags in her arms, preferring, it seemed, to carry them all in one trip rather than make repeat trips up the two flights of stairs. Damn, she was cute.

Despite the fact that he was immensely enjoying his glimpses of her tight little body, he didn't know why he sat outside her building the rest of that day, or why he followed her to a restaurant downtown later that night and sat in his car with a fierce scowl on his face while he waited to find out who she dined with. And he certainly didn't understand why he felt so relieved to discover her dinner companion was another woman.

Nope, there was no good reason why he continued to watch over her. Except maybe he owed Owen more than a cursory "yep, she's still alive." When Leo's life had spun out of control, the guy had been rock solid, and now Leo wanted to keep his shit together long enough to pay back the debt.

So he followed Prue home from the restaurant, and stayed until the light went out in her bedroom window. The next day he returned in time to track her Monday morning commute through the city streets, over the river, and into downtown Cambridge to the parking lot of the Cambridge Science Institute.

While she ducked inside the large glass and stone structure, presumably to start her workday, he set about doing his job. His recon of the neighborhood was made complicated by the urban setting, and as he moved through the city, the sweltering sun beat down on him. The task combined with the summer heat wave worked to remind him of the region in Afghanistan where he'd been stationed the majority of his years in the military, and to summon memories he'd rather forget.

His recon complete, he returned to his rental vehicle, parked in the shade on a side street. There he remained for the rest of day, keeping watch on her office building and reading through more of her social media archive.

Sometime in the midafternoon, his cell phone rang and he accepted the call from Gideon.

Once close, Leo hadn't spoken to Gideon in years, not for any reason other than he hadn't talked to any of his old friends in years.

"How you been?" Gideon asked.

Leo rolled his shoulders. "I'm... fine. You?"

After a beat, Gideon coughed up a reply. "Fine. I'm fine, too."

Leo shifted in his seat. "You, uh, still in Chicago?"

"Sometimes," Gideon said. "I'm a lot of places these days."

"Me, too," Leo said. "I like the travel."

"Yep," came Gideon's quick reply. "And the freedom."

"The freedom is great," Leo agreed.

An awkward silence dropped between them.

Gideon cleared his throat. "So, you're with Owen's sister now?"

Leo choked on the sharp inhalation of air. "I'm, um, *near* her right now, yeah. Not with her."

"Did Owen mention he asked me to look into her troll problem?"

"He did. What did you find out?"

"Most of the harassment is coming from bot accounts," Gideon said. "Though there are some trolls joining in the fun."

"Bots? They're not real people?"

"They're real, but one or two people might be behind hundreds of accounts. All coming from the same IP address overseas. It's a coordinated attack."

When they disconnected, Leo returned to his study of her social media account with a renewed focus. By the end of the day, he had some questions.

Climbing out from behind the steering wheel, he dialed her cell phone and crossed the street. In his ear, the phone rang as he entered the Institute's parking lot and headed in the direction of her car.

Just when he decided she wasn't going to take his call, she answered.

"Hello?" Her voice was filled with uncertainty.

"Why did you delete your social media accounts?"

"How did you get my number?"

A kick of satisfaction thumped in his chest that she knew his voice. After only one night.

"I had your phone in my hand."

She hesitated. "But you didn't write down my number."

"I didn't need to write it down." Arriving at her car, he pulled up.

"I told you not to call me," she said.

Bending at the waist, he peered through the windows. "Did you?" he murmured distractedly. "I only remember you saying you weren't going to call me."

"The point is I don't want to talk to you."

"Then tell me why you deleted your social media accounts so I can hang up and go get a beer."

Through their connection, he could practically hear her mind choosing and discarding plausible answers.

Finally she made her choice. "I don't want Owen to worry."

Leo leaned against her car. "You don't want him to worry, or you don't want him to know what you're doing?"

"Both, I suppose. He needs to be focused on his work, not mine." An intriguing softness came into her voice. "Distractions are dangerous for him."

He liked that answer.

"Will there be anything else?" Her clipped tone drove out all the softness.

"What time are you off work?"

"Five."

"It's five fifteen."

"So?"

"So why are you still at work?"

"How do you know I'm still at work? I could be on my way home."

"You're not on your way home. I'm sitting on the hood

of your car and you're not in it."

Within moments, she shot through the glass doors of the large office building.

Today, she'd twisted her hair into a braid that wound around the crown of her head, and wore a flimsy, pale pink sundress that skipped and danced around her body as she marched across the parking lot. When the warm summer breeze licked at the dress's hem and revealed one long, toned thigh, he held his breath, silently praying for a glimpse of what lay hidden higher up.

She came to a stop before him. "What are you doing here?"

The question caught him off guard. He knew there was a reasonable answer, but at the moment, all that came to mind was the truth—that he'd been driven mad trying to recall the color of her eyes. He had a guess, but he needed confirmation.

Those very eyes narrowed to angry slits.

Blue. They were blue.

"You know what's weird?" He straightened away from her car and folded his arms across his chest. "Your apartment was all neat and tidy, but the inside of your car is a pigsty. What's up with that?"

"I'm surprised you remember my apartment." A golden brown strand of her hair had worked its way free of the braid, and she pushed it back from her face. "After all, it's been three long days since you were there."

He nodded. "Okay, I deserve that. Feel better?"

She lifted her small shoulders. "A little."

Seeing her up close for the first time, without alcohol or panic clouding his perception, she was prettier than he recalled. A lot prettier, with attractive coloring and small, delicate features.

"What happened to your car?"

She squirmed beneath his gaze.

"Just say it," he said. "It's the quickest way to make me

leave."

Sucking her plump bottom lip between her teeth, she glanced through the glass. His gaze followed hers.

"Someone broke into it."

His head snapped around. "When?"

"Friday."

"Where?"

"Here."

"Here?" His arms fell to his sides and he cut quick glances over his shoulders. "While you were at work? In the middle of the day?"

"I guess so. I don't know exactly what time they did it. I worked late that night and didn't see the damage until I was leaving."

"How late did you work?"

"I don't know. Seven, I think."

Pop! Bang!

The sound exploded behind him and he lunged, wrapping her in his arms even as he took her to the ground with a leg sweep. They hit the asphalt hard, though his hand cradling her head protected her from the worst of the impact.

He covered her with his body and braced for the madness. For the screams that would rain down on them. For the chaos and darkness. He held her in his arms and waited. He wouldn't let go of her. Not this time. No matter what they did to him.

"*Leo!*"

Her cry punctured the haze of fear ensnaring him.

He blinked several times until her face came into focus. Big blue eyes, full of shock and sorrow, stared up at him.

"It was a car backfiring." Her fingers trailed across his forehead. "It was only a car."

He dropped his head to her shoulder and sucked large, searing gulps of air into his lungs.

Her arms circled around his neck and she whispered soft, soothing nonsense in his ear. Like he was a scared child.

He needed to get up. Instead, he buried his face in the hollow between her neck and shoulder and tightened his arms around her.

"We're okay." Her lips brushed his earlobe. "It's okay now."

When he lifted his head, his mouth touched hers. The life flowing through her tasted sweet on his tongue. Refreshing, renewing. Holding his mouth against hers, he squeezed his eyes shut and willed the panic away. He wasn't dead. He wasn't dead.

But *she* was.

With a wrench of agony, he rolled off Prue. While his heart tried to pound its way out of his chest, he shoved to his feet, then hauled her up off the pavement.

She rubbed her elbow as she eyed him, a concerned frown touching her small features. "Are you okay?"

His hands shaking, he fumbled for the phone in his hip pocket and scrolled through his contact list.

"Wh-what are you doing?"

He hardened himself against the soft catch of vulnerability in her voice and speared her with a hard glare. "I'm calling your brother."

Chapter Six

She gasped. "What? Why?"

"Because he needs to get his ass back here and deal with whatever it is that's going on with you."

"But–" She bit off her protest when he pressed the phone to his ear. Folding her arms over her abdomen, she arched an eyebrow at him. "What are you going to tell him? That you don't remember sleeping with me?"

Light glinted in his eyes and a muscle ticked along his jawline while he stared her down.

The seconds ticked away until finally he spoke. "Owen, call me. It's about your sister."

He disconnected, and Prue threw her hands in the air. "Why did you do that? That's going to freak him out."

"I'm okay with that."

"He can't do anything to help me from the other side of the world."

"Which is why he needs to come home."

"No, he does not." She shook her head, adamant. "I can handle this on my own."

"You can handle what?"

Doubt constricted her throat and her protests jammed in the narrowing passageway. At dinner the previous night, Faith had tried again to convince Prue to stop investigating Aron King's activities. In stating her case, Faith had utilized a range of biting remarks that left Prue feeling bashed and bruised.

Still a little raw, she wasn't sure how well she'd endure another tongue-lashing. Especially one delivered by a former Marine.

She scratched a spot on the tip of her nose. "Uh, it's complicated."

His glittering green eyes held her captive. "Try me."

"I was being targeted by some online trolls, but it's over now. I've taken care of it."

"You already told me that. How did you take care of it?"

"What is this, an interrogation?"

"I'm just getting started," he said coolly.

"I deleted my accounts." A sour taste flooded her mouth with the words. "No account, no trolls. Simple."

"What about the person, or people, who broke into your car?"

She clenched her teeth against the upheaval his questioning stirred inside her.

"You know who did it, don't you?" His unwavering gaze remained fixed on her face. "Do you also know who's been threatening you online?"

"No. Well, not exactly," she admitted. "But it doesn't matter. They were just trying to scare me."

"Oh, is that all?" The bite in his tone stung. "Intimidation, harassment. Shit, what's a little aggravated felony when you need to make a point?"

Misery pressed down on her. Everyone was either

against her or racked with worry. Or suspicious of her mental state. Her brother on the other side of the world was so concerned he'd sent a bodyguard from God knew where to deal with her. A bodyguard who was either neurotically jumpy or suffering some serious post-traumatic stress.

Her quest doomed, defeat clamped like a vise around her heart.

"Look, it worked, okay?" Her vision blurred with tears of frustration. "I'm done. I'm out. They win."

Suspicion touched his features. "Are you just saying that to get rid of me?"

"No, it's true." Her shoulders sagged. "I can't stand the thought of Owen worrying. My sister thinks I'm—"

"Your sister thinks you're what?"

"Nothing. She wants me to back off, so that's what I'm going to do."

He studied her, his expression serious, and the urge to confess to crimes she'd never committed nearly overwhelmed her.

"Okay," he said finally.

She released the breath she'd been holding.

Then, drawing her shoulders back, she gave a firm nod. "Okay."

Her heart in her throat, she reached for her car door, but his body blocked her from pulling it open. When he refused to yield ground to her, her startled gaze flew to his face.

The breath snagged in her lungs to see the lean restlessness lurking in him, just under the surface. An electrical charge arced between them and for a moment, she wanted to draw back, away from the danger, but the look on his face wouldn't let her move. It was as if he hadn't had enough to eat, or enough sleep, and suddenly all she wanted to do was reach out and touch him. Maybe stroke the side of his face or press a kiss to the lines of sorrow bracketing his eyes and mouth.

Of course, she didn't do any of those ridiculous things.

When she found her voice, she spoke to his shirtfront. "Thanks for trying to help." Then she risked one last glimpse into his eyes. "Goodbye, Leo."

Yanking open the door, her legs gave out and she collapsed in the driver seat.

As she drove from the parking lot, she refused to glance in the rearview mirror, certain that if she had to watch Leo Nolan disappear from her life again, she wouldn't be able to hold back her tears.

☙

Naturally, he followed her home.

It was his duty to do so, but also, he knew she was hurting. The truth was stamped plainly on her face.

But why? Fear he could understand, but why so much hurt?

It didn't matter, he supposed. At least she'd agreed to walk away from whatever trouble had been drawing near.

She was sensible. Smart. He admired her for that.

From his spot parked under the oak tree, he watched her water and care for her plants before disappearing indoors. Later that evening, she reemerged, a book in hand, and settled in the lone deck chair. He'd never been so entertained watching someone read.

So much so, he frowned when his cell phone vibrated on the console, wrenching his attention from her.

With a tap on the screen, he accepted Owen's call. "What the hell, man? You said she was fragile."

Owen's soft laughter rumbled over the connection. "She's my kid sister. What can I say?"

Leo bit down on his tongue. There was nothing childlike about her. It probably wouldn't be wise to

53

inform his friend that his "kid sister" had a hot ass and a mouth more luscious than a succulent peach. Yeah, that'd be weird. And possibly life-ending.

"What did you find out?" Owen asked.

Leo filled him in on the details, minus the one rather significant fact of their hookup. Once Owen was back in the States and safe, Leo would find a way to tell his friend that he'd defiled his baby sister.

"You think the break-in is related?"

"I don't know, but she seems to think it is." On the balcony, Prue stretched out her long legs and propped her bare feet atop the railing. An image of those legs wrapped around his naked waist knocked into Leo with enough force that for a moment he struggled to regain his focus. "Any idea what she did that riled up the Twitter crazies?"

"None," Owen said. "When I saw the threats and asked her about them, her reaction let me know something was up."

"Well, she's taken down her accounts now."

"Good, that's good. When I'm done here I'll head straight for Boston."

"Where are you, anyway?" Leo didn't know why he asked. He didn't care.

"Ukraine. We're guarding a diplomatic envoy that's here through the end of the month. Hopefully Prue can sit tight for the next two weeks."

Leo was unable to tear his gaze away from her and the long length of her smooth legs when he said, "I'll keep an eye on things until then."

"You've done enough already," Owen said. "I owe you one."

Leo would be sure to bring that up when Owen found out the truth about the night Leo met Prue in that hotel bar.

"I don't mind."

"Honestly, it's not going to be necessary." A hint of humor infected Owen's voice.

"What makes you say that?"

"I got a call from my dad last night. He was upset because my mom is upset, because she talked to my other sister, who told her Prue has a stalker, and what the hell am I going to do about it anyway?" Owen chuckled softly. "Something tells me Prue's going to be well guarded until I get back."

As he disconnected the call, a splash of fading sunlight washed her in its golden warmth.

He was off the hook. If he wanted, he could drive back to the hotel, pack his bag, and leave town that night.

Still, he remained parked outside her apartment until she retreated indoors and, a few hours later, her bedroom light winked out. He then completed a neighborhood recon and, back behind the wheel of his car, maneuvered the vehicle through the darkened city streets.

He'd fulfilled his duty to his friend. His conscience was as clear as a cloudless sky.

So why did he feel so damned dark and gloomy?

Chapter Seven

Quitting "Project Aron" turned out to be harder than Prue ever imagined, taking nearly as much willpower as the crash diet she'd attempted in the ninth grade. Back then, she only lasted a day before she caved to the hunger. Now, well into day two with zero work given to her research, the hunger was all-consuming.

Maybe Faith was right. Maybe it was so difficult to walk away because, deep down, a part of her wanted to get back at Aron for what he'd done. The part of her that still felt humiliated by his betrayal. The part that never wanted to get close to another man for fear she'd put her trust in him and have her faith destroyed, once and for all. Or maybe she wanted revenge for the teeny-tiny part of her that would forever doubt herself.

When she returned home from work at the Institute, she settled on the sofa with her laptop. The craving to go to her files nearly overwhelmed until she recalled the panic on Leo's face when he thought they were in danger. The fear rioting in his eyes. The helpless, hopeless expression contorting his beautiful features. Then her regret was manageable, and her hunger worth the payoff.

Her kitten, Arlo, perched on the sofa back and Prue scratched his head. Then she opened her email and typed a short message to Paul Cook, a journalist she'd met online who had also been digging into the merry band of mobsters surrounding the controversial politician from Eastern Europe.

Over the past few weeks, she and Paul had attacked the research together, sharing notes and documents as they tried to piece together the vast web of connections. As Paul had experienced a rash of hacking attempts, they were extremely careful when sharing files, and they never uploaded anything anywhere online that they didn't want others to see, which meant she held most of her work locally on her laptop and backed up to an external hard drive. He was a sharp, thorough researcher, an incredible writer, and she'd loved working with him. But, as she explained in her email to him, she needed to step away from the work for a while. Then she offered to send him all her notes and the trove of records she'd gathered.

The moment she hit Send on that email, she had to blink away a sudden upwelling of tears, but a knock on her apartment door cut short any pity party she might've thrown.

She dumped her laptop on the coffee table and shuffled to the door. Pulling it open, she recoiled to find her parents standing in the hallway.

Scowls of disapproval marred their faces, and for the next several hours, she defended herself against their twisted logic which centered on the bizarre notion that she had a stalker. *Thank you, Faith.*

After she finally shooed them away, she collapsed on the sofa, wired and exhausted at the same time. Her laptop beckoned like a piece of moist chocolate cake, so she distracted herself with junk food and mind-numbing television. It was no use.

Frustration spurring her on, she shoved the computer to the back of her closet, beneath a pile of shoes and hand-me-downs from Faith, and slammed the door closed. Then she retreated to her bed and flipped off the lights.

If there were any justice in the world, she'd be rewarded for her strength of will with a few hours' reprieve from the torment.

But it was not to be.

☓

A sound pulled her from sleep.

Her eyes blinked open, but the room was shrouded in darkness.

Arlo's silhouette sat primly at the end of the bed, watching the bedroom door with raised ears. He tilted his head and her heart lurched when another muffled noise sounded, this one closer.

She reached for her cell phone on the nightstand, but her fingers brushed over the smooth wood surface. The device wasn't there. She must've left it in the living room when she came to bed.

The figure of a man appeared in the doorway.

Fear arrowed to her heart. He was short, but broad, and he wore a ski mask. Too terrified to move, she froze while desperate prayers began running through her mind. She prayed he didn't know she was there, and that if she remained still in the darkness, he wouldn't see her. Arlo slunk to the edge of the mattress and dropped silently to the floor.

Then the man stepped into the bedroom and her breathing stopped. Her heart thundered beneath her breastbone, but she didn't move. She didn't twitch or even blink.

From the doorway, he scanned the room, then strode toward her desk.

But at the foot of the bed, he pulled up abruptly. Slowly, he turned his head in her direction.

She'd been detected.

A force overcame her, whether instinct or adrenaline or simply the will to survive, and she charged. When she crashed into him, his curse shattered the quiet, and he stumbled back. In that split second when she knocked him off-balance, she spotted an opening between him and the bedroom door, and she shot through it.

Behind her, he burst into the hallway. Footsteps hounded her, and she erupted into the living room as his meaty hands clamped onto her shoulders. With a brutal shove, he slammed her into the wall. She twisted around, and his hand crushed her throat in a vicious grip.

Oxygen squeezed through her constricted airway when he leaned close.

"Where is it?" His breath smelled stale.

Pale light from the bathroom filtered across his face, and shock jolted through her when she peered into his eyes. Though she wouldn't recall the color of his irises, she'd never forget the remarkable absence of emotion in his dead eyes. They held none of the panic she'd expect of a desperate thief, or the mania of a deranged killer.

Indeed, there wasn't a single shred of fear or insanity in him. This man possessed all his faculties, and nothing desperate or crazed drove him. He was in complete control and knew exactly what he was doing. He knew that he was hurting her and that she was terrified. He knew, and he didn't care.

When she didn't supply him with an answer, his hand shot out and cracked into her cheekbone. Pain exploded inside her skull and white noise filled her head with the force of the blow.

Terror fueling her, she mustered all her strength and jammed her knee to his balls. He yelped and his grip loosened.

Then fresh rage contorted his face. "Fucking bitch."

Before he struck her again, she pressed her palms to his barrel chest and shoved. He rocked back and she stumbled from his grasp on weak legs.

But she only made it a few steps before he tackled her, landing on top of her when they hit the ground with a jarring collision. A piercing agony sliced into her side and tore a cry from her. Her body contorted and her elbow connected with some part of his face. Pain shot up her arm even as the sound of something clattering across the hardwood floor drew him toward it.

On her hands and knees, she scrambled away, but with a grunt, he lunged and his large hand clamped around her ankle. With a hard jerk, he dragged her toward him. The skin on her knees and thighs scraped across the wood floor and she twisted onto her back.

Her body worked without her conscious choice. She kicked and punched, screaming until her vocal cords burned. When her heel caught his chin, his arm came up to cover his head.

She kept kicking, fighting through pain and exhaustion. More grunts and curses sputtered from him. Suddenly, he lifted his head and turned. Then he was retreating.

Darkness hovered at the edges of her vision when she touched the searing pain in her side. Wetness seeped through her T-shirt to drench her hand, and she pressed her palm over the wound.

When she rolled to her stomach, the pain wrenched

another cry from her. The room spun as she raised up on her haunches. On the coffee table, she spotted her cell phone. Her fingers fumbled with the device, dropping it once before she managed to bring up the number pad to make an outgoing call.

Blackness invaded the edges of her vision, and she stabbed blindly at the screen where she hoped the digits 911 would be located. But before she'd punched the last number, ringing sounded on the other end.

The tunnel around her line of sight closed tighter, and the device slipped from her trembling hands.

One more ring reverberated in the dark silence before she collapsed to the floor.

Chapter Eight

Leo had intended to leave town that morning. Instead, he made the visit he'd dreaded making since his return to Boston. After he left the cemetery, rather than hit the road as planned, he'd gone back to his hotel room and gotten shitfaced drunk.

Sometime in the early afternoon, he'd passed out, and he didn't wake again until the sound of his cell phone roused him from sleep.

In the dark hotel room, he fumbled for the device on the bedside table and tipped it so he could read the display.

Seeing her name, he shot upright and swung his legs off the bed as he connected the call. "Prue?"

Silence on the other end drove him to his feet. "Prue, are you there?"

The clock on the nightstand screamed the time in bloodred digits: 2:17 a.m.

He closed his eyes, listening. Something, someone, was there. He could just make out the faintest of sounds. Soft, rattling breaths.

It was her, he knew it.

The phone pressed to his ear, he yanked on a pair of blue jeans. "Prue, if you can hear me, hang on. I'm coming."

He plucked his backpack off the floor at the end of the bed, which he'd crammed with his belongings the night before in preparation for his morning departure, and burst through the door. At a full sprint, he careened down the long, empty corridor.

In the parking ramp, he vaulted behind the wheel and jammed the keys in the ignition. He refused to disconnect Prue's call, switching to speakerphone before he laid the device on the dashboard. The engine roared to life and the tires screeched when he punched the accelerator.

His heartbeat hammered inside his skull with sickening thuds. This couldn't be happening. Not again.

In case she could hear him, he talked to her while he sped along the narrow city streets, which were mostly quiet at the late hour. He broke several traffic laws to arrive at the Victorian home in half the normal time, then he parked illegally in front of the house and darted up the front steps two at a time.

As he approached the front door, he reached for his gun, which of course, he wasn't wearing. Just one more way in which he'd struggled to adjust to civilian life. He slipped inside the building.

Head up, he hugged the wall and scaled both flights of stairs. On the landing, he crept toward her apartment door. It stood open, the interior dark and quiet.

Just then, a door across the hall creaked open and a woman's head poked through the crack. When her gaze landed on him, he froze. Her eyes went wide and she whisked the door closed.

Through the door, her muffled voice possessed a shaky warning. "I–I've called the police."

Silently, Leo stole inside Prue's apartment. He crouched with his back to the wall and waited while his eyes adjusted to the darkness. Soon, he could make out a form heaped on the floor.

Nausea twisted his gut and he expelled a slow breath as he moved toward it. Relying on his memory of the room's layout, he found the table lamp and flipped it on. Soft light flooded the space and confirmed his worst fear. She appeared unconscious, and dark red stained the nightshirt over her stomach.

A curse shot from him and he hurled toward her, falling to his knees as he reached her side. "Prue?" He smoothed his palm across her cheek. "Oh shit, Prue. I'm sorry. I'm so fucking sorry."

Her eyes blinked open. Glazed with panic, they fastened on his face. "Leo?"

"Where are you hurt?" he asked, even as his hands searched her body.

She winced and lifted a hand to touch her side. "Here."

"Who did this?"

She sucked in a sharp breath when he pulled the fabric from her skin. "I don't know him. A man...."

Leo's gaze swept the room. "Is he still here?"

"I don't think so."

With the outer edge of his own T-shirt, he gently wiped the blood away from the spot of the wound, trying to assess the damage.

Another curse ripped from him. "He had a knife?"

This was his fault. He was the reason this had happened to her. Once again, his failure caused others to suffer.

"I don't.... It was dark. I couldn't see...."

When he'd cleaned away enough blood to examine the

cut, relief flooded him.

"It isn't bad. He just caught the surface." But there was so much blood. He rechecked the wound. "Did you fight him?"

If she'd struggled, that might explain the amount of blood.

"I was trying to get away, but he kept coming."

Leo squeezed his eyes shut briefly. The struggle might explain the amount of blood, but knowing that did nothing to calm the fear that choked him.

With the tips of his fingers, he touched her cheek. "You fought well."

Her chin quivered and her eyes shimmered. "It doesn't feel like it."

A lump lodged in his throat. "I'm sorry I wasn't here."

"I didn't call you." Her tone held a defiant ring.

He peered into her eyes, checking her pupils for symmetry. "Maybe you don't remember."

"Well, I didn't mean to call you. I said I wouldn't and I didn't." A frown puckered the spot between her brows. "But you came anyway."

At the softness in her voice, the lump sitting inside his throat swelled. "Do you have a first-aid kit?"

"In the bathroom."

He did a quick sweep of the apartment to make certain the attacker had fled before he returned to her side with a wet, warm towel and the kit.

He'd cleaned the wound and was dressing it when two policemen appeared at the apartment door he'd left open.

Prue dragged her gaze from the officers at the door back to him. "That's who I was trying to call."

Leo pulled the hem of her nightshirt down to cover her and, with a hand under her arm, helped her sit. She took a moment, and once steady, climbed slowly to her feet. He refused to let go of her arm until she was safely seated on the couch.

Sitting on the solid wood coffee table, he listened as she relayed to the officers the details of the incident. When she stated that she'd woken up to find a man standing in her bedroom, and described how he'd hunted her throughout the apartment in a prolonged assault, the room started to spin around him.

Guilt and fear threatened to swallow him. He should've taken her protection more seriously. After he found out about the car break-in, he never should have left her alone. He didn't know who was after her, or why, but at this point he had to assume her attacker would be back.

Clearly he couldn't protect her and he had no business pretending that he could. So what could he do? Ask the cops to lock her in a jail cell where no one could get near her?

The hand he hauled through his hair stilled when a thought struck. He might not be able to lock her away, but he could hide her. Just until they figured out what the hell was going on.

While the officers set about their work of fingerprinting and combing for evidence, his mind raced to fill in the details of a hazy plan.

He twisted on the table to face her. "I think we should get you out of town for a few days while we sort this all out. What do you think?"

She frowned. "Where would I go?"

"I don't know." He grimaced with the admission. "Right now, I think any place might be safer for you than this town. Why don't you pack a few things while I finish up with the officers?"

Leo gave his cell phone number to the cops and explained he'd be taking Prue out of town for a few days. In exchange, they left him with their contact information and a promise to call him if they discovered the identity of Prue's attacker.

While he waited for Prue, he moved through the apartment, closing up and securing every window and the terrace door, which she'd left open to let in the cooler night air. When she reappeared, he plucked the suitcase from her grip and opened the apartment door for her.

But at the doorway, she hesitated. "Is it all right if I bring Arlo?"

He frowned. "Who's Arlo?"

"My kitten. He's kind of dependent on me, and if anyone tries to break in again...."

With a sigh, he jerked his chin at her. "Get the cat."

She found the fur ball under her bed and, amid his mewing protests, dragged him into her arms. Once there, the little beast quieted and settled in the cradle of her breasts. Lucky bastard.

Downstairs, Leo's car remained in the illegal parking zone, hazards blinking. He held open the passenger side door while Prue climbed gingerly into the cab and cuddled Arlo in her lap.

Sunrise still a couple of hours away, the city streets remained free of traffic and light rolled through the car's interior in a steady pattern as they passed under the streetlamps.

"Where are we going?"

At the lack of strength in her voice, a frown pulled at his features. "Someplace safe."

It wasn't an answer, but he wasn't yet prepared to commit to his plan. Not when he still had several hundred miles to come up with an alternative.

She laid her head on the headrest. "I've never been to the Caribbean." The tinge of humor in her voice did much to soothe the soreness in his chest.

"Did you happen to grab your passport on the way out?"

She shook her head. "I think it's expired anyway."

"It's fine. We don't need to leave the country." Yet.

"Hawaii?"

"No way are we getting on a plane." He glanced over his shoulder before easing the car into the other lane.

"Why not?"

"Makes it too easy to track our movements."

Her brow puckered. "Is that legal?"

"No."

A hiss of air escaped her, and he looked over to see her biting down on her bottom lip. She pushed out a long, steadying breath.

"We should get you to a hospital." He reached for his cell phone to look up the nearest location.

Her fingers brushed his hand. "Oh please no. We'd be there for hours. I'm fine. I just forgot and moved too fast."

He refused to relinquish his phone.

"If it's still bothering me when we get wherever we're going, I'll go. I promise."

He returned his hand to the steering wheel and immediately mourned the loss of her touch.

"So, you still haven't said where it is we're going."

Dread tasted bitter in his throat. "Michigan."

"What's in Michigan?"

"No bad guys."

"I'm going to hide out there? In Michigan?"

He shot her a sidelong look. "You sound skeptical."

"I am," she stated matter-of-factly. She turned her face to the window and gazed out at the scenery for a time. "I've never been to Michigan."

When he'd left his brother's place the week prior, he hadn't planned on returning so soon. As hard as it was to witness his brother's wedded bliss and impending fatherhood, the test that awaited Leo now would challenge everything in him.

"So no tropical island getaway, then, huh?"

Though she tried to inject her words with a lighthearted tint, he could hear the fear in the vulnerable catch of her voice and see it in her trembling hands. In her sky-blue eyes, he could all but touch it.

"Well," he said lightly, "it's an island, anyway."

Chapter Nine

The soft sway of the vehicle wrung the adrenaline from Prue's body. She wanted to know more about where Leo was taking her, and if he intended to stay there with her or not, but exhaustion dragged at her and she couldn't muster the wherewithal to question him further. Soon, she dropped into the shelter of sleep.

Sometime later, her attacker returned to haunt her dreams. His cold eyes ravaged her. The crushing weight of his body on hers revolted her.

She jolted from sleep, frightened and disoriented.

The first thing she saw was Leo, alert and focused on the road before them. Her panic eased immediately. As long as she gazed at him, the grip of fear around her heart and lungs steadily weakened. She studied his steady profile, and his hands on the steering wheel, sure and strong. The way the muscles in his forearms and biceps reacted with his movements set off a whisper of flutters in her stomach while the artistry of the small shamrock tattooed on the inside of his left wrist delivered a faint smile to her lips.

Watching him, her eyelids grew heavy. She dozed again, but restful sleep proved elusive. Every time she opened her eyes, Leo was there, calm and vigilant. Constant.

When she next awoke, they were parked in front of a gas station and bright sunlight blanketed the earth.

Leo wasn't in the driver seat beside her.

Her heart lurched, but before panic took hold, she spotted him through the car's windshield, leaning against the hood with his cell phone pressed to his ear.

When she climbed from the vehicle, the midday air was thick with heat and humidity. She lifted her arm to shield her eyes from the glaring sun as he disconnected his call.

His gaze swept over her. "How are you? You doing okay?"

"I'm okay." She leaned against the car beside him and tried to convince herself that the tenderness in his tone didn't mean anything.

He gestured with his phone. "I talked to your dad."

Surprise flew through her. "What did you say?"

"I told him that Owen asked me to get you out of town for a few days. I wanted him to know that you're with me now, and that you're safe."

Was she safe? She wanted to believe him, but the aching knot in the pit of her stomach doubted if she'd ever feel safe again.

"I should call my work," she said. "They're probably wondering where I am."

"I already called them."

"You called my work?" Sweet relief swooped through her. Then she stole a look at him. "What did you tell them?"

"I talked to... Amanda, is it?" He scratched his jaw, which had darkened with the shadow of fresh beard growth. "I told her you had a family emergency and you'd call her when you know more."

"Wow. You're a good liar."

An odd expression chased across his features, which he quickly concealed. "Can I get you anything from inside? You want something to eat?"

With the churning in her stomach, she didn't feel like eating. But when she considered that he'd go into the store without her and she'd be left outside, alone, a punch of anxiety slammed into her.

She berated herself for her ridiculousness even as she tripped forward. "I'll come with you."

Hauling open the car door, she reached for her purse on the floor but started when Arlo's tiny head peeked out from inside the roomy handbag. She snatched them both up and followed Leo into the store.

She trailed close behind him as he moved down one aisle, drawn to his solid strength as though she were a flimsy piece of scrap metal and he a potent magnet. He walked with a slight hitch in his gait and seeing it, she frowned. That night at the bar, she'd assumed the alcohol had caused his uneven stride. Maybe it was simply stiffness from the hours he'd spent sitting in the car, but the slight limp reminded her of the jagged scar on his hip.

Beneath the restroom sign, she hesitated.

Leo turned, a quizzical look lifting one eyebrow.

She pointed to the sign above his head. "I gotta pee."

A smile might have teased the corner of his mouth when she slipped past him and pushed open the door to the women's restroom, but it vanished so swiftly she couldn't be sure.

Aside from hurting, the wound in her side made her movements slow and awkward. She fumbled through, and when she reemerged, he was waiting for her.

She resisted the urge to nestle into his side, but stayed close as he navigated the aisles, accepting a bottle of water, a sandwich, and a protein bar when he handed them to her. Then he snagged a first-aid kit and a pack of batteries off the shelf and headed toward the checkout.

She dumped her purchases on the store counter and dug through her purse for her wallet, but when she slid her bank card from its slot, Leo's hand covered hers.

"I got it," he said easily, then passed a bill to the cashier.

Returning the card to its spot, she followed him outside and found a patch of grass behind the building for Arlo to explore and do his business. Back at the car, Leo helped her inside before walking around to the driver side door.

He wrestled the first-aid kit from the shopping bag and ripped into the plastic covering. Popping open the white case, he selected a small packet and tore it in two.

"Here, take these."

She held out her hand and he dropped two pills into her palm.

Then he offered her the sandwich. "Better try to eat something with them though."

"Why did you pay for my lunch?" Though the sandwich held little appeal, she took it from him.

"I don't want you using your cards."

"Too easy to track?"

He inclined his head.

"I'll pay you back," she muttered.

The pills abraded her throat when she swallowed them so she took a long drink from the water bottle. More water was needed as she forced down bites of dry bread and turkey. Soon, the pain in her side eased. She relaxed in her seat and watched the scenery change from populated urban cityscapes to the rolling hills of western Pennsylvania. When the hills flattened out into the rural farmlands of eastern Ohio, she began to doze.

When the car's lulling motion varied, she stirred from sleep. They'd exited the highway and Leo steered them into a hotel parking lot.

Rubbing her eyes, she straightened in her seat. "We're stopping?"

"I hope that's okay." He killed the engine and gave her a long, assessing look. "I need to make some more calls and grab a couple hours of sleep."

She lifted her shoulders. "I've never been on the run before. This is all new to me."

There it was again. The almost-smile.

He grabbed their bags from the back seat and she scooped her purse off the floor at her feet, which still sheltered a cowering Arlo. Sore from her injuries and stiff from lack of movement, she walked slowly. Leo shuffled along beside her, a deep scowl on his face.

While he disappeared indoors, she hung back to let Arlo down in a grassy speck of lawn. When Leo returned for them, she followed him inside, through the hotel lobby, and down a long corridor of doors to arrive at the last one on the right.

With a card key, he let them into the room, which had no view and only one bed, but was quiet and clean. After spending the previous thirteen hours in a car, her body begged to stretch out on the double bed.

But first, she needed a shower.

"Do you mind if I have a look at your cell phone?" Leo asked. "I want to make sure you don't have any apps running that can track your location, or anything else that might cause us problems we don't need."

She pulled the device from a side pocket on her purse and handed it over. "Do you mind if I shower?"

A flicker of something flitted across his features, but he shook his head and stared down at her phone. "Not at all."

She plucked her suitcase off the bed and retreated to the bathroom.

Not until she was in the shower and soaked through did she realize she'd handed her phone over to him without a moment's hesitation. Not one suspicious or cynical thought had entered her head before doing so, even though her entire life was on that phone. One app opened directly to her email account, which contained her credit card and banking statements, and access to all her research on Aron King.

And she'd just left Leo alone with the device. As though she trusted him completely. Implicitly.

Damn, she was bad at this.

With a defeated sigh, she shut her eyes and let the warm water pour over her.

But as soon as her eyes closed, memories of the assault sprang from the shadows in her mind to torment her. The terror hit her all at once. The utter helplessness she'd felt to realize she couldn't match his power, or his ruthlessness. The panic that'd gripped her when she stared into his cold, dead eyes. The devastating certainty that she wouldn't survive the attack.

Tears streamed down her cheeks and she swiped at them, but she couldn't stem the onslaught. Fear rose up to choke her and she slapped a hand over her mouth to muffle the wrenching sobs that racked her body.

Sinking to the tub floor, she pulled her knees to her chest and wept.

CƆ

He awoke with a start. That was how he always woke up, as if he hadn't meant to fall asleep and yanked himself awake, ready to fight.

At his side, the soft, delicate sounds of Prue's snoring

told him she slept.

Daylight persisted at the edges of the drawn curtains, and the clock on the nightstand informed him that he'd slept nearly an hour. He rubbed a hand over his face and braced himself for the next phase of their journey.

Unable to come up with a better strategy, he'd resigned himself to the course he'd chosen. Two weeks. That's all he could give her. He'd keep her hidden, but only until Owen returned. And not one day more.

While Prue showered he'd called the power company to have service switched on as soon as possible. Some instinct, or maybe it was just plain old-fashioned paranoia, told him not to stay in one place too long. They needed to keep moving, and if they were going to make it to their destination yet tonight, they needed to hit the road within the next hour.

Just then, movement at his elbow startled him, and he jolted. In turn, a gray puffball launched itself a foot into the air.

Leo stifled a curse and collapsed back in the bed as the cat landed gracefully in the covers. Prue's cat was charcoal gray, except for the splotches of white on all four of his paws and his tiny chest. He sidled closer and placed a white paw tentatively on Leo's rib cage. Then he looked at Leo, with only one eye.

The little guy was missing his right eye, which lay uselessly shut, the small slit nearly lost amidst gray fur. With one finger, Leo scratched him under the chin and the cat stretched into his touch. The soft hum of his purring motor revved.

Once satiated, Arlo curled up next to Prue and Leo climbed from the bed. He set the alarm on his cell phone to make sure they left on time, then headed into the bathroom for a quick shower.

Afterward, he pulled on a clean pair of shorts and used the towel to scrub the water from his wet hair.

When he returned to the main room, Prue still slept, so he retrieved the first-aid kit from the console and approached the bed. Her dark lashes lay on rounded cheeks flushed pink with sleep. A pang wrenched his insides when he noticed the shadow of a bruise forming on her cheekbone.

He trailed his fingertips over her skin, careful not touch the tender spot. She was warm, but not feverish.

His fingers lingered on her unbearably soft skin.

Dammit, but he should've been there for her. With a sharp bite of regret, he pulled his hand away and knelt on the floor beside her.

He lifted the hem of her shirt to reveal the site of her wound, then gently peeled back the bandage. A huff of breath he didn't know he'd been holding rushed from him. The cut looked good, clean and healthy. He placed a blob of antibiotic ointment on the gash and applied two butterfly bindings before covering the area with a larger bandage.

His work done, his gaze wandered over her body. Over the smooth skin of her abdomen to the dip of her waist. A deep, primitive sensation tugged at his groin. It'd been so long since he'd experienced it, he'd almost forgotten the feel of his own arousal.

Madness took hold and he flattened his palm over the rounded swell of her belly. The night he spent in her bed, had he taken the time to explore her body? To taste her skin? If he had, would another taste now return his memory to him?

He wanted to remember being with her. To recall the feel of losing himself in her warm, soft flesh. What sounds had she made when he'd entered her body? He'd been dead so long, he'd forgotten what it felt like to partake in life. Suddenly, he wanted to remember that, too.

He bent his head over her and searched out her scent. With a mere sliver of space between his face and her skin, he inhaled deeply. Then he pressed his lips to the unharmed flesh on her abdomen.

Her soft gasp reverberated through him. Without lifting his head, his eyes met hers over the plane of her stomach. A primitive, possessive need took control. His grip on her waist tightened and he rose up, ready to claim what belonged to him.

Then his gaze landed on the darkening shadow under her left eye.

He touched her cheek, beneath the budding bruise. "He hit you?"

She nodded, and her eyes clouded with The Fear. He recognized it instantly.

"What if he comes back?" Her throat worked when she swallowed. "What if he finds us?"

"I'll kill him."

His response didn't dampen the terror. Might've increased it, actually.

"But you won't be with me forever," she said softly.

His chest ached. "Prue, I know I let you down. I'm sorry."

Her brow crinkled with equal parts confusion and heartbreak. "You didn't let me down. You came even though I told you not to. You came when I didn't call you."

"You're not going to let that go, are you?"

A hint of a smile touched her lips. "No. I'll never forget what you did for me."

"I won't leave you again unless I know you're safe." Emotion thickened his voice. "I promise."

Oddly, that statement *did* dilute some of her trepidation. A soft hum of gratification ricocheted through him. More than anything, he wanted to banish that last shadow of fear from her eyes.

Of its own volition, his hand on her stomach rubbed in slow, soothing circles.

When her mouth formed a sexy little O of surprise and her breathing hitched higher, his hand stilled. Their gazes tangled.

Then he watched in horror as her hand slipped down her body, over her stomach, where her fingers snagged on the hem of her shirt. With an aching, sensual slowness, she inched the fabric upward.

She. Inched. The. Fabric. Upward.

The punch of lust that struck him was so strong it knocked the air from his lungs. He wanted to fuck her. The wanting was visceral. All-consuming. God, but he wanted to know what it was like to bury his cock in her wet heat.

She was the first thing he wanted from this world in so fucking long that his body began to tremble with the pain of holding himself back. His breath shuddered through him.

"Leo?" Her eyes pleaded with him, and fear shifted to something more like hope.

Correction: Arousal.

He gulped.

She's vulnerable, he reminded himself. He'd be the worst kind of monster to take advantage of her.

Then she touched his hand, and her eyes turned soft and imploring.

Owen was going to kill him.

For crimes already committed, the devilish voice whispered inside him. What was another wrongdoing added to the first? Especially if he restricted it to a lesser crime?

After a gluttonous feast, what was one more little taste?

He dipped his head, and his mouth brushed the skin near her naval. His fingertips touched where his mouth had been and a breathy moan escaped her.

Standing at the precipice, his gaze sought hers once

more. He didn't know what he sought from her. Affirmation? Permission? Some sign that what he was about to do wasn't the stupidest, most self-destructive thing he could possibly choose to do just then?

But when he peered into her face, he didn't see any of those things. He glimpsed instead the shimmer of fear, and he knew what he would do.

While he couldn't fight her battle with The Fear for her, he could help her deceive it, at least for a time. He could stoke her pleasure to the point where no room remained for fear.

If he hadn't already made his decision, Prue, in her maddening sweetness, would have pushed him to it when she reached for him with one small, trembling hand and slipped her fingers through his hair. Tenderly, she fondled the dark locks. Then, with gentle but firm pressure, she nudged his head back down to her body.

Something inside him, way deep down in the darkest corner of his soul that'd been despaired without light for all the ages, sparked.

His hand slipped to the delicate skin of her inner thighs.

She appeared mildly alarmed, and confused, but as his hand inched higher, she slowly parted her legs. He hooked a finger beneath the crotch of her panties and pulled the fabric aside.

With the tip of his index finger, he traced the opening of her sex. She gasped, and he experienced a flash of primitive pleasure. Taking his time, he toyed with her curls until they grew moist. Then he pushed a finger inside her warm hollow. He stroked and teased, and soon her arousal made his fingers slippery.

Her soft moans pulled him under and the last clear thought he remembered having was that, while he was sorry for betraying his friend again, he wouldn't regret giving Prue anything, everything, she asked of him.

She wiggled her hips, chasing the pleasure he gave her, and her breathing came in sharp, quick pants. Her eagerness devastated his control. Settling more deeply between her thighs, he dipped his head and took a long, slow lick of her.

She tasted of heat and honey. He lapped up her flavor while her soft cries tore him apart.

He was unraveling.

Then she lifted her hips, and something uncoiled inside him, near his black center. Something soft and wild where it should be wound tight and hard, and safe.

Before he was ready for her pleasure to end, her body clenched around his fingers. He slid a second finger inside her and stroked in counterpoint to his tongue.

She cried out with her release, the sound throaty and uninhibited. In that moment of her unguarded ecstasy and ultimate trust, she was a goddess. Her cheeks flushed pink and the lips of her plump mouth parted with her spent arousal. When she blinked open her eyes and offered him a shy smile, the blue irises shone like buffed jewels.

For his part, he'd never been so hard.

With a piercing wail, the alarm he'd set on his cell phone shattered the quiet in the room.

He left the cradle of her thighs, pushed to his feet, and silenced his phone.

His voice rasped harshly when he said, "We better get going."

Chapter Ten

In the confines of the car, her awareness of him took on a new potency. His scent assailed her. His hands on the steering wheel whipped the odd little flutters in her stomach into a whirlwind.

The dark scowl on his face hurt her heart.

As they hit the highway and headed north, leaving the small Ohio town behind, his dark mood seemed to grow darker. Indeed, the farther north they drove, the more she sensed him pulling away. He was turning inward, away from her, and after their intimate interaction in the hotel room, she didn't understand why.

They passed over the border into Michigan, and for the next three hours, they drove north and west. Cities faded into rural landscapes and the sun dipped low in the sky. By the time the sun slipped behind the earth, cloaking them in a blanket of darkness, the change in him from the hot, attentive man in the hotel room to the cold, withdrawn one behind the wheel of the car was complete.

She stared out her window and watched small snippets of scenery pass by in the car's headlights. Nearly four hours after leaving the hotel, Leo steered the car from the highway. They journeyed along a rural road, deeper into the night. After a time, they passed through the smallest downtown she'd ever seen and then, at the end of a prototypical main street, turned the corner.

A large ship loomed before them. Leo maneuvered into a small gravel parking lot and joined a line of cars waiting before the boat.

"What is this?"

"A car ferry. It's a short ride out to the island."

"Wait, you were serious about the island?"

The ship's hull opened and the first car inched forward, disappearing inside the boat's dark underbelly.

"I was serious." He inched the car forward.

Curiosity overcame her. "What's the name of it? How big is it?"

His scowl deepened. "Thief Island, and it's small, but the population swells in the summer now that the damned tourists have discovered it."

He eased the vehicle up a gently sloping ramp and slipped inside the steel ferry. They filed with the other cars into parking spots, and then he switched off the car's engine.

"We've got to go above deck for the trip over."

She tucked Arlo inside her purse and followed Leo across the dim lower deck to a poorly lit stairwell. They climbed the steep steps and emerged on the boat deck, where a gusty wind lifted off the lake to whip at her hair and the hem of her top.

Passengers gathered at the deck rails and she squeezed into an open spot while Leo hung back. Far below, water lapped at the boat's sturdy sides while in the far distance, a few lonesome lights twinkled in the dark.

A low rumble soon sounded, and beneath her feet, the floor began to vibrate as the ferry's engines powered on. Minutes later, the boat began to pull away from the dock. She crept slowly through the water until they reached the edge of the harbor. Then, with the blast of a horn, the engines thundered and the boat set out into the night.

She had no sense where they were headed. No light guided them. No moon or stars dotted the sky. Behind them, land fell away.

Amazed by it all, she turned to Leo with a smile.

But he wasn't there.

A brief search of the small crowd tracked him to a white bench a few feet away where he sat with his elbows on his knees, staring down at the concrete flooring.

Feeling the loss of him acutely, she turned toward the darkness. She stared into the black void, which her fears rushed forward to fill until, in the distance, lights winked to life. The railing pressed into her chest when she leaned against it, desperate to catch more glimpses of lights.

Soon, the shadowy form of a landmass rising from the sea took shape in the night sky.

When the boat eased into a harbor much like the one they'd departed, she followed Leo back downstairs into the ship's hull. In the car once more, he steered them onto land, but while most of the other cars leaving the small parking lot exited to the right, he went left.

They drove for a time along another dark, rural road. Towering trees sprang up around them and the darkness became stifling, suffocating. The smooth stretch of road became rough and bumpy, and she grabbed onto the handle above her door.

Deep in the woods, he turned up a rocky path and when they came to a seemingly random spot, he slowed the car to a stop. He switched off the engine and she peered through the window into utter blackness. Instinctively, she shrank back in her seat.

When he shoved open his car door and the overhead light winked on, she could make out the form of a small building in the woods. A house maybe? Was it his home?

He stepped into the abyss and slammed the door shut behind him. A moment later, the car's interior light faded and she was alone in the darkness. With extreme reluctance, she left the safety of the vehicle and stumbled along an uneven path after him.

Using the light from his cell phone, Leo fumbled with the door while she shot quick glances into the black night surrounding them. A shiver passed through her. Then he pushed open the door, and with a bracing breath, she followed him inside.

He moved into the home's interior and in the next moment the pitiful light from his phone vanished.

Total blackness engulfed her, and panic closed around her throat. Noises sounded in the dark as he rummaged through a closet. More rustling sounds reached her as he fiddled with something. Then suddenly, the dim glow of bobbling light splashed across the room and she could breathe again.

Flashlight in hand, he crossed to her and handed her a second flashlight, which she quickly flipped on. Pointing the light around, she discovered they were in the living room of a small house. A bungalow.

At the back of the house stood a wall of glass, through which the black void of nothingness loomed while the other end housed a tiny kitchen. The white paint on the walls must've been put there several decades prior, and the dark wood ceiling, although vaulted, did little to add a sense of space to the room.

Two darkened doorways sat on either side of the living room, and Leo shined his light in the direction of one of them.

"You can sleep in there." His eyes wouldn't meet hers. "There are blankets in the closet."

But his fortress wall suffered a crack when he thrust a hand through his hair and she saw that it trembled. Then he turned abruptly and stalked to the doorway opposite hers.

The beam of his flashlight flickered off the walls in the dark room before he lifted a foot and kicked the door shut with an unqualified bang.

℃

His heart raced, pounding with painful thumps against his breastbone. In the past twenty-four hours, he'd slept little, and fatigue clawed at him. Drained and exposed, the burden of standing in this house again hit him all at once.

He sat on the edge of the bed and dropped his head in his hands. What the hell had he been thinking, coming here?

That someone was trying to kill Prue.

Even after avoiding this place for the past four years, it was harder than he expected to come back to it. So much harder.

Everything inside him snarled and twisted with grotesque anguish. He couldn't make sense of it, except that it all pointed back to one thing. It always came back to this. They were gone, and he was the reason why.

Under heavy assault, he wanted to fall back, to retreat from the threat of his own mind, but there was nowhere to run. Nor was there a drop of alcohol within reach to dull his awareness of the mutilation taking place inside him.

He collapsed back on the bed, defeated, and closed his

eyes, trying not to see her face.

It was no use. He was dead to rights. There was no hope, and running only ensured he'd die tired.

God damn, but it was so fucked-up. He was so fucked-up.

His last thought before exhaustion claimed him was how desperately he needed a drink.

The lack of alcohol proved to be the fatal blow. Sober and weakened, he couldn't fight off the memories, which slipped past his defenses at the first chance.

CB

Four years earlier

The moment he saw her, he knew he would marry her. One day.

Her hair and makeup were overdone, the way all TV reporters overdid it, but her smile and her excitement for her first real assignment with a major TV network were genuine. She lit up the room full of seasoned military men. The brightest star in the sky, she sprinkled her stardust on everyone she encountered.

Leo was just one of the grunts assigned to the crew's security detail as they arrived in Syria to cover the escalating civil war. She paid little attention to the six-man team, preferring the company of her coworkers instead.

Until their second day in the city center, when a fight erupted between some locals. Leo moved to shield her from the shoving while Owen and Claymore broke up the brawl and dispersed the gathering crowd.

Leo eased away from her. "You okay?"

She snuck a glance at him from beneath the sweep of her eyelashes and nodded.

Later that night, she approached him while he ate dinner alone at the hotel.

She slipped into a chair across from him and regarded him with huge round eyes. "I wanted to thank you for today."

He finished chewing and swallowed. "Just doing my job."

She fiddled with a corner of the tablecloth. "How long have you been a security guard?"

"You're my first."

She managed to blush and frown at the same time.

He didn't bother to hide his grin. "Don't worry. It's not my first rodeo, only my first private security gig."

"It's my first international reporting gig." Her brilliant smile appeared then. "I guess we'll be virgins together."

Oorah.

"I guess we will," he said.

☙

Prue wasn't tired.

And she was seriously creeped out.

She refused to switch off her flashlight, and directed its beam around the small bedroom. Light touched every surface and pushed into every corner until she felt certain no bugs or critters occupied the space with her.

The strange, rickety old house made weird sounds, not at all like the creaks and groans made by the historic house she lived in in Boston. Noises outside kept her on edge, the worst offender a sustained, low-level rumbling. It wasn't a roar, or a hum, but a growl that never stopped. The leaves rustled in the trees as though they, too, were agitated by the monster grumbling in the dark.

Along with a thick layer of dust, her bedroom boasted the same washed-out white paint as the living room. It, too, featured one wall made almost entirely of glass and beyond the fragile barrier, the black abyss loomed.

Turning her back to the disturbing void, the opposite wall contained built-in bookshelves, which sat empty. A row of boxes lined the floor in front of them.

She plucked her cell phone from the pocket of her purse and thumbed through her apps. After her attempt to log in to her email failed, she searched for a Wi-Fi connection.

There was none.

If he didn't have Wi-Fi, maybe he had a cable connection? Curious, she poked her head through a crack in her bedroom door and shot her flashlight's beam around the main room for signs of the hookup. But she spotted no wires or evidence of any internet connection at all. In fact, she found no signs of any technological device whatsoever. There was no TV. No laptop or PC. No stereo, or radio, or tablet, or mp3 player. Nothing.

Indeed, she would be surprised if the home had been upgraded from candle to electric light. What was the point?

With a sigh, she dropped her phone on the bed. Then she went over to one of the boxes and lifted the dust-covered lid.

It was stuffed full of books. Tilting her head, she read their spines.

Books on military history and weaponry abounded. With a flip of her wrist, she flicked up the lid on the next box, and the next. All full of books, on every topic from world history and philosophy, to political theory and psychology. One entire box was crammed with classic fiction novels.

In all, there were hundreds of books.

Sitting in boxes.

Were they Leo's books? Had he moved in recently? Maybe the home was a fixer-upper that he hadn't yet fixed up?

Selecting one of the novels, she settled on the bed and flipped it open.

After she'd been reading for a while, a sound pulled her from the story. She grew still, listening.

There it was again.

Arlo hopped down off the bed and slipped through the small crack of the door's opening. Prue tossed the book aside and pushed up off the bed to scurry after him.

By the time she caught up to Arlo, he sat in front of the closed door Leo had disappeared behind. He peered up at her and meowed.

She inched closer but drew up at the harsh sound of Leo's voice. She leaned forward until her ear almost touched the door, trying to make out his words, but the words coming from him were mumbled and jumbled together.

Was he on the phone? Or was he dreaming? She recalled the night he'd slept in her bed in Boston. Was he having another nightmare?

Reaching out, she twisted the knob on his bedroom door.

Arlo bounded into the room and onto the bed. Prue hesitated, but when Leo whimpered, the sound filled with agony, she sidled closer. In sleep, he grimaced as though he were in pain, and his hair appeared damp with sweat.

Her heart throbbed. She wanted to help him but knew of no way to do so. When he flinched in his sleep, she went around the bed and drew back the covers. Climbing beneath the sheets, she snuggled close to him and laid a hand on his spine.

When he didn't wake or startle, she rubbed his back in light, slow circles. Motor humming, Arlo settled into the crook of Leo's knees.

She didn't speak or whisper reassurances. Considering

she knew nothing of what troubled him, she didn't have any reassurances to give anyway.

Eventually he calmed and his breathing evened out. The tension left his body.

But Prue didn't leave his bed.

Chapter Eleven

He slipped his arm around her waist and pulled her tight against his chest. She was soft and warm, and he buried his face in her hair. A lazy contentment seeped into his bones.

Then something cold touched his bare arm, and he lifted his head to find a one-eyed cat staring at him.

Leo reared back with the violent blow of reality that crashed into him. His head snapped around and he gaped at his arm hooked around Prue's waist, his hand inches from the heavy underside of one breast. The sound of her soft, peaceful snores, now almost familiar to him, ripped a hole wide open inside him.

He'd imagined this very moment a million times and more. Waking up here, in this house, but with a different woman tucked inside his arms.

He jerked his arm away as though he'd been scalded and stumbled from the bed, tripping when his feet tangled in the sheets.

Prue stirred and stretched. With her knuckles, she rubbed her eyes, then blinked several times into the bright sunlight. Her dark hair adorably disheveled, a soft smile curved her mouth when she looked up at him.

Grief and fear and anger, so much fucking anger, pounded into him, like the unrelenting breakers rolling off the lake outside the patio doors. He was defenseless against the torrent of emotion.

It wasn't Prue's fault, he knew, but in that moment he didn't particularly care if his aim wasn't true. Everything had been taken from him, and his helpless fury couldn't be contained any longer.

He loomed over her. "What the hell are you doing in my bed?"

But rather than answer, her gaze snapped to the glass doors behind him and she bolted upright as a cry of surprise tore from her. Throwing back the covers, she shot from the bed and over to the patio doors where she fumbled with the lock before bursting out into the warm morning sunshine.

At the edge of the patio, her toes sank into soft sand and she gazed at the clear blue expanse of Lake Michigan stretching beyond the horizon. She made a slow turn that took in the exterior of the small cottage and her pretty face filled with wonder.

The air wheezed from him, as though he'd been punched in the gut. Once, he'd hoped to behold that exact expression on Lauren's face the first time she saw the house he'd bought for her.

Prue's laughter bubbled up. "It's a paradise." She gaped at the lake another moment, then stepped back inside and blasted him with her bright smile. "This place is incredible. Is it yours?"

Her words struck him like a knife lodging in his sternum. It wasn't supposed to be his house. It should've been hers. Theirs.

With an agonizing wrench, he twisted away and stalked from the bedroom.

She pursued him. "How long have you lived here? Did you grow up on this island? Is the weather always so perfect?"

Every one of her questions landed as a brutal stab on his scarred heart, and he struggled to gain ground against the assault.

"Why didn't you tell me to bring my bathing suit?" Her light, lyrical laugh twisted the knife in his chest.

It should have been Lauren standing in his living room, overcome with joy and excitement and asking him a thousand questions.

Fresh blood flowing from his wounded heart, he snapped, "Who gives a fuck about the house? We need to figure out how to fix this mess you're in and get you out of my house. Out of my life."

She sucked in a sharp breath, and the hurt his words caused her showed plainly on her face. Unable to bear the sight of her pain, he shoved to his feet and turned his back to her.

Regret churned and an ancient resentment flowed through his veins when he dragged open the refrigerator door. Seeing it was empty, he slammed it shut again.

He was so tired. Tired of the bitterness. Tired of the war. He opened the cupboard doors, one after the other, hoping he'd stashed a bottle of liquor somewhere. Despite the fact that he knew he wouldn't find any alcohol, at the last vacant cupboard, he kicked the door shut with a frustrated growl. He never left a drop in any bottle. If he had it, he drank it.

Flattening his palms on the island countertop, he dropped his head while his untethered emotions wrought havoc in him. When he looked up, she had retreated to the other side of the room. Her arms folded protectively over her abdomen, she stared out at the lake.

"What do you eat?" he asked.

She half turned and eyed him with suspicion. "What?"

He scooped his car keys off the counter. "I need to pick up some supplies in town. What can I get you?"

Her arms dropped heavily to her sides as she twisted to face him fully. "You're leaving?"

The vulnerable catch in her voice gutted him. "I won't be gone long."

He had to get away, even if only for a few minutes. Enough time to catch his breath. The desperate need to escape the torture of being back here even outweighed the pain of watching The Fear take hold in her eyes.

"I'll search the property before I go, but we're completely alone out here. You're safe." *For now.*

The struggle to believe him played out on her features. Finally, with a firm nod, she accepted his assurances. She chose to trust him.

Something soft and slippery niggled in the center of his chest, but he ignored it.

"When I get back, we'll sit down and figure this thing out, okay?"

She pulled her hair over one shoulder and worked it into a braid. "Okay."

"What can I get you?"

Her small hand flitted through the air. "I'm not picky."

The wide neckline of her T-shirt slipped to expose her bare shoulder, and the surge of longing that curled through him nearly dropped him to his knees. He yearned to go to her, to touch his mouth to her skin and take away the hurt he'd inflicted.

Instead, he fled.

⁋

She gaped at the door he'd disappeared behind with a resounding bang. Again.

What the hell had just happened? He was upset, yet again, but why now?

Her heart sick, she looked out at the stunning view. The lake stretched endlessly toward the horizon and sunlight danced on the water's surface, twinkling like cut diamonds among the waves.

Turning back, she considered Leo's home. White paint on the walls appeared faded from the abundance of sunlight pouring in through the patio doors, and the wide-plank hardwood floors were worn smooth, probably from years of being buffed by the beach sands carried indoors.

She couldn't believe this was the same dark, creepy house she'd experienced the night before. In the light of day, the home's charm was evident. No longer did it seem old and unloved. It was quaint and enchanting, as much a product of the sea as the rocks being eternally pulverized to sand mere steps outside its doors. Both yielding and stubborn.

And she'd fallen instantly, completely in love with it.

She frowned. How could he own a place like this and be so unhappy? *Well, get over it.*

"Jerk."

But the truth was, after his self-imposed isolation the night before, the outburst stunned her. And, well, it stung.

She tried to will her hurt into anger, but it was no use. Not after she'd glimpsed that hitch of heartbreak in his eyes and detected the teardrop of pain in his voice. What was that? Did it have to do with her? What was the name he'd said, that first night?

Rose.

She recalled the way he'd begged her stay with him

and how he had clutched her hand, as though he'd die if she let go. With the memory, whatever emotional hurt she might've harbored evaporated like a puff of campfire smoke.

A weary sigh pulled from her. She'd been so caught up in the miracle of this magical place, and the magnificence of his bare chest, lean and muscular with the dark markings of a tattoo flaring across his right pec and shoulder, that she hadn't heeded the grumpy scowl marring his well-formed features.

She didn't heed it, though she should have.

She really, really should have.

Sliding open the glass door and screen, she stepped onto the wooden deck nestled between the house and those first soft ripples of soft sandy beach. Once again, the sound of that rumbling monster from the previous night greeted her, having been revealed as nothing more than the low, steady roar of the lake's waves crashing ashore.

Beneath her feet, the sun-warmed wood was hot, and she scrambled to a shaded area beneath the pergola perched outside the slider door off her bedroom. Overgrown with greenery, the nook felt like a hidden sanctuary, complete with a tattered hammock hanging between two pillars. Discovering a bravery she didn't know she possessed, she climbed in.

She didn't risk her good fortune by swinging, but lounged and listened to the waves dipping and diving toward shore while she absorbed her surroundings. Three sets of glass patio doors ran the length of the house, and weathered cedar shingles covered the remainder of the home's exterior. The lush greenery sheltering her from the sun was mostly weeds, but in a broken pot in the corner of the patio, a half-dead non-weed plant gasped for life.

Bounding out of the hammock, she rescued the plant

from its spot in the sweltering sun, and then she found a place for it in a patch of rich soil tucked alongside the northern ridge of the decking. Likely, the plant was too far gone, but she had to try to save it.

A search of the kitchen turned up no utensils that might be used to shovel a hole, so she dug with her fingers and set the plant into the nourishing ground. Then she packed dirt around its base and, using a shard of the broken pot, fetched water from the kitchen sink. Lost in her work, the nervous tension and angst that'd been spiraling through her began to loosen their hold on her.

Her task complete, she reclaimed her place in the hammock, sinking carefully down into the cloth sling. More tension eased from her as a contented sigh. If she owned a place like this, she'd never want to leave. Except maybe to get some Wi-Fi.

As the sun marched toward its apex, the day's heat grew steadily warmer. Despite the shade, moisture glistened on her skin and when she could no longer stop herself, she clambered clumsily to her feet and set off for the water.

The sand burned beneath her bare feet and she scurried along, hustling into the cool and refreshing waves at the water's edge. She waded in up to her knees and bent over to drop her hands beneath the surface. She rolled the hem of her baggy cotton shorts up as high as they'd go and roamed farther out to meet the surf rolling in.

The water grabbed hold of the angst that had been roiling inside her the past day, months, years, and drew the turmoil from her body, dragging it all out to sea with its retreat. Her heart lightened. She lifted her face to the sun and closed her eyes.

Just then, a large wave rolled in and knocked into her with such force that she fell back into the water.

Her indignation quickly washed away with the receding water. She clawed her way to her feet and plunged headlong into the waves as they rushed forward. The cut in her side ached, but the pain didn't bother her enough to stop her fun. Not until she was soaked through and out of breath did she turn back and trudge toward shore.

But she stumbled to find Leo standing on the beach, the fierce scowl still marring his striking features. As she emerged from the water, her drenched clothing clung to her and his gaze swept like seeking hands over her body. With the heat in his eyes, a delicious tension coiled low in her belly. Immediately her mind returned to that hotel room in Ohio.

She'd never spent much time thinking about her figure, or her sexuality, but it was suddenly all she could think about. The sweet tease of his fingers had sparked something too long ignored inside her, and the way he looked at her now, his hot gaze caressing the contours of her body, making sure to touch every dip and swell, set her heart racing.

Emboldened, she didn't try to hide herself, though she knew the thin fabric of her wet sleep clothes must reveal... everything. When he finally dragged his eyes from her breasts to her face, she offered him a knowing smile.

His frown deepened. "You should come inside."

Then he twisted around and strode toward the house, but not before his bold gaze took one more long, hungry appraisal of her body.

A thrill chased through her, touching all the places that had longed for him all the years he was away.

Aron had never looked at her like that, and when he'd told her she was too puny and inexperienced for his tastes, the hit had left a permanent mark on her self-esteem. She hadn't felt sexy since. Instead, she'd been frozen for six aching years, convinced she wasn't attractive to men. All these years, she'd believed she wasn't sexy or sexual.

But Leo's hot gazes, along with the incredible thing he'd done in that hotel room, had set afloat a balloon of hope inside her. Maybe she wasn't deficient. Maybe, with a little study and practice, she could overcome her inadequacies.

A light wind kissed her wet skin and hair as she followed him up the gently sloping beach. She let her fingers graze the tops of the beach grasses as she passed by. In both directions, sandy beach extended as far as she could see, and not a single other house or building was visible anywhere along the shoreline. Behind Leo's home, the large trees she remembered from the drive in swayed in the breeze. It was as though the house was tucked away among the treetops, in a secret world known only to them.

He slid open the patio door and waited for her to enter the house before him. When she slipped past him, she risked a glance at his face. His green eyes captured hers and she froze, halted by the force of his compelling gaze.

Searching his eyes, she spotted a touch of the panic she'd witnessed in the parking lot at her work the day that car had backfired.

She swallowed convulsively. "It isn't safe to go out there?"

His gaze dropped to her mouth, setting off a flurry of flutters in her stomach.

"It's okay," he said. "But I should be with you next time."

He shut the screen with a soft thump that caused her to jump. Then he crossed to the kitchen where a mountain of grocery totes lay in a haphazard heap on the island countertop.

Had he dropped everything to go in search of her?

His head bent, he rummaged through a few of the sacks before plucking a beach towel from one of them. He tossed it to her, then continued to unpack the shopping bag.

She used the towel to wring the moisture from her hair as she approached the kitchen island. When she'd finished, she draped the towel over a barstool and turned to the nearest tote. She kept a close watch on Leo, trying to assess his mood as she set a container of strawberries, a melon, and a head of lettuce next to a bag of apples on the counter.

From the next bag, she retrieved a loaf of bread, hamburger buns, three bags of varying kinds of chips, and a variety pack of cheese slices while across the island, he produced boxes of cereal, several packs of meat, and tubs of peanut butter, yogurt, and ice cream.

"Wow," she said. "This is a lot of food."

Sheepishly, he shoved a hand through his hair. "I didn't know what you like."

She stared down at the array of frozen vegetables and dinner entrees he'd unpacked. He didn't know what she liked, so he'd bought a little bit of everything. For her.

A silly bubble of pleasure expanded in her chest. "I like all of this. Thank you."

For emphasis, her stomach released a noisy growl.

Hearing it, he offered her a box of cereal. She bit down on her bottom lip and she took the box from him. While she worked at opening it, he pulled a package of plastic bowls from one of the other bags and ripped into them. He handed her a bowl before rifling through another bag to produce a gallon of milk.

But he didn't slide the carton across the counter to her.

Instead, he pinned her with a solemn look. "I'm sorry."

"For what?" she asked cautiously.

"I shouldn't have brought you here." The torment behind his eyes landed like a blow on her heart. "I thought I could handle it, but... I misjudged."

Questions piled in her throat. *Why is it hard for you to be here? Don't you like it? Is that why you haven't moved in? Are you going to move in? When? Is it because of Rose? Why don't you ever smile?*

But instinct, and the dark shadows stalking his expression, warned her against asking even one of them.

"You don't have internet," she said instead.

He pushed the gallon of milk over to her.

"I never got around to setting it up." A frown touching his features, he flicked the switch next to the kitchen sink and the overhead light flickered on. "At least we have power now."

She poured cereal into her plastic bowl and passed him the box as he handed her a plastic spoon.

"Who's Paul Cook?"

At his unexpected question, the milk nearly slipped from her grasp. She returned the jug to the counter, but hesitated to answer. What if she told him what she was investigating and, like Faith, he thought she sounded crazy?

"Prue, I want to help you, but I can't if you don't tell me everything."

"Everything, huh? That could take a while."

Nothing. Not even a lip twitch.

He dropped his head and stared down at the counter. "I'm sorry, but you can't stay here. I can't stay here."

Her heart plummeted like a stone sinking to the sea floor. He was going to make her leave?

His head came up and he regarded her with grave eyes. "The sooner we figure out who's trying to hurt you, the sooner we can put an end to all this and go back to our normal lives."

Suddenly, her heart raced for a reason other than the

way Leo was looking at her. Well, the reason was still because of the way he looked at her, but he no longer appeared to want to gobble her up, as he had in the hotel room and on the beach only moments ago. Now, he considered her with a calculating gleam.

"He's a journalist," she said. "A few months ago, he wrote a profile piece about a foreign politician. After I read it, I wanted to know more, so I contacted him to ask some questions. One thing lead to another and pretty soon, I was down the rabbit hole with him, digging into this hopelessly corrupt politician–who is also a drug trafficker, it turns out–and the ginormous network of mobsters and criminals he does business with. I haven't sorted it all out yet, but–"

She stopped speaking when he straightened away from the counter and stumbled back. His hand rubbed the center of his chest.

"What is it?" she asked. "What's wrong?"

"You're a journalist?"

At the look of horror contorting his features, she laughed. "No. Not at all. I stumbled onto something that confused me, and bothered me, and I had no idea what to do." She lifted one shoulder. "But I'm a researcher, so I started researching."

"Is that what you do at the Institute? Research?"

She shook her head. "No. I make coffee. Answer phones. That sort of thing."

"I don't get it."

"The research is something I used to do. A long time ago." She snuck a sideways glance at him. "I studied physics and chemistry at MIT."

After a lengthy pause in which he studied her intently, he asked, "Why did you give it up?"

Emotion squeezed her throat and she knew she'd never be able to tell him the truth of it. But he waited, expectant, and she had to tell him something. So she settled on an age-old wound that, although it'd left an ugly scar, didn't hurt quite so much anymore.

"My parents didn't approve."

His eyebrows inched upward. "How the hell could anyone's parents disapprove of an education at one of the best universities in the world?"

"They didn't mind that so much, but as a kid, I asked a lot of questions. They're... kind of religious, and I think they thought I was... I don't know, attacking their beliefs or something."

The hard set of his features seemed to soften. "You were a heretic, were ya?"

Her jaw dropped slightly ajar. Was that...? Was he... being funny? On his cheeks, two dents flirted with forming, and if his smile ever broke loose, she suspected she might glimpse two of the sexiest dimples imaginable.

She attempted a smile of her own, but in the end, it faltered. "I guess so. All I wanted to do was study. To figure it all out, you know? To find the truth."

His eyes probed her face, reaching into her thoughts. "The truth, with a capital *T*?"

Her cheeks warmed. "It was dumb, I know."

"It's not dumb," he said softly. "You wanted to find God."

Startled, her head snapped up. "How did you know that?"

His expression, open briefly, suddenly shuddered. "It's something I used to do. A long time ago." He lobbed her own words back at her.

"Why did you give it up?" she volleyed.

A light glittered in his eyes for the briefest of moments before it sputtered out. "I got the answers to my questions."

His tone held a lightness she'd never heard from him before, but it didn't quite manage to disguise the sadness in his eyes.

With a sudden shift in his posture, he cleared his throat. "So we have bots, an overseas crime ring, and a real-life deranged criminal. What am I missing?"

"I don't understand it fully myself yet." With Faith's pessimism still fresh in her mind, she opted for a different entry point into the tale. "When I started researching this corrupt politician, I discovered he was involved in several business ventures with lots of prominent people, but something wasn't adding up."

At first, she picked her words carefully, delving into the web of connections she'd uncovered, but soon her caution caused her to trip over names and provide stilted explanations. Once, she stopped midsentence and changed track entirely.

He frowned.

She talked faster, and when she realized in her effort to talk around one thing–or person–she was rambling, she pulled her bottom lip between her teeth to cut off the painful chatter.

The pucker between Leo's eyebrows deepened. "It's a money laundering scheme?"

"Yes." She pushed out a sharp breath. "A massive one."

"Makes sense," he said. "What good does smuggling all those drugs do you if you can't spend your ill-gotten gains?"

"Exactly. Oh, and guns. Drugs and guns."

"Of course." His mouth pulled into a thin line. "Is our corrupt politician behind all of this criminal activity?"

"Well, it's a massive group of bad guys," she hedged. "But... one other name does keep popping up."

"What name is that?"

Beneath the sweep of her eyelashes, she risked a glance at him. "Aron King."

Leo went still. "The security contractor?"

She nodded.

"He's not an enemy you want to have." His eyes

narrowed as he watched her reaction to his words. "But you already knew that."

Her gaze slipped away. "Given his history, it's a safe assumption."

"You know him, then?"

When her hands started to shake, she buried them in her lap. "Not anymore."

She should have told Leo the truth about her history with Aron, and everything that followed, but she couldn't find her voice. Would he view things differently if he knew she and Aron had dated? If you could call the scam that was their relationship dating. Or would he, like Faith, assume a host of corrupt motivations drove her pursuit of the truth?

Rather than poke at her evasive answer as she expected him to, he granted her a reprieve, asking instead, "Your plan is to take them all down?"

Though it sounded ridiculous to hear it spoken out loud, she didn't deny it. "I thought if I could expose one or two of the key players, the entire network might be jeopardized, and possibly collapse."

He leaned against the counter and folded his arms over his chest. Head down, he studied the floor tiles. "We'll need help."

Her eyes flew to his face. "You would help me?"

"I would, and I am."

"But what if I'm wrong?" She couldn't keep out the hint of challenge that crept into her voice. "What if I'm just making it all up?"

"Are you making it all up?"

"No, but you have to admit, a gang of politicians and mobsters and mercenaries all working together to create so much chaos sounds a little crazy." She watched him closely. "Like a ridiculous conspiracy theory."

A touch of exasperation crept into his expression. "Someone tried to kill you."

Her stomach wrenched. No longer hungry, she pushed her bowl away.

"Look, you don't sound crazy," he said softly. "What you're talking about sounds like a fairly typical organized crime ring, to be honest. And besides, all investigations into conspiracy start with a conspiracy theory, don't they? There should be records—banking transactions, shell company filings, lawsuits—to help separate fact from fiction. Do you have anything like that?"

"So that guy—" Her words rasped with the memory of her attacker's hand closed around her throat. "The one that broke into my apartment. I don't think he was trying to kill me."

His sharp focus remained tight on her face.

"I think he was looking for something," she said. "And I just got in the way."

"Looking for something, such as...?"

"My laptop."

"Why? What's on your laptop?"

"Records. Lots and lots of records."

Chapter Twelve

While Prue slipped off the barstool and scurried to retrieve her laptop, Leo frowned after her. She'd been cautious in her responses to him. He'd listened to the particular way she'd parsed her words, seeking clues about what she wasn't telling him, and why, but he hadn't been able to identify the reason for her secrecy.

Though if he were a betting man, and he was, he'd wager his life savings that it had something to do with Aron King.

Founder and former owner of the private security firm where Leo once worked, Aron was widely regarded as power hungry and ruthless. Leo had met the man on a number of occasions and basically agreed with that assessment. He was also a conceited prick.

After Leo had left the company, King drew it into scandal by authorizing a chemical weapons strike in a small village in Iraq. Use of the chemicals, strictly prohibited by international law, led to a trial and conviction of the men on the ground carrying out the attack. The controversy had forced King to leave Blackstone, and last Leo had heard, he'd started a new company training police and military in developing countries.

Prue returned to the kitchen and settled at the island while he worked on putting away the remaining items from the grocery bags.

"What do you want to see first?" Even as she brimmed with eagerness, her eyes held a guarded tint.

This was important to her. Sensing that it somehow mattered to her what he would say and do in the next moments, he went around to stand beside her and peered down at the computer screen. She'd opened a folder, and a long list of documents ran the length of the display.

"Wow, is this all related to our bad guys?"

"Pretty much." Her smile had a way of taking him by surprise, every time. "It's amazing what you can find on the internet."

"Give me the quick overview so I can get a sense of how deep this thing goes, and how much you've already got on them."

She lifted a pair of eyeglasses off her lap and slipped them on her face. They were dark-rimmed and oversized, and transformed her from sultry and sophisticated to cute and vulnerable so fast that a bemused smile touched his lips.

Over the next hour, they sifted through her files.

Her mind was sharp, hyperfocused, and almost turned him on more than her sweet moans in the hotel room, or her delectable curves, visible through her sodden clothing as she emerged from the lake. Almost.

When he leaned close to read the file she'd opened, her breathing hitched a little higher and at the sound, a tug of primal satisfaction pulled at his groin. But she was talking, and saying important and interesting things, so he slammed the door on his wayward thoughts and forced his attention back to her words.

Problem was, she wore short shorts, and her long legs kept distracting him. Soon his mind was jumbled with four years' worth of sexual fantasies and foreign-sounding names and meaningless corporate acronyms.

"This is incredible." *You're incredible, and so fucking hot.* "I can't believe you found all this."

Pink rushed into her cheeks, his compliment visibly flustering her. He marveled at the way the pink color set off the bright blue of her eyes and at the attractiveness of her neat features. Cute no longer captured her appeal. There was too much passion and knowing behind her eyes.

As he stared down into her face, the now-familiar current arced between them, drawing them closer. His head dipped, and her lips parted. If he could have but one taste of her–

What the hell was he doing? He had no idea what was happening to him. He'd gone years without wanting a particular woman. Not one. And now suddenly he wanted her. Owen's baby sister.

At once, they pulled apart. Hands on his head, he retreated to the living room while she slipped off her stool and rounded the island.

From the one remaining grocery tote, she removed a bottle of shampoo and a can opener. Then a frown touched the corners of her delectable mouth as she peered down into the bag. Reaching inside, she pulled out the scrap of black fabric and held it up, trying to make out its shape.

Her gasp of excitement filled the room, and his heart.

"Is this for me?" She clutched the women's swimsuit protectively to her chest.

"Oh, uh, yeah." He rubbed the back of his neck. "It's the only one they had."

Was he blushing? What the actual fuck?

He twisted away and, bending at the waist, shoved the coffee table across the room and against the wall.

She started toward the bedroom. "Do you want to go for a swim?"

He groaned at the images that sprang to mind. Of Prue, naked.

Under him.

Moaning.

Coming.

"No," he snapped. "Not yet."

She tripped to a stop and her gaze slid between him and the coffee table, and back again. "What are you doing?"

"Not me, you."

Her eyebrows shot up. "Me? What am I doing?"

"You're going to learn how to fight."

Her eyes bulged, and then she was backing away. "Oh no, I don't think–"

He snatched her hand before she could escape.

She dug in her heels. "But you said I have to tell you everything. I was only getting started."

"We'll finish that later."

"You know, my side is hurting a little." She stopped abruptly, wincing. "I wouldn't want to re-injure it."

He pinned her with a look. "You didn't seem all that concerned about it when you were frolicking in the lake."

"Frolicking?"

"Prue, you were attacked." His words, meant to puncture her reluctance, twisted around and pierced him instead. Bile rose in his throat. "The bastard might've killed you."

She groaned. "But... I'm a pacifist," she said weakly.

"He could've killed Arlo."

A flash of terror chased across her features.

He turned smug. "I knew it."

"You knew what?"

"I've met a bleeding-heart pacifist or two in my time, and you're all alike."

"Is that so?" she asked wryly.

"Yes, that's so. You're all sweet and tree hugging... until you're not."

A frown puckering her brow, she launched one last counterstrike. "I'm not very athletic. Reading is really more my thing...."

No matter how much she protested, he wouldn't relent. Not as long as the fear still shimmered in her eyes.

Gently, he traced the bruise on her cheek with his knuckle. "No more fear, Prue." He let his hand fall away. "It's time to get pissed."

Her shoulders sagged with her defeat.

Apart from his noble intentions, when he'd suggested they train, he'd needed something uncomplicated to divert his thoughts away from all the things his body wanted to do to hers. From the prettiness of her face and the lushness of her shape. From the memory of her moans of pleasure in that hotel room.

His plan backfired. Miserably.

When she mimicked his movements, thrusting her palm into the center of his chest as he instructed, her breasts jiggled tantalizingly and his concentration snapped. When he asked her to turn around so he could approach her from behind, as a perp might, the dry pair of shorts she'd changed into molded to her tight, round ass with a perfection that momentarily mesmerized him. When she arched her back to take hold of his wrist as he coached her to do, her tank top strained across her chest and the straps of her bra peeked out to tease him with fantasies of ripping the holster away from her body to set her glorious tits free.

Indeed, rather than taking his mind off her body, their workout placed her hot little form front and center. Now he had a raging hard-on and a headache forming between his brows from the lack of blood feeding his brain.

"No, like this." He demonstrated the move again, careful to show her with slow, deliberate movements. The heel of his palm brushed the swells of her cleavage and he nearly groaned with thwarted desire.

She imitated his movements again, but his gaze remained riveted to her chest when her hand crashed into his sternum with enough force to knock him back a step.

"Sorry." She rushed forward. "Sorry, I didn't mean to do that."

"Nice shot. Do it again."

She squared up and repeated the strike.

"Perfect," he said, rubbing the spot.

Her smile flashed quick and bright, and suddenly his chest ached for a different reason than the blow she'd landed there. They'd been practicing for more than an hour, and if the delectable jiggling had been too much, he didn't stand a chance against her smiles.

"I wish I'd known that move a couple of days ago," she said.

His gut churned. "You think it might've helped?"

A self-deprecating smirk twisted her mouth. "Would've been better than what I did."

"What do you mean?" Lord help him, he didn't want to know what she meant.

"I ran." Her soft chuckle lacked the richness of her true laugh. "And when he caught me, I tried to punch him. You know, they make it look so easy in the movies, but holy crap, did that hurt. I thought I broke my hand. After that, I just tried to kick him in the crotch."

With a scowl, he reached for her hand.

She pulled it away. "Oh, it's fine now."

He refused to relinquish his hold and dragged her small hand beneath his critical gaze. Cradling her fingers in his palm, he fingered her knuckles and the other fine bones of her hand, pressing and wiggling as he checked for mobility and pain.

"It only hurt for a few hours," she muttered.

Satisfied she hadn't broken any bones, he released her. "When overpowered, you should always try to evade your opponent. There's no shame in that. But if that doesn't work, kicking a man in the nuts is a solid strategy."

A pure smile worked its way to her lips. "Is that the next lesson?"

His throat tight, he snagged his water bottle off the coffee table. "I think that's enough for today."

"Oh okay." She relaxed her stance.

"It's a good start." He held her bottle out to her. "You're a natural."

She took the water and untwisted the cap. "It's physics. Like you said."

"Pretty sure I never said that."

It was incredible the way her smile lit up her entire face. "You did. When you were talking about how it doesn't matter if I'm not the biggest or the strongest, or even the fastest. That if I understand the ways the human body can and cannot bend, and exploit those weaknesses, I stand a good chance in any fight."

If he wasn't so jaded, he might've believed her smile existed for him and him alone.

"See? Physics." She took a long, slow drink of water. "Oh, and you were right about the anger. That changes everything."

Damn, she was beautiful. Dewy moisture clung to her skin and when she reached up to release the heavy mass of her hair, which she'd piled on top of her head, the dark tresses shimmied around her shoulders.

"Mind if I go for a swim?" she asked.

Hell yes, he minded. As it was, he was hanging by a thread, calling on every ounce of willpower he possessed to keep himself from snatching her to him and sucking on her plump, pouty mouth.

With his grunt, she disappeared behind her bedroom door, reappearing a few agonizing moments later. At the sight of her, a growl of frustrated desire ripped through him.

The swimsuit was not particularly revealing, in a throwback style of the forties' pin-up, but she had enough flesh to give the vintage bombshells serious competition. The fabric cradled her breasts, which were round and full, before dipping halfway to her naval, and her hips flared generously from the inward curve of her small waist.

As they walked toward the lake, he tried to focus on the landscape, but the hypnotic sway of her hips pulled him in a little deeper with each rhythmic undulation until he was drowning in lust and carnal need.

While she ventured into the water, he reclined on the beach, willing his erection away. He'd almost managed the feat—until she emerged from the lake to walk back to him. Her dark hair slicked black with wet and water sluiced off her body. Through the bathing suit, her nipples, pebbled with chill, beckoned.

Oorah.

With a sharp motion, he sat. He'd never experienced anything like this. The want was all-consuming. Maddening. How was it he'd gone so long without hunger only to be suddenly, desperately ravenous?

She bent to pluck her beach towel off the warm sand, and her breasts swayed with her movements.

A pucker appeared on her forehead. "Are you okay?"

Unable to drag his gaze from her lush curves, he

swallowed with a painful gulp. "I'm starving."

She moaned. "Me, too. Want me to fix us something to eat?"

He nodded, or maybe he was only tracking the soft jiggle of her amazing breasts too rigorously. "I think there's a grill in the garage."

"Seriously?" She waved a hand at him. "Go. Get it. I'll get the food."

He didn't own much stuff, mostly just some books and the things leftover after Shea cleaned out their dad's place, so he located the grill easily enough. He found a wooden table he didn't recall ever seeing before and pulled down a couple of beach chairs he spotted hanging from the rafters.

On the patio, she set out a fat cluster of grapes and a bag of potato chips while he lit the grill and tossed on the chicken breasts and veggies she'd prepared. Then he sank into the empty beach chair beside her just as she lifted a grape to her mouth. With a flash of small, even white teeth her plump lips wrapped around the juicy fruit.

Hell, even the way she ate grapes made him hard. Her lips parted for the next bite and his mind rocketed back to that hotel room, where she lay before him, her legs spread and her soft moans of pleasure raining down on his head. If she fellated one more grape, he was going to explode.

Her eyes touched his face, and when she saw his expression, she froze. On a quick intake of breath, her blue eyes darkened.

With arousal.

He wanted to fuck her so badly his cock ached. If only he could recall the night he'd spent in her bed, maybe he could go on with his life, content with the memories. As it was, he had nothing but a hunger so fierce it drove his every thought and feeling.

He wanted to stop wanting her.

But more than that, he wanted to never stop. The wanting was delicious and maddening. Deliciously maddening.

Despite the clash of opposing wants—and because, apparently, he'd lost his ever-loving mind—he drew closer to her. Just one touch, he told himself, though he understood, even in that moment of crazed lust, that she'd be harder to quit than any bottle of liquor he'd ever done battle with.

At the last possible moment, he wrenched himself away from her, collapsing back in his chair. A hard scowl on his face, he stared out over the lake. How in the hell was going to get through the next few days without touching her? Without kissing her, on her mouth and everywhere else also. Again.

He needed a distraction. A better distraction than teaching her to fight, or anything that involved her wearing that swimsuit, or those short shorts, or the nerdy eyeglasses.

Maybe he needed some time alone. That was it, he needed some time alone with the mobsters and the bad guys trying to kill her.

Turning his head, he asked, "Can I see your laptop?"

Throughout the remainder of that day, Leo hunched over her laptop, combing through the morass of records and notes she'd gathered the past few months. Mostly he kept to himself, stopping only once in a while to ask her questions about the disparate puzzle pieces in his careful, comprehensive effort to make order out of the chaos.

At some point, a warm sensation began to spread through her. It felt a little like love, but she knew that wasn't it. That'd be silly. It was just so nice to have someone to share her work with. Someone in addition to Paul Cook, who she'd interacted with only through emails and social media. Someone real. And not just anyone, but Leo.

Her Leo.

Her heart full, she became obsessed with watching him. The way he moved around the house and patio as he studied her work, smooth and light-footed. His muscular chest and flat stomach, left exposed by the unbuttoned shirt that he wore with his shorts. Even his bare feet were sexy. And his dimples. Were they real? She hadn't imagined them, had she? What could she do to draw them out? Was there anything that might him smile?

The warm day ebbed into a balmy dusk, and as the sun barreled toward the horizon, she dropped into a beach chair in the sand to watch its final descent. Far off shore, the boats floating by throughout the day moored to take in the view as well.

As Leo planted a chair in the sand beside her, she looked up. He cradled Arlo in the crook of his elbow and his shirttail flapped in the gentle breeze, permitting her more mouthwatering glimpses of his bare torso.

She dug her toes beneath the top layer of warm sand and tried to focus on the glowing orange ball's plunge into the lake, or the waves crashing to shore with steady, unrelenting resolve. But the slow, seductive slide of Leo's hand over Arlo's fur kept drawing her gaze back to it. Little flutters tickled in her stomach at the way the muscles of his forearms rippled with his movements.

From her chair, she could hear Arlo's satisfied purr, and she experienced a stab of jealousy.

Leo stroked the cat as he stared into the setting sun. In profile, his jaw was set and she experienced a pang of sorrow to see that a touch of troubled pain had returned to his features. She knew nothing about what haunted him, and as night settled around them, her fears also wanted to creep in with the shadows.

Her mind wanted to engage with them, calling up memories of her assault. Tossing out hand grenades to detonate inside her head. Had her attacker followed them to the island? Did he lurk in the shadows, waiting for the cover of darkness to strike? Would she be able to sleep? In her own bed, alone? She shivered and tried to push away the brain bombs.

Since the attack, the only time she'd managed to truly leave behind her terror was in the hotel room. When she was with Leo.

Sneaking a glance at him, she chewed on her bottom lip. His gaze had dropped to a spot in the sand a few feet in front of him, and for a moment, he appeared as lost and broken as he had that night at the bar.

The darkness in him scared her more than the memories.

She wished she knew a way to help him, as he had helped her. Coming for her when she didn't call him, whisking her away to this secret haven, what he did for her in the hotel room....

A thought struck. What if she could help him, by doing for him what he'd done for her? Okay, maybe not *that.* She'd never pleased a man that way before. But she was willing to try, and she was a fast learner. Everyone said so.

Her heart kicked in her chest, but this time, a different kind of fear stirred inside her.

Leo's skillful fingers teased Arlo's tiny kitten ears, and the cat's one eye fell shut with his shameless hedonism.

She swallowed the ball of nervousness rising in her throat. "You sure know how to satisfy a pussy."

Leo choked on the swig of water he'd just swallowed.

"Cat," she finished. "Pussy cat."

Shock receded, and then he smiled.

Oh. My. God.

He.

Smiled.

And oh, what a smile it was. Beautiful and breathtaking. With a flash of white teeth, two deep dents appeared on his cheeks, partially hidden in his dark scruff. A smile worth the wait and the work to draw it out.

But as soon as his lips curled up, they mashed back down into their customary pouty frown.

When he looked at her, his eyes burned with a fire rivaling the sun's magnificent dying blaze. "I haven't satisfied a pussy in a long time."

"Don't you remember the hotel room?"

He bent his head, slicing her with a look. "That never should have happened."

The stern disavowal tore at her heart. "Wow, you sure have a way with the ladies, you know that?"

"I'm not saying I regret it, or that I didn't enjoy every fucking second of it, but it was a mistake."

"I don't regret it either, nor do I think it was a mistake." She risked a glance at him out of the corner of her eye. "I'd do it again."

With a grunt, he rocked forward, visibly impacted by her words. "Don't say that."

"Why not?" Her voice carried a plaintive tone that she hated but couldn't restrain, not with the flood of heartbreak and humiliation that swamped her.

He'd said he enjoyed it, hadn't he? But then why wouldn't he want to do it again? Was it because of her? Had she done something wrong? Something he didn't like? Maybe Aron had been right all those years ago. She was too inexperienced. Too unappetizing to men. Just plain bad at sex.

He lurched to his feet and she stood as he paced to the slider door. Whipping open the screen, he set Arlo carefully inside the house, then slammed the screen shut and stalked back across the patio to her.

But when he reached her, he didn't stop. He kept right on coming, pushing his hands beneath her hair and cradling her head in his palms.

"Because if you keep talking about having sex, I'm not going to be able to stop myself from doing this."

Then he kissed her. His mouth came down on hers hard, but quickly gentled. With tender nips and slow, lingering caresses, he explored her. Somewhere along the way, the last sliver of sun slipped behind the earth, and she couldn't care less to have missed the miracle.

When the tip of his tongue stole inside her mouth, a tingling sensation shot from her heart to the spot low in her belly.

"This," he murmured against her mouth. "I remember this."

"Hmmm?"

He pulled her bottom lip between his teeth. "Your taste." He moved to nuzzle the sensitive skin below her ear. "Your smell. I remember it so clearly. And yet... I can't remember *you*. The feel of being inside you." His thumb scraped across her bottom lip. "Prue, I have to have you again."

A dizzying rush swooped through her and she gripped his wrists to steady herself.

"If I could take back our night together, I would."

She crash landed from her blissful flight with a dull thud.

His thumbs traced soft circles on the side of her face. "You deserve so much better than sex with a drunk asshole who can't remember anything the next morning."

"Uh, Leo—"

"And your brother deserves a better friend than me." The green in his eyes glittered like gemstones. "If I had it to do all over again, I'd make it right, but it's too late for that now."

She wanted to pretend she didn't hear him.

Instead, she squeezed her eyes shut and pressed her forehead to the center of his chest.

He dropped a kiss on the top of her head and her heart wrenched. Once she told him the truth, would he still want to be with her? Or was her appeal wrapped up in the mystery of his lost memories? If he had it to do all over again, would he choose her?

"Leo?" She spoke into his chest, which muffled her voice. "There's something I have to tell you."

Chapter Thirteen

A rush of words poured from her. "There's a reason you don't remember that night. I mean, a reason that's different than the one you're thinking."

Over his eyebrow, a pucker appeared.

Her nerves stretched tight and she licked her suddenly dry lips. "It's because... well... we didn't... do it."

His jaw slackened with his astonishment. "I don't understand."

"We tried. You wanted to," she was quick to add. "But you passed out before we got to the really good stuff."

For several irregular heartbeats, he appeared frozen in time. She braced for his anger, or his accusations, but he didn't lash out at her. Instead, he dropped his head and dragged a hand over his face. His shoulders shook, and she realized he was laughing.

At the deep, husky sound, her heart took flight.

His arms came around her. "Oh, Prue, I'm so sorry."

He pulled back and peered down into her face. "I've been such a jackass to you. Can you ever forgive me?"

His words pulled a frown from her. "You apologize to me too much."

"Do you want me to stop apologizing?" A faint ring of amusement crept into his tone.

She pondered his question. "Only apologize for the things you could have prevented. You couldn't have not passed out any more than you could have stopped that man from breaking into my apartment."

His arms fell to his sides and he backed away from her. "I've been careless with you, Prue, and for that I am sorry. If I was that drunk, I can only imagine how badly I behaved." He pinned her with a sober look. "If I hurt you–"

Shaking her head, she cut him off. "It wasn't like that."

He slipped his hands into the pocket of his shorts and regarded her with a skeptical scowl.

"You didn't, Leo. Please believe me." That he even considered he might be capable of such a thing caused her heart to ache. "That night, you were sweet to me. So much so, you were the first guy I'd wanted to be with in a really long time."

His scowl deepened. "How long?"

"Six years." Furious heat burned her cheeks. "I hadn't been with anyone in six years. I hadn't *wanted* to be with anyone. Until that night."

His Adam's apple bobbed. "What were you waiting for?"

"For you." She lifted one shoulder. "Someone worth the trouble."

"You were wrong about me." His voice sounded unsteady.

"I wasn't wrong."

A hint of exasperation touched his features. "I disappointed you."

"No, you didn't."

When Aron King seduced and betrayed her, she'd been disappointed. Devastated in fact, and disheartened that she'd been too naïve to sense the threat. Now, six years after Aron shattered her world, she was no longer that naïve girl. Except when it came to sex. In that regard, she was as naïve as ever, and painfully gun-shy to boot.

But Leo could change all that.

"Okay, maybe I was a little disappointed," she teased.

Despite her attempt at levity, his gaze slid away.

She inched closer to him. "But the disappointment I felt was from not being with you."

Without lifting his head, his eyes found her face.

"You were right when you said I deserved better that night." The intensity of his fierce gaze set off a trembling in her hands and voice. "The way I see it, you owe me."

His head came up slowly. "What do you think I owe you?"

"S-sex."

He concealed his reaction to her words behind an inscrutable mask. "We settled my debt in that hotel room."

With the sharp bite of her mortification, heat rushed into her face.

"So the way I see it," he began in a low voice, "it's you who owes me."

Her eyes flew to his face. The cruel glint she expected to see in his eyes was absent and her breath caught at the heat and hunger that shimmered among the green-and-gold jewel tones.

The soles of his flip-flops scraped on the wood deck when he drew a step nearer to her, and then stopped. "But as much as I want to call up your debt, Prue, I can't do it. Your brother would never approve of me with you."

She blinked away a sudden surge of irrational tears, drawing instead upon her anger, the way Leo had taught her. "Owen has no say in who I do, or do not, sleep with. Zero. You forget, I left that bar knowing exactly who you were, and that Owen might one day find out about it. I thought you knew who I was, too, and that you felt the same."

"I don't need Owen's permission to be with you, but he's my friend and I prefer to keep it that way."

His unaffected calm only added to her upset. "He wouldn't stop being your friend if you and I were... together."

"He would if he thought I was going to hurt you."

"So don't hurt me."

"I can't help it. It's what I do." It was a statement, and she detected nothing casual or callous in his tone.

Her mind reeled with confusion. "You hurt people?"

"I don't set out to do it, and I don't want to hurt anyone, especially not you." Regret clung to him. "I just don't know how not to. It's who I am. I break things. People. I break people."

"Why do you do that?" she asked softly.

The shadow of a humorless smile touched his lips. "Well, if I knew the answer to that, I'd stop doing it, wouldn't I? Until I figure it out, I won't get involved with anyone."

"Get involved? You mean get into a relationship?"

"Definitely no relationships. It's a lot harder to break someone if you're not in a relationship with them."

"You don't have to be in a relationship to have sex, do you?"

A light in his eyes sparked. "It's often better that way, but no, it isn't required."

"So you won't do relationships, but–theoretically speaking, of course–you would consider an arrangement?"

The spark flared. "Depends on the arrangement."

Her courage faltered, but her heart refused to retreat.

"How about a hookup? A short-term, sex-focused nonrelationship. Isn't that what everyone our age is doing?"

A full-fledged green-gold firestorm raged in his eyes now. "Not many women are okay with that."

If given a choice, Prue doubted many women would turn Leo down. Her expression must've said as much.

"They might agree to the terms and say they don't want a relationship either," he said. "But it never works out that way in the end."

"You're just too irresistible, I suppose."

His mouth tipped with a sensual curve. "When two people are compatible, it's natural to want more."

Her heart, already pounding, tripped over in her chest. "Natural for them, but not for you?"

"No. Not for me." The invisible shield went up, shutting her out before she got even a fraction of an inch closer.

With a frown, she contemplated him. She didn't like the barrier. She liked the real Leo and wanted to talk more to that guy.

"So that's it? We're never going to happen, and I'm stuck with these impure thoughts I keep having about you?"

His eyebrows climbed. "Impure thoughts?"

Just like that, her Leo was back.

She bit back a smug smile. "I grew up in a religious household, so it was probably inevitable."

"I'd like to hear more about these thoughts. Are you naked in them?"

"Do you want me to be naked?"

He made a sound in his throat, sort of like a whimper of pain.

With it, a memory bubbled up from the night they met at the hotel bar. When he kissed her, he'd murmured something about it being so long since he'd seen her.

Well, she'd thought he was talking about her, but as she found out the next morning, he hadn't remembered her at all. So what had his words meant? Could it be, like her, he hadn't been with anyone else in too long?

"Uh, Leo, how long has it been since you've, you know, been with someone?"

He hardly hesitated. "Four years."

"Four years?" She couldn't swallow her gasp of surprise. "Sorry, but wow. Four years? That's like twenty in guy years, isn't it?"

"At least," he said dryly.

The mellow breeze pushed a strand of hair across her forehead, and when she reached up to tuck it behind her ear, her hand still shook. She'd never propositioned a man before, and never in all her years of secretly being in love with Leo did she imagine she'd ever actually get a chance to be with him.

She pushed aside the tempest of emotion swirling inside her. There was no need for sentimentality. This was a puzzle she could solve with logic.

"You know, I think we're each exactly what the other needs."

He watched her with hooded eyes.

She plunged ahead with her thesis. "You break people, right? Well, I can't be broken, because I'd never be so stupid as to put my trust in you in the first place—no offense. And even if we did fall in love, we have no chance at a future because Owen would never approve and I know you're not going to pick me over him, which means I can't even be hurt or mad at you for not choosing me because I knew upfront that'd be the outcome." With a sharp intake of air, she stated her summary conclusion. "So there's no risk for either of us. We can just have sex without worrying about all that other stuff."

A grimace bracketed his eyes and mouth. "I don't like several things you said just now."

She bristled. "Tell me, where am I wrong?"

"For one, and this is just for starters, if you don't trust me, why would you want to sleep with me?

She waved a hand dismissively. "Oh, it's not you personally. I don't trust men. Any man. Not completely. At least not one who wants to sleep with me."

"Any particular reason why?"

"*Lots* of reasons why."

"Care to share any?"

"No, I'm good."

His eyes narrowed to slits. "Why not?"

"Probably the same reason you don't want to talk about your allergy to relationships."

His mouth thinned with his displeasure, but he didn't argue.

Fearing a stalemate, she offered a compromise. "Maybe we could agree not to talk about the past?"

"Deal."

With his quick agreement, she frowned, suddenly beset by curiosity. Why was he so eager to bury the past?

But before she postulated a working theory, he launched his next line of questioning.

"Why are you so certain you'd come out on the losing end of any choice I might make between you and your brother?"

"I grew up surrounded by military men," she said. "I'm fully aware loyalty to the brotherhood is stronger than anything else."

"The 'brotherhood' is strong enough that choices like the one you're describing don't have to be made."

"You think Owen wouldn't mind?"

Leo recoiled at the mere suggestion. "Hell yes, he'd mind. But the choice I'd be given is to have my balls cut off and either fed to his dog or tossed in the lake. My balls, my choice. See? Brothers."

"The male species is far more complicated than I

realized," she said dryly. "Nonetheless, it's a moot point because Owen will never find out about us. I'm not going to tell him, and as part of the terms of our arrangement, I'll swear you to secrecy, too. Problem. Solved."

"There is no such thing as sex without the other stuff."

Her shoulders sagged. "There isn't?"

"Prue, you have had sex before, haven't you?"

Okay, screw logic.

"Leo, look. I like you. And I really liked what we did in that hotel room." Her heart throbbed in her ears. "I promise I won't fall in love with you, or try to extort a marriage proposal out of you, or whatever else it is that you're so afraid of happening–"

"I am not afraid."

"If you say so."

"I do."

"I won't make you own up to your hang-ups–that's between you and your conscience. But as long as we're stuck on this island together, why shouldn't we enjoy each other's company?"

"You sure you didn't study to be a lawyer? A prosecutor, maybe?"

His nearness overwhelmed her senses. "We can help each other."

"I don't need help." A muscle ticked along his jawline.

"You do. You're a man in his prime who hasn't had sex in four years."

"I don't like the turn this conversation has taken."

"If you want to stop talking, that's fine by me. We could go inside and...." She tilted her face up to his.

He didn't budge a centimeter. "We're not done here yet."

She bit back a groan of frustration. "What's left to talk about?"

"You haven't told me how I would be helping you."

"I've got hang-ups, too. You'd be helping me get over

them."

"What hang-ups?"

She eased back. "Yeah, I'm not going to tell you that."

One of his eyebrows inched upward. "What if it's one of my conditions?"

"Not admissible. Hang-ups fall under the no talking about the past clause."

With a smooth, nearly imperceptible movement, he closed the space between them. "Overruled."

She swallowed convulsively. "M-my issues are really none of your business."

His mouth near her ear, his voice dropped into that husky register. "If we're sleeping together, they sure the hell are."

"I don't need help either." With his scent tormenting her senses, she failed to filter her words before they fell out her mouth. "All I need is sex. A lot of sex. All the various kinds of sex."

He closed his eyes and a hiss of air wheezed from him. "So, me personally, you have no use for. You just want to use my body?"

"Yes," she breathed. "Just your body."

"Sounds kinky," he rasped.

"Is it?" She turned her head infinitesimally, bringing her mouth a whisper from his. "I was hoping we could try some kinky stuff."

"Jesus Christ, Prue." His hands stroked up her arms.

"And all the normal stuff, too. Any and all of the stuff, I want to do it. With you."

A painful sob sounded in his throat when he pressed his forehead to hers.

She trailed her fingertips down the side of his face. "Are you okay?"

"Just tell me one thing," he said. "How am I supposed to help you with your hang-ups if I don't even know what they are?"

"You being you is all the help I need."

His grip tightened around her arms. "I don't understand you."

"No one does." A tiny pang struck her heart with that truth. "It isn't necessary for a nonrelationship, is it?"

"No. I don't know." He shook his head. "I'm sorry, the blood left my head hours ago." Then he set her away from him. "Can you explain one more time what it is you want from me?"

Nervously, she licked her lips. "I want to have sex. Sex that is... that isn't...." She ducked her chin. "I want to be with someone I know isn't going to try to hurt me afterward."

"Hurt you?" He angled his body closer, as though to protect her from some immediate threat. "Who? How?"

"It's nothing. Really." Her stomach in knots, she pressed her fist to her abdomen. "I only mean that... I want to enjoy sex. That's it. Just pure physical pleasure."

"You don't enjoy sex?" At the tenderness in his voice, her heart lurched.

"I...." Her mouth moved but no words came out.

Gently, he brushed that wayward strand of hair off her face.

She lifted her shoulders and then dropped them heavily. "I don't know if I enjoy it. It's been six years and I don't... remember... much that was good about it."

His expression twisted with pain.

"It's not as bad as it sounds." She was making a mess of this, she knew, and frustration tinted her words. "Everyone else seems to like it a lot, you know? I mean, it's, like, a really big deal, and I want to know what they know. I want to know what it's like when it's good. At the hotel, I think I started to understand, but it was over so quickly that I'm not sure, and I want to do it again. A lot. With you."

He fell quiet, and the moment stretched out. The

crippling insecurity had begun to take hold when he leaned closer. With his nearness, her heart tripped over in her chest.

"I don't want to hurt you," he said thickly.

"You can't." A smile found its way to her lips. "But if it makes you feel better, we'll use a safe word."

His brows slammed together. "What now?"

"You know, like they do in the sex clubs. A safe word, like banana or Oklahoma."

His rusty laugh carried on the night air. "Holy shit, this is the most fucked-up conversation I've ever had sober."

Her laughter mingled with his. "Have I managed to convince you yet?"

"I don't know what's happening. I just keep hearing the word 'sex' and everything else is a drone."

"Okay, then hear this: Leo, I want you. For sex, not marriage. Maybe friendship, but that's probably a slippery slope. When this is over, we'll go our separate ways, as if we never met. What do you think?"

He snagged the zipper of her sweatshirt and tugged her across the last whisper of distance between them. "I think I'm in trouble."

Shock crashed into her with the force of a tidal wave. "Really?"

One hand slipped around her waist while the other stole beneath her hair to grasp her nape. "I want you, too, Prue. More than I've wanted anything in a very long time."

His words, words she'd fantasized about hearing but never believed this man might actually utter to her, made her head spin.

He took one small, tender nip at her mouth, then another. "I can't wait to finally feel you naked under me. Tomorrow can't get here soon enough."

The sensual haze his kisses stirred up evaporated. "Tomorrow?"

"I don't have any condoms. The island's only store is closed for the night by now. The gas station, too." He removed his hand from the tangle of her hair.

She snagged his wrist to stop his retreat.

He stilled, but he didn't return his mouth to hers.

While she adored him for his thoughtfulness, now that she knew his sexual history, and he hers, were such precautions necessary?

A sudden stab of awkwardness struck her. "Neither one of us have been with anyone else in years."

"I know, and I'm not worried about that," he said softly. "But there are other reasons we need to be careful."

"I'm on the pill." At his confused scowl, she rushed to explain. "I've been on it for years. Not for birth control, but for medical reasons."

His warm palm cupped the side of her face. "Are you okay?"

When his thumb stroked across her cheek, she turned into his touch. She nodded.

A long, slow breath rattled through him, and then he pressed two fingers to her throat, stroking the rapid throb of her pulse. Her heart slung itself painfully against her breastbone, and as he brought his head down, her chest rose and fell with her rapid breathing.

His lips brushed over hers with feathery strokes before deepening into soothing nibbles. She mimicked his movements, and a dizzying rush swooped through her with the first tentative taste of him. She took another nip, and another, and even took a tiny lick inside his mouth.

With a growl of surrender, he consumed her. His mouth and hands were everywhere all at once, shoving her tank top up and over her breasts and tugging on her bra. One breast popped free, and he sucked the sensitive bud into his hot mouth. She arched into his touch.

Beneath the wildness, he caressed her with gentle hands and kissed her with a tenderness that clogged the back of her throat even as it stoked the arousal building between her legs.

He backed her to the patio door and fumbled with the latch until it gave way. They tripped into her bedroom as they clawed at each other's clothing with breathless urgency. They were both naked when they tumbled onto the bed.

His body covered hers, and every one of her nerve endings relished the weight and feel of him on top of her, skin to skin from their shoulders to their toes. His mouth dragged down the side of her neck. His hard thigh nudged between her legs, brushing against her, and suddenly she realized she had no idea what to do.

Uncertainty swamped her.

Sensing it, he lifted his head and peered down into her face.

Propped on his elbows, his fingers lightly traced her features. "You're worried. Why?"

"I don't know what to do." With the confession, heat rushed over her chest and face.

His mouth curved into a soft smile. "You don't have to do anything except enjoy yourself. That's our deal."

His fingertips trailed lightly over one of her breasts, and a wave of erotic tingles rippled through her.

"Will you tell me if I do something w-wrong?" she asked.

Then she gasped with pleasure when his fingers danced across her stomach and pushed through her curls.

"Believe me when I say that isn't possible. Everything you do makes me hard."

His inquisitive fingers slipped to the spot of her most aroused flesh. With the first stroke, a moan vibrated in the back of her throat. As he did in the hotel, he fondled her until her body made his fingers slick with moisture. He rubbed in slow, erotic circles, occasionally dipping his fingertips into her entrance. A wild, reckless arousal built inside her and just as the sensations threatened to overcome her, he pulled his hand away.

Rising to his knees, he raked his bold gaze over her naked body. At the unmistakable appreciation on his face, a thrill chased through her. His hard shaft pressed against the flat plane of his abdomen, and she marveled at it. At him. All of him. He was beautiful. Long and lean, with rounded pecs and a ripple of muscle visible over his stomach. Her lips parted as her eyes explored him. Even his hips were sexy, the bones forming a V.

Then her gaze landed on the angry welt on his left hip.

Her heart snagged. In the bed, she pushed upright and tucked her heels under her. As she traced the path of the old wound with her fingers, she looked up at him.

His eyes blazed in his shadowed face.

Slowly, she leaned close and touched her lips to the scar.

He sucked in a hiss of air and his hard shaft jerked, brushing against her hair.

"What happened?" Sorrow softened her voice.

His throat moved with his hard swallow. "Shark bite."

She wasn't sure if he joked, but saw no hints of humor in his expression. Only a stormy hunger.

His hands slipped into her hair and he tilted her face up for his kiss. Then he lifted her bottom and pressed her back to the mattress with his body. She parted her legs for him, and he settled between her thighs. His hardness nudged at her core, but he didn't plunge or force his way inside.

Poised at her entrance, he stopped.

"Prue." His husky whisper was thick with want and need. "It's been so long, I can't go slow. I'm sorry."

The head of his shaft pushed a fraction inside her.

Despite his warning, he didn't shove deep and instead waited for her to accommodate him. When her body opened for him, he slid a little deeper.

With excruciating gentleness, he worked his way inside her inch by inch. The delicious tension between her legs shot directly to her heart. It was happening. It was really happening. Leo Nolan was going to make love to her. Leo Nolan *was* making love to her.

Her heart tried to beat its way out of her chest.

"Prue, sweetheart, are you okay?"

Unable to speak, she nodded.

"If you need me to stop, you just say so. The last thing I want to do is hurt you."

Emotions filled her chest and she wrapped her arms around his neck. Lifting her knees, she took him deep, and a wave of fire engulfed her.

A sob built in her throat. "I won't ask you to stop, Leo. Not ever."

With a fierce groan, he wedged deeper and her body relented until she swallowed all of him. When he retreated, she cried out, and he slid home again.

Sensation swelled and expanded with every slow thrust. She raised her arms above her head and gave her body over to him. She wanted more of him. Everything he could give her. His teeth scraped along the side of her neck as he pumped into her. His pace increased and one hand clutched her nape while the other gripped her hip as he moved inside her with fierce urgency.

He fucked her with deep plunges and lazy slides that might as well have been earthquakes. She should've grown self-conscious, her breasts bouncing with his thrusts and her body fully exposed to his questing gaze, but she was too far gone to care. Helpless to the pleasure he was giving her. A slave to the sensations coursing through her body.

She gasped his name again and again, unable to stop

the desperate sounds pouring out of her. He pulled everything from her. From the deepest depths of her soul, he extracted all the hot, carnal hunger she possessed, and she gleefully gave it to him.

It was a frenzied race to fulfillment. With each next thrust, exquisite sensation rolled through her and the shackles of the past began to break away. She wasn't an inexperienced and awkward girl, but a sexual woman unafraid to claim her pleasure. Joy swamped her, filling her heart and healing that wounded corner of her soul that had grown warped by self-doubt and fear.

When her orgasm crashed over her, she rode the sensation higher and higher, until she reclaimed her womanhood, and as the sweet, relentless pleasure shuddered through her, she knew she would love him forever.

His mouth a whisper from hers, he continued pumping his hips. When his hand slipped between their bodies and his fingers danced over her swollen flesh, a gasp rasped from her. Soon, her arousal was building again.

With each deep plunge, she rose to meet him, rushing toward another release, desperate for it. Then he pulled taut and high, and a guttural groan rumbled in his chest when he crested. His head fell to her shoulder and she pushed her hands through his hair, holding him to her as a second climax swept over her in delicious, drugging waves.

Their breathing slowed and soon the only sounds in the room came from the lake outside her bedroom doors.

He pressed a quick kiss to her bare shoulder. "Thank you."

Then he rolled away and shoved to his feet.

He dragged his shorts over his slender hips and bent to pluck his shirt off the floor. When he wouldn't meet her gaze, a cold hurt slithered through her. She scooted to a sitting position in the bed as he shoved his hands through the shirt's armholes.

Then he dropped a kiss on the crown of her head and crossed to the bedroom door. Without a word, he slipped through the door and closed it behind him.

Chapter Fourteen

Four years earlier

He fell in love with her that first day. She, however, took more convincing, and it wasn't until that first assignment ended and they'd returned home to Boston that she gave in to his needling.

Fourteen days. That's how long it took her to admit she was in love with him, too.

Three months later, when the network sent her back to the region, Leo demanded he be assigned to her security detail. Going forward, he would always demand it. After all, he couldn't sit back and let her, his heart, walk into a war zone alone and unprotected by him.

But the situation in the country had changed drastically in those months, spiraling into a full-fledged civil war. She struggled with the realities of combat.

At the end of their first few days in Damascus, the

conditions worsened and had Leo on the phone with his supervisor in Arlington.

"We need more men."

"How many?"

"Two, at least," Leo said. "Four would be better."

"I'll see what I can do."

But when, the next day, Jim called with the decision, Leo exploded. "What the hell do you mean the request is denied? This isn't up for debate. We can't keep these people safe without the extra men."

The day before, a crackdown on protesters by the authoritarian regime had erupted in chaos and now, outside their hotel's security gates, bodies littered the streets.

"Then you'll need to come home," Jim said. "Mr. King was clear—the priority right now is not civilian security. With the new contract in Afghanistan—"

The stream of expletives coming from Leo drowned out the bullshit Jim was shoveling, and it marked the beginning of the end of Leo's employment with Blackstone.

After the call, he returned to the hotel room he shared with Lauren.

Her eyes glassy and her cheeks flushed with her emotion, she stared blankly ahead.

He set a tumbler of whiskey in front of her.

She drank, and though she rarely consumed liquor, she didn't flinch or show any reaction when the fiery liquid slid down her throat.

Her voice when she spoke sounded strained and hoarse. "No one ever talks about the smell."

"I was warned about the smell," Leo admitted. "But the dogs surprised me."

Her eyes moved to his face. "Where do they all come from?"

He didn't know if they were wild animals or pets that

lost their civility right along with the humans, but they always seemed to appear to scavenge when the body count started to rise.

For a week, up until that day, she'd reported the chaos and despair of the escalating war dutifully and professionally before the TV cameras. But back in their hotel room that night, she'd reached her breaking point. He'd never seen her so upset. So heartbroken. It was the boy. Seeing his small body discarded along with the others had sent her to a dark, terrifying place.

"I'm so sick of war," she whispered. "I'm so sick of reporting about that horrible man and everything he's doing. No one is going to stop him. They don't care that he's killing his own people."

"They care."

"Not enough to do anything about it."

"It's complicated."

"It's not." A sob broke from her. "People are dying. Children are dying. Why aren't people angry? Or horrified? Why won't they do something?"

Leo struggled to keep himself from unraveling along with her. "I don't know the answers, but I believe if they understood what was really happening, and what needed to be done to stop it, they'd do it. That's why what you're doing here is so important."

She collapsed into him. "I hate it."

"You're making a difference."

"Really? You're not lying to me, are you?"

"I never lie." It was a new truth for him. He no longer had the stomach for deception, and he had nothing to hide from her anyway. "Not to you."

She tilted her chin to gaze up at him with huge brown eyes. "I know."

The certainty in her words uncurled a ribbon of calm inside him.

"But it's only because you don't care what anyone

thinks," she added, her tone teasing but affectionate.

"I care what you think." He dropped a kiss on the top of her head. "I love you."

❧

Leo woke to a room full of bright daylight. His head didn't ache, and his stomach wasn't churning with nausea. He couldn't remember the last time he'd truly slept, or woke feeling rested. Kicking off the sheets, he climbed from the bed and pulled a pair of shorts on over his boxer briefs.

In the living room, Prue's bedroom door remained closed.

His mind pounced on the memory of last night. Her naked body beneath him. Her soft heat and vulnerable eyes. The exquisite slide of his cock through her wet heat.

The pained expression on her face when he'd coldly left her bed.

That look had gutted him, and he'd wanted to apologize to her, but she'd made him promise not to say he was sorry for something he couldn't prevent.

So he'd kept right on walking. If this nonrelationship was going to work, he needed to set some boundaries, and after what had transpired between them, it was essential that he do it. Indeed, going forward, he would need to defend the borders of their familiarity with one another, or he risked a swift and resounding downfall.

He wasn't lying or being melodramatic when he'd warned her about his bent for hurting people. In that one, and only one, respect, he was exactly like his dad. Inevitably, he destroyed everyone and everything he cared about.

Which wasn't to say he didn't hate himself for it, or that he didn't regret the hurt he'd caused her so soon

143

after their physical connection. But ultimately it was an act of kindness. He was trying to save her from a more severe injury later.

Arlo, curled into a tight ball on the couch, lifted his head groggily and greeted Leo with a croaky meow.

With one hand, Leo scooped up the fur ball. "C'mon, guard kitty, time to make the rounds."

At the sliding glass doors, Leo stepped into his flip-flops while Arlo climbed up his shoulder and settled like a mantle around his neck.

Outside, the day was already hot, with a bright sun blazing in a cloudless blue sky. As he did the previous morning and night, and periodically throughout the day, he walked the perimeter of the property, checking for any signs of trouble or unwanted visitors.

Convinced no one besides he and Prue had been on the property, he returned indoors.

In the kitchen, he filched a can of tuna fish that never found its way into a cupboard off the counter. With the first couple of cranks on the can opener, a whiff of tuna wafted on the air and brought Arlo scrambling to him. The cat wove between and around Leo's legs, his meows growing more impatient with every second that passed.

After delivering Arlo's feast, Leo settled on a barstool at the kitchen island with his cell phone. A few minutes into his call, while the operator had him on hold, Prue's bedroom door opened behind him.

He swiveled in her direction, and when he saw her, the punch of lust nearly knocked him off his stool. She was dressed in her bathing suit, and the tiny scrap of fabric only hid a few key places on her body from his probing gaze. His tongue slipped out to lick his bottom lip as he recalled what lay beneath the scanty material.

He dragged his eyes to her face. Their gazes collided, and his lust shifted into a longing so raw and visceral he gasped with the force of it.

In her eyes, hurt and confusion swirled.

He opened his mouth—to explain, to apologize, to say I told you so—but no words existed that could chase away her wounded look. It was like those months after his mom died, when he was too young to understand what had happened, and why everyone around him appeared so lost and broken. The fear had boiled up to choke him, and for months, or maybe years, he couldn't speak. Everyone worried that he wasn't talking, and their worry only tightened the stranglehold of fear around his throat.

On his phone, the operator returned to the line and he blinked away the memories. He gestured to Prue that he'd be a minute longer.

When she passed by him, her light scent teased his nostrils. His attention riveted to her backside as she moved about the kitchen. The soft sway of her hips transfixed him, and filled him with satisfaction when he recalled the way he'd gripped those hips as he'd eased inside her.

At the toaster, she shoved two slices of bread into the slats and pushed down the levers. A grape disappeared inside her mouth and he studied the puffy outline of her lips as she crammed a plastic cup full of ice from the freezer.

While he answered questions about his address and billing information, she buttered the toast and slathered strawberry jelly across the surface, her small hands moving with light, graceful motions. She set the plate of toast in front of him and dropped two more slices into the toaster.

When the operator put him on hold again, he lifted a slice of toast to his lips and bit into it with a crunch. The shock of sweetness erupted inside his mouth and he frowned, trying to recollect the last time he'd tasted any of the food he ate.

With her toast and ice water, she crossed to the patio

doors and stepped outside, leaving him to finish his phone conversation in private.

A technical glitch meant the call lasted another half hour before he joined her outside. The refreshing breeze that often blew off the lake was absent that morning, and the sun's heat baked the wood decking.

He moved to the shade but pulled up when he ducked beneath the alcove. Lounging in the hammock, she'd hooked her dark, wet hair over one shoulder and worked at braiding it in a long rope. Water still clung to her body from the lake, and the few fingers of warm sunlight peeping through the canopy kissed her smooth skin.

But her beauty wasn't even the sexiest thing about her just then. She was lost in her thoughts, and a soft, serene expression played across her features. At the sight, his breath caught in his lungs. All the blood rushed to his cock.

He wanted her again. What would it be like to make love to her slowly? To orchestrate her arousal, keeping her high and tight until he was ready to bring her to completion, only after a long, slow torture of pleasure?

He couldn't wait to find out.

"What are you thinking about?" The question was out before he'd formulated it in his mind and deemed it too dangerous to speak.

She started to find him standing so near. Pink touched her cheeks. "Oh, nothing."

"It didn't look like nothing."

Apprehension glittered in her bright eyes. "Uh, well, I was wondering what's at the bottom of a black hole."

That surprised a smile from him. "Why didn't you want to tell me that?"

"I didn't want you to be mad at me."

At the catch in her voice, a pang struck him in the center of his chest. "Why would I be mad?"

"I don't know." Some emotion chased across her face

too quickly for him to read.

Except it was obvious she knew exactly why she feared his reaction, she just wasn't going to tell him.

He held out her cell phone. "We've got internet."

An irresistible smile playing on her kissable mouth, she cradled the phone between her breasts. "Thank you."

He watched the smile reach her eyes, and he suddenly found himself wanting things he couldn't have. Things that were dangerous to him. It felt a little like standing at the edge of a pier while the waves crashed over the boardwalk to knock into him and trying not to fall into the water. For surely if he fell, he might not survive the crushing force of the churning sea below.

Standing beneath the low-slung pergola, he raised his arms and gripped one of the wooden crossbeams. In the distance, the waves crested and receded in their rhythmic dance, but without a breeze, the summer heat was oppressive, stifling and unrelenting.

"I was wondering, what happened to Arlo's eye?"

"I don't know," she said softly. "I went to the shelter to adopt a dog and they were taking him to be put down. He'd already lost the eye and no one wanted to adopt him."

Oddly, Leo's heart thundered against his rib cage. With a scowl, he moved to lean against a pillar, his bare back pressed to the weathered wood post.

"He's a great cat. I'm glad you believed he was worth rescuing."

Her eyes went all soft and watery. "Me, too. He's such a sweetie."

Pushing away from the post, he moved to the hammock and climbed in on the opposite end, carefully entwining their legs, bare skin to bare skin.

Catching one of her feet, he rubbed the arch with the pad of his thumb. "How long have you had him?"

"Only a couple of months." A charming blush touched

her cheeks when her foot brushed against his erection. "He was so skittish when I brought him home, I think he lived under my bed the whole first month."

His hand smoothed up her calf. "He's lucky to have you."

When his fingers danced along her inner thigh, the color on her cheeks heightened. "I think I'm the lucky one."

Compelled by the look in her eyes, he sat. "How so?" he asked, his voice shaky.

"It took a while, but eventually he let me love him."

Leo stilled, frozen by her words and the delicate smile pulling at the corners of her plump mouth.

He placed his foot on the ground, careful not to tip them out of the hammock, and draped her legs across his thighs. His cock strained toward her but he ignored it, taking a moment to drink her in. Fascinated by the color of her hair, his hand came up to touch the strands of rich brown and burnished gold.

"You're so beautiful," he said.

She laughed as though he'd made a joke.

With the tips of his fingers brushed the spot between her breasts where the swimsuit plunged low. In the wake of his touch, goose bumps rose across her fevered flesh. Her nipples pebbled and his cock jumped.

He ached with wanting her. He couldn't recall ever wanting a woman so much. Honestly, he couldn't imagine a time when he wouldn't want her, or when his body would have its fill of her. Probably because he'd gone so long without sex.

That had to be it. Nothing else could explain how she'd managed to hijack his every thought and emotion, despite his resistance. He was the best resister. He'd resisted every woman, every pleasure for four years.

Now she was all he could think about. All he wanted. All he'd ever want again.

He smoothed his palms over the soft skin of her inner thighs. Her gaze found his and she pulled her bottom lip between her teeth. Hooking the crotch of her bathing suit around one finger, he pulled the fabric aside and, with one fingertip, traced the crease of her opening.

A sound vibrated in her throat and her eyes fell shut. His fingers worked her body, searching out her pleasure points. She angled her hips upward for his touch and he rewarded her, which pulled more enthusiastic sounds from her.

God, he loved her sounds. As if she couldn't decide what surprised her more—his bold touches or the way her body reacted to them.

Every single time.

Her breathy moans sent a hot lick of fire spiraling through him as he stroked her. When her body opened for him, a primitive groan ripped from his chest.

"That's it, baby." He urged her on, his voice not entirely steady.

The intoxicating musk of her arousal danced around him as he continued his tender assault. He felt himself falling, pulled under by her scent and her little noises. By the way her body wept for him. By her faith and freedom as her arousal climbed higher. By the way she forgave him when he lashed out at the world.

Struggling to maintain control of himself, he tugged the straps of her swimsuit down her shoulders to reveal her plump breasts. He cupped her and kissed the sweet, puckered flesh around her nipples as he helped her wiggle the suit over her hips. When the bathing suit hung around one ankle, she kicked and the scrap of material landed on the deck with a sodden squish.

He plucked kisses from her mouth, soft, slow kisses sprinkled with warm sighs and little laughs for their precarious placement in the hammock. He hadn't had fun with a woman in as long as he could remember. Maybe ever.

A devilish plan formed in his mind.

"It's so hot out here." Arousal thickened his voice. "Are you hot?"

"Yes." She sounded out of breath.

Stretching, he reached for her water and snagged an ice cube from the glass with two fingers. When he touched the ice to her nipple she sucked a sharp gasp between her teeth. Circling the peak, the bud puckered and she lifted her arms above her head, giving him free rein over her body. Rivulets of water soon trailed down and between her breasts to her stomach.

He lapped at the stream with his hot tongue.

She guided him with her throaty moans and desperate pleas. He trailed the ice around her naval and then dragged the cube through her soft curls. Her eyes flew open and the haze of arousal clouding their pure blue depths nearly shattered his fragile control.

She whimpered and he pressed the frozen cube to her core. The shock tore a cry of pleasure from her throat, and she threw her head back. Her chest rose and fell with her rapid breathing while he played with her, teasing her until melted ice trickled down her slit to pool under her bottom.

With his tongue, he reached inside her. His name shot from her as shock and pleasure. She thrust her hands through his hair and rolled her hips with gentle gyrations while he licked and ate, sucking in freezing water along with the moisture from her body.

Fire and ice.

When the cube had melted to a small nub, he withdrew it. He kissed her again, savoring the coolness that lingered on her fleshy lips. Then, over the plane of her stomach, his gaze captured hers. One corner of his mouth lifted with his smile as he sucked the ice cube between his teeth.

Her eyes went wide.

The smile still playing on his lips, he moved over her and with one languid glide, nudged his thick shaft inside her. The feel of her sent a painful rush of pleasure through him, the bliss so pure and perfect that it seared him.

Suddenly he wasn't smiling. She moaned his name and he squeezed his eyes shut, absorbing the feel of her sweet flesh, so snug and soft. Then he started to move.

He pumped his hips, withdrawing only so that he might melt into her softness again, and again. Alarm bells were going off inside his skull, but he was helpless to react to them with her feminine moans cascading down on him.

She was supposed to be the inexperienced one, and he the one in command, but she'd taken control of him, wringing more out of him than he had to give.

A sob gathered in his throat and he pressed his forehead to her shoulder. Their fire was too bright, too hot. It scalded, but he couldn't turn away from her. She was the light after so much darkness. Redemption after the fall.

His thrusts became urgent, her power holding him to her. Commanding his need and want, and lust and love. Urging him even past the point he was willing to go. No matter how much he might want to, he couldn't escape her, or this moment.

Goddammit, but she would take everything.

He plunged his hips, burying himself deep, but it wasn't enough. It would never be enough. Again and again, he withdrew and returned home, driven by the will to make her his. For that's what she was—his. As he was hers, whether he wanted to be or not. Whether he deserved to be or not.

And no matter what happened to them in the coming days, that fact would forever remain. They belonged to each other.

She clamped her arms and legs tight around him. Their ragged breaths filled the alcove along with the soft, slippery sound of their bodies joining. When her sex contracted around him and she cried out with her climax, her ecstasy appeared as fierce and bright as the burning sun.

Her blue eyes filled with an unbearable softness when she gazed up at him while he throbbed inside her. She touched the side of his face and lifted her knees.

A guttural groan ripped from him and he came, emptying his soul into her with his release.

Beneath his ear, her racing heart slowed while the thread of chaos continued unraveling inside him.

With a lingering kiss that spoke of things left unsaid, he climbed unsteadily to his feet. "I'm going to dive in the lake. You want to come?"

"I'll join you in a bit." She looked as shaken as he felt.

In the cool water, he dove headfirst into a wave, wanting to wash away the sudden turmoil in his mind. He'd never experienced sex like that before, so carnal and honest.

But it was only sex, he reminded himself.

He was out of practice. He'd been isolated so long, keeping himself away from others, that he didn't know how to handle it now that he'd gotten intimate with someone else.

It wasn't a big deal. She was his friend's sister, a consenting adult, and they were slaking each other's needs for a while. So what if he liked her? A lot. The sex was better that way, and damn, the sex was good.

But only because it'd been so long since he'd been with a woman, any woman, let alone one as pretty and as fiery as Prue was. And sweet.

Lust was a powerful drug.

Though his lust didn't explain the sudden urgent need

that overcame him to figure out who had tried to hurt her and put an end to them. As he walked up the beach toward the house, his mind turned to his top priority–her safety–and away from all the ways that existed to bring about her next orgasm.

When he returned to the patio, she'd dressed in her swimsuit and was reclined in a beach chair.

Bending over, he plucked a kiss from her hot mouth, then filched his cell phone from the table. "I think I know someone who might be able to help us figure out what this network of criminals is up to."

She straightened in the chair. "Who?"

"Just an old BRC buddy."

"What's BRC?"

Scrolling through his contact list, he waved a hand distractedly. "It's a Marine training course."

"So he's a Marine, too?" she asked, a frown in her voice. "How is he going to help?"

"Claymore is a different sort of cat than most, but he knows his shit and is well-connected. It's probably a long shot, but I just want to see what he knows, or can find out, if anything."

"Claymore? Is that his name?"

"It's a nickname." Leo found the number and selected it. "After the Scottish broadsword. Double-edged and lethal as fuck when wielded by someone who knows its power."

His words failed to bring a smile to her face. He sent the call and pressed the phone to his ear.

Looking up, he found she hovered at the patio door to her bedroom. With a tilt of his head, he waited, but she didn't speak. Instead she watched him with large, lucid eyes, a concerned frown puckering the spot above her brow.

When she caught his questioning gaze, a weak smile flitted across her face, but then she turned her face away.

He almost didn't catch that her smile crumpled when she stepped through the screen door and closed it softly shut behind her.

The phone ringing in his ear, his mind searched for clues to her reaction.

Then she reached behind her and unfastened the strap to her swimsuit. His thoughts scrambled when the fabric fell away from her body. His cock jerked. There was no way he could go again, but damn, he wished he could. He craved her like a junkie craved his chosen vice, or an alcoholic his spirits.

Just as Claymore's gruff voice crackled across the line, Leo realized that he'd gone all morning without thinking about having a drink.

Chapter Fifteen

Prue had never heard Owen mention anyone named Claymore. She had no idea who he was, or what he could do to help them. The sudden uncertainty played tricks on her mind, causing her to do battle with the shadows, both real and imagined.

Whatever Leo wanted Claymore to do, would it involve digging into the past? Her past? What if Claymore found out about her and Aron King? Would he share that information with Leo? How would Leo react? Would he think less of her? Would he be mad or disappointed, like she was? Would he be angry that she'd lied to him?

With a steadying breath, she pushed aside her troubling thoughts. What did any of that matter? She and Leo weren't a couple. They didn't have a future she needed to protect, and which might be jeopardized by her deception. And if exposing her secrets meant Aron was stopped from hurting more people, she'd suffer the consequences without complaint.

Outdoors, the sun hovered a few fingers above the horizon, and this time she didn't want to miss its dramatic plunge into the sea. Hurriedly, she finished carving up a hunk of cheese and added the slices to the paper plate already loaded down with crackers and grapes.

On the patio, Leo lounged in a beach chair, his long legs stretched out in the sand and her computer balanced on his lap.

She set the plate on the table between their chairs, and when he reached for a cracker, a smile pierced her heart. He hardly ate, and never seemed to think of food, except when he wanted to make sure she had enough. But she had a theory that if she placed food in front of him he'd eat it. Twice now, her theory had proven correct.

The cracker disappeared into his mouth, and then his gaze snagged hers. The warm glow of the sunset cast him in a soft light that picked out the green in his eyes and a shadow of a smile touched his lips. With his smile, an unexpected sensation swelled inside her, a mix of joy and certainty. She'd never experienced anything like it.

The disquiet she'd felt only moments before suddenly seemed like a distant memory. She could stay here forever—even without the Wi-Fi. With him.

"Do you mind if I send Claymore some of your files?"

A sliver of unease returned to her. "Which ones would you send him?"

"Everything you have on King. As a US citizen, he's the one we have the best chance of nailing."

"You think we can?"

"Yeah, I think we can." His eyes shone with a conspiratorial light. "With as much as you and Paul already pieced together from publicly available sources alone, imagine what the NSA and CIA must have on him."

"Do you think they know about his, uh, freelancing?"

"By law, he has to tell them." He reached for a wedge of cheese. "And if he hasn't told them by now, that in and of itself might be a crime."

She nibbled on a cracker while she chewed over that information. After a moment, she realized he watched her, his expression thoughtful.

"If you don't want me to share your work with him, that's okay, too," he said softly.

That he cared, once again, to protect her wishes soothed her worries.

With a smile, she gave her head a small shake. "If you trust him, then so will I."

An odd look touched his features, but he turned away as the last slice of fiery orange disappeared beyond the horizon.

"Does Claymore work for the NSA or the CIA?"

In the fading light, white teeth flashed in his dark face. "I'd tell you, but then I'd have to kill you."

A laugh startled from her. She couldn't believe she was there with Leo, and that he was making jokes.

He pushed slowly to his feet. "I'm going to grab a water. You want anything?"

"I'll take a water."

But at the patio door, he froze. His turned his head and gazed down at the pitiful plant she'd stuck in the ground the day before.

"It was dying."

His head snapped around. "What?"

At the desperate edge in his voice, she sat forward in her chair.

"The rose bush." She pointed at the scraggy shrub. "I'm going to try to save it."

His lips parted and an odd sound eased from him, as though she'd struck him and he couldn't catch his breath.

But he didn't say anything before he slipped silently

inside the house.

⚃

Four years earlier

She'd told him early on that she didn't want kids. Her career was taking off, and the frequent travel to the world's most dangerous hotspots didn't allow room for children.

For his part, Leo hadn't given much thought to parenthood. It'd always been a far-off concept, and without anything concrete to hold on to, not one worth investing too much energy in.

Still, when she told him, he felt a pang of loss in the center of his chest. For in that moment, the idea of having children with her appealed. Very much. She was concrete. That something, someone, he wanted to hold on to, to belong to, finally. Forever.

But he hadn't argued with her, because he wanted to be with her more than he wanted kids.

After Jim refused his request for more men, Leo made the decision to pull out. Beyond their hotel gates, the violence raged on and without the extra men, they were unable to flee through the fighting to reach the airport safely. So they waited while chaos unfolded around them.

In the end, hundreds lay dead in the city streets.

Raw emotion choked him. Helplessness and anger lashed at his control. The Fear took hold.

Sitting on the floor in their hotel room, between the beds, they passed a bottle of the local moonshine back and forth between them. Lauren's TV makeup ran down her cheeks in dark streams forged by her tears, like the hollow blackness of despair tunneling through them both.

She took a nip from the bottle. A sharp hiss escaped her and she handed the decanter back to him.

He drank deeply, relishing the lick of fire burning down his throat to spread through his roiling stomach. Regretfully, he eyed the container. There wasn't nearly enough alcohol remaining in the bottle to offer anything close to oblivion.

"After this is over and we're back home, I want to have a baby."

Her softly spoken words hit him like a punch to the gut. A sharp longing stole his voice.

"I know it's not what we talked about. It's just–" She ducked her chin and her light hair shimmied with her head shake. "I don't know."

He swallowed hard to dislodge the lump in his throat. "I know why."

Her head came up. "You do?"

"Of course I do."

"Then tell me, please, because I don't understand any of this."

He paused, searching for the words. "After so much death, you want to create life."

Silent tears flowed down her cheeks. Curling her legs under her, she crawled to him and collapsed into his side.

She buried her face in the crook of his neck. "I want to go home, Leo."

He dropped a kiss on the top of her head. "We'll need to buy a house."

She drew back enough to look up at him. For the first time in days, her eyes shone with something other than her devastation. "Where should we live?"

"Anywhere you want."

"I don't care as long as you're there, and the baby."

"We'll need a big yard, for the kids."

Her head on his shoulder moved with her nod of agreement.

"Is there anything else you want, Lauren? Name it and I'll get it for you."

"Someplace quiet. Not in the city. Maybe with a view, if we can afford it."

He knew the perfect place.

Leo jerked from sleep. Sweat clung to him, and his heart thumped inside his chest cavity.

In the dark room, he reached for the bottle of liquor that'd been a mainstay on his nightstand for years. But there was no bottle, and he managed only to knock his cell phone off the table.

He dropped back on the pillows. Flopping an arm across his forehead, he stared at the ceiling.

The last couple of years hadn't been pretty, but at the very least, he'd managed to grow some scar tissue. But since being back in this house, the old wounds ached, like an embedded sliver finally working its way to the surface and breaking through the healed over skin.

He couldn't go back to those days when all he did was bleed. He wasn't strong enough.

A noise brought his head instantly up off the pillow. With a soft creak, his bedroom door cracked open. His muscles bunched. The gap grew several inches wide, then halted.

He waited, and then Arlo launched himself onto the bed, landing in the blankets with a soft trill.

Leo collapsed back on the pillows. But before his heart rate had returned to normal, the door budged again. It slid open and Prue tiptoed into the room.

He didn't speak or move, or even dare to breathe, as she crawled beneath the sheets and snuggled as close as to him as was possible without actually touching.

What the hell was she doing in his bed?

Again?

He should send her back to her own bed. Tell her that while fucking her wasn't a problem, sleeping together went too far. It was too personal. Too intimate. That's what he should've done.

But he didn't.

He rolled to his side, turning his back to her. Hadn't he made it clear to her that there were boundaries? Did he need to draw a big red line around his bed? He frowned at the wall.

He never should have agreed to her outrageous proposal. But it was too late for that now. Now, he had to summon the resolve to guard against her.

Behind him, she cuddled closer.

All the pent-up angst inside him escaped like the air in a leaky car tire. There was no way he was getting out of this nonrelationship without hurting her. Likely, it was already too late.

The only right decision he could make was the one that involved sending her back to her bed. Alone.

Of course, sending her away would hurt her, but not sending her away would hurt a thousand times worse. It'd hurt *him*.

As good as it'd felt getting lost in her sweet little body for the last twenty-four hours, somehow, inexplicably, it'd torn him apart. The pleasure stung like the cutting gash of a betrayal. A betrayal of his friend's trust. A betrayal of *their* memory.

A betrayal of Prue's non-trust.

Even if he didn't care to protect himself from her, he owed it to all of them to shield her from him.

So why was she still in his bed?

And why did he let her stay?

Twisting toward her, he wrapped his arm around her waist and held on tightly.

Chapter Sixteen

"**B**etter. Do it again."

Prue drew back her elbow, then drove her fist into Leo's chest.

He shook his head. "Center your hips." Moving to stand behind her, his hands clamped around her hip bones. "Again."

She punched the air. It was becoming her thing, taking swings at ghosts she couldn't see.

After his odd reaction to the rose bush, he hadn't returned to the patio, and she'd spent the rest of the evening wondering what she'd said or done to upset him, her heart aching at the return of his cold disposition.

But in the night, the sounds of his nightmare had dragged her from sleep, and she went to him. Soothing him in the dark, her wounded anger morphed into merciful anguish.

She didn't know what demons haunted him, but she

couldn't escape the sense that his battle was becoming hers.

When morning dawned, his fierce scowl eclipsed the sun's bright light, and an hour of training hadn't taken the bite out of his mood.

"Okay, that's good," he said. "Let's work on something else."

"Making coffee?" she asked hopefully.

His hands moved to her shoulders. "I want to show you some things you can do if someone grabs you from behind."

"Now this sounds promising." Craning her neck, she looked up at him over her shoulder, hoping to catch a glimpse of his dimples.

Instead, he gripped a fistful of her hair.

"Reach back with both of your hands." He spoke near her ear.

When she obeyed, he guided her so that one hand held on to his wrist while the other encircled his thumb.

"Now it's all a matter of physics," he said. "Try to bend my thumb back while holding my wrist in place."

When she struck, he moved with her. "That's it. Keep going."

She ducked under his arms and with a controlled wrench, twisted free of his grip.

Facing him, a startled laugh burst from her. "I can't believe that worked."

"That was good," he said, a huskiness in his voice. "Let's do it again."

Prue turned her back to him as he repositioned himself behind her. His fist tangled in her hair, and she reached over her head to grip his wrist. Stretching, she arched her back and her bottom brushed against his hardness.

At the evidence of his erection, a triumphant thrill shot through her veins. She did that. Prudish Prue

Lockhart made Leo Nolan hard.

She wriggled slightly, pretending to adjust her stance. "Are my hips centered?"

"Prue...." Her name held a warning.

But she was tired of his warnings, and his grumpy faces. She wasn't afraid of him, or the darkness inside him. Not anymore.

Her fiery hunger emboldened her, prodding her to draw his shadows out into the light so that she might have him all to herself, at least for a little while.

She leaned against his chest. "You know, I might not fight you off if you wanted to bend me over the–"

His possessive growl rumbled in her ear, and then he was corralling her toward the sofa. She lifted her arms as he raked her T-shirt up her body and over her head. The flat of his palm pressed between her shoulders blades and he bent her over the arm of the sofa. He yanked the waistband of her shorts and panties down, and cool air prickled over her skin a moment before his heavy shaft brushed against her backside.

A tremor of fear snaked through her.

Standing behind her, his hand ran down her spine and smoothed over her bottom, then slipped around her waist to her stomach. He wrapped his body around hers and his hot mouth took nibbles of her shoulder, her spine, the back of her neck.

Fear faded, driven away by the clever play of his fingers between her legs and the tender brushes of his mouth across her skin. At first teasingly elusive, his fingers soon probed her boldly in a slow, repetitive rhythm. Seeking all her secrets. As her body yielded to his touch, her breath came in short gasps and she clawed at the sofa cushions.

He pressed his legs between her thighs, widening her stance, and centered himself. Her awareness zeroed in on the place where his body invaded hers with an unhurried thrust, filling her in one long, smooth glide.

He was moving inside her and with every delicious push, her heart expanded to swallow his demons. She tilted her hips, exposing her sex to him.

"Prue, Jesus–"

He lifted her from the sofa and turned her, pinning her against the wall with his body. His hand hooked behind one of her knees and then the other, and he wrapped her legs around his lean waist. Gripping her bottom with both of his large hands, he parted her with his thick length.

Too soon, her inner muscles clenched around him.

While she came, he pumped into her with fierce, wild thrusts, and she flung her arms around his neck, holding fast as he drove his darkness into her. His mouth burned her lips. His touch seared her skin. When his heartbreak became hers, tears prickled behind her eyes.

"I love the way you fuck me, Prue." He throbbed inside her. "I love everything about you."

At her startled gasp, he froze.

The terror filling his eyes broke her heart. "Prue... I...."

If he spoke, she feared what he might say, so she wriggled against him.

He gasped and closed his eyes. "Maybe we should stop."

"We don't have to stop. I know you didn't mean it." Her weak laughter rang hollow. "I love the way you fuck me, too."

His frown conveyed his doubt. "Even if Owen would let me near you, I can't...."

She rotated her hips in a slow circle.

With a moan, his head dropped to her shoulder. "I'll never be the guy you want me to be."

If that were true, then why did her heart hurt every time he put up barriers to keep her out? And why did the thought of leaving him in a matter of days or weeks, when all this was over, make her want to cry?

But she didn't argue with him. Words would never change his mind, or his heart.

"Okay, Leo." She rose up and dropped down the length of his hard shaft.

A guttural groan tore from him, and his hips started to move inside her once more. "Just... don't forget that. Please."

"I won't, Leo. Please don't worry."

His palms hit the wall and he plunged into her. After a series of hard, furious thrusts, he growled and ground against her, holding deep with his release.

He gripped her nape and captured her mouth for a savage kiss, his puffy lips flavored with desperation.

When he broke away, his chest heaved with his labored breathing. "I didn't hurt you, did I?"

She shook her head. "No."

"I didn't mean to be so rough with you."

She touched his cheek. "I liked it, Leo." *I like you.*

Cupping her face with both hands, he brushed the pads of his thumbs across her cheeks. His expression somber, he searched her eyes, and she braced for the apology that'd break her heart.

"Thank you," he said.

She tried to bite back a smile, but it was no use. "You're welcome."

He withdrew from her body and set her carefully on the floor. Then he plucked her T-shirt off the sofa back and handed it to her.

She tugged the shirt on and dragged it over her body. "Any chance that could be considered kinky sex? I want to be able to say I've had kinky sex."

His rusty laugh rumbled in his chest. "We can look it up later on the internet."

"Really? I'll go get my laptop."

He backed toward his bedroom door. "I'm going to

grab a quick shower. Don't you dare start that internet search without me."

A goofy smile plastered to her face, she went into the kitchen to start some coffee. After setting the pot to brew, she turned toward the refrigerator.

And gasped to see a man standing at the patio doors.

Fear ricocheted through her and she dropped to her knees behind the kitchen island. Pressing her back to the wood cabinets, her heart thrummed wildly in her chest.

With the soft squeal of the screen door sliding open and then snapping shut, panic turned to ice in her veins.

He was inside the house.

He'd walked right in, without knocking. Who did that?

Tears and panic rose to choke her. This couldn't be happening again. Was it the man from her apartment? Had he found them? Could she stay there, hidden, until Leo was out of the shower?

Or would the intruder find him in the shower first, unsuspecting and defenseless?

Frantically, she looked around for a weapon. As silently as she could manage, she opened the cupboard and pulled out a short stack of cooking pots with shaking hands.

His footsteps grew near, and before he spotted her, she decided on a preemptive strike.

With a primal scream, she leapt to her feet and launched the pots at him one after another.

His sharp curse rent the air, and he ducked to avoid the first missile. The second hit him in the thigh, and the third, he knocked down with a swipe of his arm. The pans clattered to the floor with a series of resounding clangs.

Prue snatched the can opener off the counter and drew back her arm.

"Wait!" The man held his palms face out on either side of his head. "Don't throw that. Please."

She blinked at him rapidly. "Who are you?" Shock

mixed with her biting demand.

Shock not at the stranger's sudden, unexplained appearance, but at his uncanny resemblance to Leo.

"I'm Noah. Who are you?"

He had a thick accent, and her mind struggled to catch up with his words. "Prue."

"Nice to meet you, Prue." Slowly, his hands dropped to his sides. "Don't take this the wrong way–typically I'd be thrilled to stumble upon a half-naked woman alone in the woods–but what the hell are you doing here?"

"I'm here with Leo."

"Leo?" Surprise rippled across the man's attractive features and he shot a few quick glances around the room. "He's here?"

"He's in the other room. Cleaning his gun." She cleared her throat. "One of his many, many guns."

One of Noah's dark eyebrows inched upward.

"I'm sorry, but I didn't catch it the first time." She surveyed him through narrowed eyes. "What did you say you're doing here?"

"I heard a rumor my brother was spotted in town." He lifted his shoulders. "I wanted to check it out for myself."

"Your brother?"

"My brother. Leo."

Her pounding heart stopped. "Leo is your brother?"

"He is, yes."

"Leo has a brother," she repeated, her heart sinking to the floorboards.

"Four of them, actually."

She gasped and sputtered. "Four brothers?"

Behind Noah, Leo appeared in the bedroom doorway. He'd wrapped a towel around his lean waist and his wet hair stood on end. His gaze moved from her, to Noah, and back to her.

"You have a brother." She could hardly lift her voice above a whisper.

"Yes," he said. "This is Noah."

"You lied to me?"

Noah backed toward the patio door. "I'll come back later—"

"No." Her face on fire, she froze Noah to the spot with a look. "You stay. I'll go."

She rounded the island and, shoulders back, chin held high, stalked to her bedroom.

This time, *she* slammed the door on *him*.

℁

Leo wanted to charge after her, and that's exactly why he didn't.

That and the low whistle leaking out from between Noah's teeth.

Leo's gaze swung to his brother. "What the hell are you doing here?"

"I wanted to see you."

"Why?"

"You're my brother. I don't need a reason."

They might be brothers, but Leo and Noah knew next to nothing about each other. To be fair, Leo hardly knew any of his brothers anymore.

He preferred to keep it that way.

"Look, I'd love to chat, but I'm right in the middle of something here."

"Right. Prue, is it?" Noah rubbed his elbow. "She's got a good arm."

With a frown, Leo noted the trio of pots that littered the living room floor. "She threw these at you?"

"Oh yeah." A deep chuckle tumbled out of Noah. "Connected two out of three."

"We'll have to work on that," Leo muttered.

The humor left Noah's face. "Why? Are you in

trouble?"

He was treading water, and the sharks were circling. "Nothing I can't handle."

"Are you sure? If you need anything—"

"I'm sure." Leo scratched a spot on his bare shoulder, but the itch moved and he chased it to the back of his neck.

"So, there's this thing I've been trying," Noah said conversationally.

"What's that?" Leo asked, hoping to speed up Noah's departure.

"I've been a shitty brother to you. To all of you, but especially to you." Noah's dark eyes regarded him with sober frankness. "I'm trying to do better."

Leo itched all over now. "Let me know how that works out for you."

A surprisingly genuine smile lit up Noah's features. "If you're in town for a few days, why don't you stop by? Mind you, I'm not asking for any of us, but the girls would love to see you. I think you're their favorite."

The girls? Noah must be referring to his brothers' wives or, in Haven's case, soon-to-be wife.

"I doubt that's true."

Noah shrugged. "Come by and see for yourself."

"Haven likes having me around because she thinks she can beat me at poker, but I've been letting her win." He tried to joke, but a raw and abrasive shame swept through him and he risked a glance at his brother's face. "Emily should hate me."

"Emily doesn't hate anyone." Noah's smile lingered. "You should see her. She looks ready to pop."

And just like that Leo was drowning. The waves crashed over his head, pressing down on him until the air squeezed from his lungs and the fight left his body.

"I don't mean to be a dick," he said, "but I want to put on some clothes and make sure Prue is all right."

"Yeah, okay," Noah said easily. "You know where we are, if you need us."

I won't need you, he wanted to say. Instead, he watched Noah step through the patio doors and disappear around the side of the house.

The rest of the day, she remained secluded in her bedroom. It wasn't until the sun began its downward slide that he found her outside, on her knees in the dirt, picking dead leaves off the sickly stalks of the rose bush. As if the plant might sprout new growth once freed from the shackles of decay.

Watching her, an ache formed in the center of his chest.

"Leave it," he said, rubbing at the tender spot beneath his breastbone.

She ignored him and focused on pushing broken eggshells into the soil surrounding the plant.

The ancient paralysis tried to freeze the words in his throat, but frustration at the reappearance of the old difficulty knocked them loose. "If I can't apologize, what can I say?"

She sat back on her heels and regarded him with her big blue eyes. "Why did you do it?"

"Why did I lie?"

"The lie itself was harmless. What does it matter to me if you have four brothers or none? So why bother with it?"

He hated how she looked at him, her delicate features full of doubt and uncertainty. In him.

Disappointment.

In him.

He wanted her to look at him the way she did before the lie. As though he wasn't a piece-of-shit loser more deserving of her scorn than her respect.

And he really wanted her to get away from that plant.

"Will you come over here and talk to me? Please."

With a harried sigh, she gained her feet only to stomp across the patio and collapse in a beach chair.

He settled in the chair beside her and took a moment to gather his thoughts. "It's my default," he said finally. "Whenever someone asks me about my personal life, I lie."

"Why do you do that?" Her voice carried a touch of annoyance.

The lie served two purposes. It kept them from knowing him, and him from forming attachments to them. What good were attachments when, in the end, everyone either died or left him?

But he didn't want to tell her that. He wanted to lie some more. Remind her, and himself, that they were only fucking, and that he didn't need to explain or justify his behavior to her.

That's what he wanted to say, but when he opened his mouth, the truth tumbled out instead. "It's better than letting them in."

Her expression softened. "Who?"

"Everyone." Looking away, he dragged a hand through his hair.

Why did he tell her that?

Damn, he needed a drink. The impulse gripped him hard, and he shifted in the chair as though he might be able to escape its stranglehold on him.

When he was inside her, he didn't think about alcohol. Or things like betrayal and dishonor. Everything melted away the instant he buried himself in her sweet heat.

He risked a glance at her.

In her eyes, some of the doubt had receded, but a touch of wariness remained. He needed to erase that last trace of uncertainty. He needed her to forget the lie, to look at him the way she did before. He needed her faith and her trust restored.

He needed her.

The need defied reason.

Kneeling before her in the sand, he brought his face level with hers. She shifted and he nestled between her thighs as his hands slipped into her hair. Unable to give voice to his apology, he pulled her to him and dropped a light kiss on her mouth. He pressed his forehead to hers while his thumbs traced the soft contours of her cheeks.

When she tipped her chin and took a tiny taste of his mouth, her softness devastated him. The feathery stroke of her tongue licked inside him, and his heart throbbed.

He slid his hands down the column of her throat to dance along her clavicle, and her head tipped to one side. The wide neck of her T-shirt sagged off her shoulder and his mouth followed the path of his fingers across her smooth skin. Slipping his hands beneath her shirt, he found the peak of one breast and brushed the pad of his thumb over the fabric of her bra, stroking the beaded nipple beneath.

A gasp slipped from her.

God, that was hot.

He released the closure of her bra and pulled the fabric away from her body.

She pushed his shirt over his shoulders and her nimble fingers grappled with the fastenings on his shorts even as she lifted her hips, allowing him to drag down the waistband of her shorts. When she was naked before him, he lifted a trembling hand to her silken curls. He teased her entrance until she opened for him.

"Prue, honey, lift your knees."

She did and he gently pushed them wider, hooking her legs over the arms of the chair.

Hectic color rushed over her face and chest.

"No, keep them there." He smoothed his palms along her inner thighs. "I want to see you."

The doubt in her eyes just then had nothing to do with his lies. "Like this?"

His heart shattered.

Damn, she was sweet. Insecure, but so fucking eager to please him. It shredded his heart. She might not want to trust him, but she'd put all her faith in him to show her what to do.

"Yes, sweetheart, that's perfect. You're perfect." The position rendered her body helpless to his touch, and emotion thickened his voice. "God, Prue, you're so fucking perfect."

He pushed a finger into her soft folds. Her sounds and scent intoxicated him, and soon the need to be inside her overcame all else. Slanting his hips, he rubbed against the wet notch between her legs. Moisture from her body made him slippery, and he poised at the heart of her for a moment before nudging inside. She moaned and he pressed deeper.

When her body sucked him in, he felt the first tremors of his release right away. But he couldn't accept an end to the pleasure, so he drew back and pulled her onto his lap.

Her eyes grew wide. "I don't know how...."

He soothed her, running his hands up and down her back, and over her hips. "Do it however you like it. There is no wrong way. Show me how you like it."

Lifting her hips, she centered herself over his stiff length and then sank slowly down. He closed his eyes to the dizzying, heady rush of her soft snugness. Sensation poured over, searing him.

At first, she moved awkwardly, but then she found her rhythm. When she began rolling her hips with erotic swivels, shudders rippled through him.

"Am I doing it right?" she asked, vulnerability shining in her eyes.

A sound like a sob tore from him. "Jesus, yes. So right."

Her bottom filled his hands as her lush body rode him, plunging him deep, and deeper, into her heat. Before his eyes, her breasts swayed with her slow movements and he dragged his tongue over their pebbled peaks. Her warm depths gripped his cock, and he heard himself muttering reckless endearments and desperate pleas, tender reassurances, and oh so many impure thoughts. Lots and lots of impure thoughts.

He groaned with triumph when she cried out with her release.

Soon Owen would return and she would leave him, but for now she was his. Helpless to his lust and the excruciating hardness of his cock, he dragged her to the sand and shoved her knees to her chest. Then he plunged into her with unrelenting strokes.

It was madness, but he couldn't stop himself.

He withdrew and pushed home, again and again. With every thrust, he wanted to lie to her. To repeat untrue words over and over, until even he believed them. Until he became them. Until falsehoods became truth, dark became light, wrong became right, and he became worthy of her.

With every pump of his hips, her name dropped from his lips until, with a gut-wrenching groan, he hurtled over the edge.

Afterward, while he lay mostly on top of her, his fingers toyed with the hair at her temples. He dropped kisses on her cheeks, her mouth, and the tip of her nose, and when he peered down into her face, his soul calmed to find only the remnants of her passion and no trace of her earlier uncertainty.

It should have bothered him more to realize that by banishing the doubt from her eyes, he'd also obliterated the distance he'd sought to maintain between them.

Chapter Seventeen

Rain moved in overnight, falling from the sky as a light but steady drizzle. Thick mugginess clung to the air, though the rainy mist provided a welcome relief from the heat.

Only a few raindrops touched Prue's hair and skin in her spot beneath the pergola. Today, the lake churned and roiled with restlessness, stirred up by the approaching storm. Today, the lake reminded her of Leo.

Like the waves in the water, he pushed her away only to pull her back in again. Hard and cold one moment, he'd turn tender and sweet in the next. He'd lie to her about little things, then make love to her in a way that only left room for fierce, searing honesty. There were times she thought he didn't even like her, but then he'd risk his life for her, or kiss her with a knowledge so intimate and deep, she couldn't believe he didn't at least care for her a little.

The tender soreness in her heart when she thought about him worried her. He obviously had issues, and was quite possibly hung up on another woman. She couldn't let herself love him. That'd be suicidal.

Behind her, the screen door opened with a soft screech. She turned as Leo poked his head outside.

His green-gold eyes alight, he held up his cell phone. "Claymore sent some information."

Her heart jumped. She scrambled out of the hammock and bounded through the doorway after him. "Can I look at it?"

He nodded. "Let's use your laptop."

While he cleared a spot on the coffee table, she retrieved her computer from the bedroom. Returning, she set it on the coffee table in front of him.

"This is just the first batch of stuff." With a cable, he connected his cell phone to her laptop. "He said there's more, a lot more, but he wants to follow up on a few leads before he sends it over."

He opened the first file, and she leaned in to read the small print on the screen.

"Hold on, I need to get my glasses."

She darted to her bedroom, but her glasses weren't on the nightstand where she'd left them. A frenzied search finally tracked them to the floor under the bed, where they must've fallen. Shoving them on, she scrambled to her feet.

When she returned to the living room, Leo sat back on the couch, his hands linked behind his head. The expression on his face slowed her steps.

She perched on the edge of the arm chair. "What's wrong? What does it say?"

"King's not *involved* in the smuggling ring." The cold fury in his voice sent a chill straight to her heart. "He's running it."

A rush of wild fury erupted from her. "I knew it!" She

swallowed the outburst. "That bastard."

"And they're not just dealing in guns and drugs."

She gave her a head a small shake, baffled.

"They're trafficking humans, too. Mostly underage girls."

The breath left her body and a sharp, revolting pain rushed in to fill the void.

Leo clambered to his feet. "Hey, are you okay?"

Her vision blurred as his fuzzy form moved toward her.

"Breathe," he murmured, smoothing a hand down her back.

She dragged gulps of air into her lungs. How could she have slept with a man who would do something so horrific? She'd thought she was in love with him, and he was a monster.

Her hands shook with the shock and repulsion banging through her body. She wanted to scream and cry and throw up, all at once.

Crouching before her, Leo peered into her face, and his fingers came up to touch her cheek. "Wow, you're really upset by this."

"I'm just so... so...." She pulled off her glasses and rubbed her wet eyes. "Angry." Her voice broke over the word.

He sat carefully on the edge of the coffee table. Elbows on his knees, his compelling gaze pierced her.

She rubbed a hand across her forehead, but when her tears escaped she used her palm to hide her face. "And disgusted. It's disgusting, right?"

"It makes me sick."

"Me, too."

Something like sorrow, or regret, touched his features. "Is that all that you're feeling?"

"Maybe?"

Reaching out, he caught a tear with the pad of his

thumb.

When he began speaking, he seemed to pick his words carefully. "I know we agreed not to show each other all our ugly parts, "but I think your ugly parts might be relevant to our current situation. Am I right?"

She shook her head, but when he frowned, her head shake morphed into a bob.

The corners of his mouth lifted and lines appeared around his eyes, but he wasn't smiling. "If you could go ahead and show me those ugly parts now, I'd really appreciate it."

She swallowed with an audible gulp.

"Would it help if I promise not to be a judgmental prick about it?"

"You can't promise that," she whispered. "You don't even know what I'm going to say."

"I don't need to know. I know you, and that's all that matters." One of his hands found hers and he laced their fingers together. "Whatever you say, it won't change anything, but I need to know the whole story."

"I did not lie to you."

"I'm not saying you did."

She squirmed. "It's so embarrassing."

"Prue, honey, I'm kind of freaking out here. Can you give me a clue where this is headed?"

She didn't want to freak him out, but she struggled to find the words. How did she relay the story of what had happened in a way that wouldn't lead him to conclude the worst about her? Her heartbeat thrummed, rushing past her ears with a deafening throb.

But there was nowhere to hide, not from him, or from the truth.

The fortifying breath she drew into her lungs wobbled. "I was a nerd."

His eyebrows shot up.

"I mean, I *am* a nerd," she corrected. "But I was one in

high school and college, too. No boys showed any interest in me. Ever."

A smug smile touched his mouth. "Morons."

"Which is why it was so bizarre when this guy in my organic chemistry class at MIT suddenly asked me out one day."

His satisfied smile mashed into a thin-lipped line.

"Aron King, he was the guy."

He quickly concealed his reaction behind an unreadable mask. "I didn't know he went to MIT."

"He didn't." The sharp bite of his treachery stung again. "It was a lie. A scam. All part of the act."

"What act?"

"He pretended to be a dual major, like me, working on his PhD. He was the first guy who ever paid any attention to me, so I overlooked the fact that he sucked at science. He sucked at sex, too, but I'd never been with anyone else and didn't know it could be so... different." Warmth touched her cheeks. "So much better."

"He's why you don't trust men." Leo's statement held a lethal edge.

"Men, yes, but also myself. I was supposed to be so smart, and when it came right down to it, I was just a stupid girl."

"You weren't stupid, you were conned."

"Is there a difference?"

"Yes. A big one. How old were you?"

"Twenty-one."

The cold fury in his eyes now seethed white-hot. "And that made him, what? Thirty-one? Thirty-two?"

"Thirty-three."

Outside, heavy rain droplets began to plop to the ground in a steady stream.

"What happened?" he asked gently.

"He fucked me and dumped me. Broke my heart. I would've gotten over him easily enough, except...." Knots wrenched her stomach. "It was three days before I realized he'd stolen my laptop."

His fingers still entwined with hers, he squeezed her hand.

"I'd finished my organic chem project early, and the first tests had gone even better than I'd hoped. I was so excited. I'd made a fertilizer that helped grow vegetation in some of the driest conditions. I thought I was going to end world hunger or something ridiculous like that." Her bitter laugh died in her throat. "I should've applied for a patent, but I didn't know what I had, and... well, he stole the formula. Made a ton of money when he sold it to a Russian lab."

Lifting her hand, Leo pressed his soft lips to her palm.

"They tweaked it a little, but it was basically my formula." She stared down at their linked hands. "They weaponized it."

"Jesus. Prue...?"

Emotion tightened her throat, and painfully, she forced out the words. "It was used exactly one time before it was banned."

"King did it. He used it in that village in Iraq."

"Almost a year after he stole my laptop. He killed eleven people. T-two children." Her tears spilled over and she wiped at them with the back of her hand. "I-I-I saw pictures."

"Oh my God, baby."

Her chin trembled as her words came faster. "After that, I sort of went into a downward spiral. Everyone assumed I was heartbroken over him, and I didn't say anything to correct them. I couldn't bring myself to tell anyone what I'd done. My doctor prescribed something to help me sleep, but one night, I was drinking and.... I wasn't trying to kill myself, but that's what everyone thought."

"Prue." Every single emotion wrapped around her

name.

"The thing is, I didn't care. I knew I shouldn't mix the pills with alcohol. The warning was right there on the bottle, on a bright yellow label. But all I could think about were those kids. Their little faces."

With a tug on her hand, he pulled her to him.

She slipped onto his lap and buried her face in the side of his neck. "I didn't care what happened, I just wanted to get those pictures out of my mind."

His fingers pressed lightly under her chin, tipping her face up, and his soft lips brushed over hers. The kiss was unbearably tender and contained more healing than the years of therapy she'd gone through.

When he broke the kiss, he pressed his forehead to hers.

"I'm sorry for what you've been through." His hand buried in her hair, he cradled her head. "Please believe me when I say, if I ever have a chance to make it right for you, I will."

She dropped her head to his shoulder and they fell quiet, listening to the rain.

"Does it freak you out?"

"That you're a chemist?" His lips touched her forehead with a light kiss. "No, it doesn't freak me out."

Her smile faltered and she pulled back so she could see his face. "It's been years. I don't see things that way anymore. I'm... stronger now."

"You're amazing." His hand massaged the tight muscles of her neck. "And you don't have to explain it to me."

"I don't?"

Intolerable pain filled his eyes, the agony so deep and dark, it snatched her breath. "I've never wanted to die, but I know what it is not to want to live anymore."

The confession notched a wound on her heart. "You have?"

"I can't describe it." He pushed his fist into his chest. "But it sits right here. All of it."

"Like a black hole," she said softly. "It sucks everything in until it's impossibly heavy. Eventually, it collapses in on itself."

"Yes." His answer leaked out as a hoarse whisper.

"You try to pretend it isn't there, or to forget about it for a while." Her voice wavered with the memories of those months where darkness and despair devoured her. "But everything that replaces the emptiness is a thousand times worse."

A flash of lightning brightened the gray sky, and an angry rumble of thunder followed.

His hands moved to her thighs and he shifted her so her legs straddled his hips. The hard length of his erection nudged against her core. He gripped her nape and pulled her head down to his.

"Not everything is worse," he murmured against her mouth.

Chapter Eighteen

Leo frowned at the computer screen. "This guy here, Alexey? How do we know him?"

Her small teeth chewed on her bottom lip. "I don't remember that name. What's he done?"

They'd spent the previous day combing through the information Claymore had sent, and started back at it first thing that morning, but by noon, they were struggling to integrate the new data with Prue's research. The web of connections overwhelmed.

With a defeated sigh, Leo tossed the notebook on the coffee table as his latest attempt to map the network of players once again trailed off the page.

"He and King met last year." On his feet, Leo pointed at the computer. "Keep reading. I'll be right back."

In the kitchen, he rummaged through drawers until he found a pad of tattered Post-it Notes. Back at the sofa, he scrawled each name from his notebook onto a separate

Post-it, then crossed to the wall on the opposite side of the room and began arranging the notes. Soon, yellow squares plastered the white wall.

He glanced over his shoulder to find Prue gaping at his handiwork. "That is so hot," she said.

A smile on his face, he surveyed the arrangement of notes as she came to stand beside him. For the next hour, they worked together, adding names and events and linking them with lines he drew in pencil directly on the wall. He needed to paint eventually anyway.

When her stomach let loose with an angry growl, they took a break to make dinner. He started the grill while she prepared the potatoes and cut up some vegetables. Food cooking, he left her lounging in the hammock and slipped inside to clean the tongs that he'd dropped in the sand.

As he headed back to the patio doors, the chime of his cell phone drew him to the coffee table.

Claymore's number displayed on the phone's screen, and he accepted the call.

"Hey, man. Thanks for the information. I don't want to know how you got your hands on so much so fast."

Claymore's deep chuckle had a sinister ring to it. "I'm about to send you the rest of it." He hesitated. "There's one file I wanted to explain to you, ear-to-ear, so to speak."

"All right." A frown pulled at Leo's features. "What've you got?"

"It's about Owen's sister. How well do you know her?"

An image of Prue riding him, her breasts bouncing in his face, came screeching to his mind. He rubbed the back of his neck. "Well enough, I suppose. Why do you ask?"

"There are some interesting rumors out there about her."

Alarm rippled through him and he stole a glance

outside to see Prue swaying gently in the hammock, her laptop propped open on her stomach. "What kind of rumors?"

"You know, the usual stuff–drug abuse, alcoholism, questions about her stability and sanity."

Leo made a sound. "What? None of that is true."

He knew what an alcoholic looked like, and she wasn't it. Had he seen her drink at all? And questions about her sanity? Seriously? It might be the most absurd thing he'd ever heard.

"I assume it's King and his bot army trying to sow doubt about her, but I wanted to get your take on it." Claymore's tone remained flat, as though he merely recited the daily brief to his commanding officer. "Though there does appear to be a history. I haven't confirmed it yet, but a few years ago, she overdosed–or attempted suicide maybe...?"

The knot twisting Leo's stomach wrenched. "It was accidental. She mixed a prescription with alcohol."

"Ah, okay. King will probably seize on that to create a narrative. He's already crying about harassment. Says she's unstable and obsessed with him, has been for years."

"He's scared shitless, isn't he?"

"It certainly smells like it. He's also threatening to sue her."

Leo exploded. "For what?"

"Who knows? I think defamation was the latest charge floating around the internet."

Curses fell from Leo's lips. "I didn't think her Twitter following was that big."

At that, Claymore snickered. "The point is to scare her, use his endless stack of dirty money to bankrupt her and generally make her life miserable. There's really no downside for him."

"He's going to file all these lawsuits from halfway

around the world?" Leo's gut churned with anger and dread.

"He arrived in the US two days ago."

Leo stilled. "Can you track him?"

"I'm looking at him right now."

"Where are you?"

"DC."

"Let me know if he moves?"

"You got it."

Leo disconnected the call and went outside to check the food on the grill. In the hammock, Prue's fingers toyed with the end of her loose braid while she stared off into space. By now, he recognized her dreamy expression and knew she worked away at one of the puzzles in her mind.

For a moment, he stared, struck by the beauty of her dainty features and the sensual promise of her long, tanned legs and smooth, bare shoulder, left exposed by her T-shirt's wide collar.

As he tended to the food, his cell phone vibrated against his hip. He closed the lid to the grill and retrieved Claymore's message. Monitoring the hammock out of the corner of his eye, he sifted through the new batch of files until he located the document titled "P.Lockhart."

He dragged and dropped it into the junk folder.

When he approached Prue, she remained lost in her thoughts, so he reached out and tapped his finger lightly on her nose.

Her eyes fluttered and a warm blush heated her cheeks as she smiled up at him.

Unable to resist the sweet bloom of her mouth, he bent down and kissed her. She tasted good, familiar, and the overpowering heat of her response singed him. He could kiss her like this forever and never grow tired of it.

With an aching reluctance, he pulled back. Big blue eyes ate him up and at the lustful yearning in them, one corner of his mouth lifted. She was lovely and passionate, and completely sane. If he was wrong, well then he'd happily drink of her madness.

Her fingers touched the side of his face. "What is it?"

"Claymore sent the rest of the files."

She sputtered and scrambled out of the hammock.

Inside, he sat on the sofa while she positioned her laptop in front of him. Connecting his phone to the computer, he transferred the files.

All except one.

He opened the first document, then stood. "I've got to get the food off the grill."

She scooched into the spot he'd vacated on the couch. When he returned with their overloaded plates of food, setting them on the coffee table while he skirted around to sit beside her, she leaned close to the computer. He pulled his plate onto his lap and started to read over her shoulder.

Just then, she lifted a hand to cover her mouth. "Oh my God," she whispered.

"What?' He swallowed his bite of potato, only half-chewed. "What is it?"

"He's a traitor."

"What?" Leo set down his plate and slanted closer to the computer.

She surged to her feet. "He's selling weapons to known terrorist groups." Her hands sliced wildly through the air as she spoke. "Terrorists who kill innocent people. Who–who–who fight American soldiers."

She exhibited none of the devastation from the previous day, when they learned about King's human trafficking crimes. Today she was simply pure, pissed-off female.

And it was glorious.

He settled back in the cushions with his dinner plate and, feet propped on the coffee table, prepared to witness the full force of her outrage. Arlo, who'd been sleeping on the sofa back, lifted his head to watch with him.

Before them, she paced. "That lying, no good, low-life traitor." She whirled on him. "Omigod, Leo, he's a traitor."

"I don't know the legal definition...."

She turned on her heel and resumed pacing. "Are all private military contractors turncoat mercenaries?"

"No. Most are patriots. Retired or former military, good at what they do, willing to risk their lives to get the job done. Aron King gives them all a bad rep."

"He was a SEAL, wasn't he? How does he go from the highest levels of our military to fighting against them? My God, he's arming the enemy."

"I've seen it before," Leo said. "Guys who feel slighted or betrayed by their country sometimes switch sides."

She stumbled to a stop. "*He* feels betrayed? What the hell did we do to him?"

"Our government put him on trial for war crimes."

A frustrated growl vibrated in her throat. "I can't believe I let that man touch me. God, I'm such an idiot."

"Stop that."

Her eyes touched his face with an unbearable softness. "Thank God I met you again. If I'd died having only ever slept with that pig, I'd be so disappointed."

The laugh that trickled from him sounded rusty from lack of use.

"What do we do now?" she asked.

He slid his plate onto the coffee table and stood. "For starters, we need to gather more facts."

A soft groan escaped her and she bit her lip. "You are so sexy when you talk like that."

How could it be that he was laughing? Their situation was growing more serious by the minute, and he had no idea how or even if he could keep her safe and unharmed.

Until this moment, the threat had been an indistinct, if

undeniably dangerous foe. Now he knew what hunted Prue. What remained to be known was how far Aron King was willing to go to silence her.

The Fear crouched in the shadows, ready to pounce. Since he'd left Blackstone four years ago, he hadn't been able to control it, and operated under no illusions he'd be able to do so now. When it struck, he'd be on his ass in a flash and useless to help her.

Rather than sit around and wait for something bad to happen, he needed to be proactive. He needed a plan. He needed information.

He needed backup.

"I've got to go out for a bit," he said.

Fear flashed in her blue eyes. "Okay," she said warily.

"You, uh, want to come with me?"

Surprise flitted across her face. "Where are you going?"

"To my brother's place."

Her eyebrows raised slightly. "Is he going to help us?"

"They, and I hope so." He gritted his teeth. "Luke is in law enforcement, and I have some legal questions for Shea."

"Luke and Shea?" She tried out their names. "Shea is a lawyer?"

"Last I knew."

"What are your other brothers' names?"

Dread gnawed at him. He didn't share personal details about his life with others. Ever.

Until now, apparently.

Inevitability settled on his shoulders. "Jack and Noah."

"Noah. How could I forget him?" A teasing smile played on her heart-shaped mouth.

While she slipped into her bedroom to change, he tried to shake off his unease. What would it hurt to talk to them? It didn't mean he'd become attached to them, or them to him.

If there was a chance his brothers might be able to help him keep Prue safe, then it was worth the risk.

Chapter Nineteen

As Leo steered the SUV along a winding coastal road, Prue relished the dramatic views of the lake and the quaint charms of the small island. The road became rural and the path more twisty before they turned up a long driveway and arrived at the doorstep of a massive, majestic estate. The home, obviously built in a different era, sat proudly atop the terrain, its soft yellow stone façade aglow in the dying light of the day.

At the base of the sweeping front porch, she bent her head back and gazed up at the grand house. A pang of insecurity struck her. Having been in the lake two, often three times a day, she hadn't shampooed her hair, so she'd pulled the dark mass over one shoulder and wove it into a braid that didn't fully contain the flyaway strands. Then she'd thrown a navy T-shirt dress on over her swimsuit and yanked a baseball hat onto her head before stepping into her flip-flops and rushing out the door with

Leo.

Nervously, she licked her sun-dried lips and ascended the stone steps behind him. When she considered his gray T-shirt and low-slung blue jeans with a worn patch on one knee, her anxiety eased a little.

Until they entered the breathtaking foyer. Black-and-white marble flooring gleamed in the soft light, and regal twin staircases soared skyward. A beautiful man sitting on one of the steps pushed to his feet.

His bright green eyes glinted when he approached them. "You must be Prue." His voice was low and a cockeyed smile lifted one side of his perfect, puffy mouth. "I'm Luke."

Leo bared his teeth. "Easy," he warned.

Luke's eyes danced. "They're waiting for us in the library."

Luke led them beneath the staircases and down a wide hallway, stopping before a set of ornately carved pocket doors. Sliding open one door, he stepped into the room and she caught a glimpse of three other men before Leo's broad shoulders blocked her view. Inside the door, he turned to her.

His green-gold eyes glittered with a light she'd never seen in them. "I'm going to talk with them alone for a minute."

"Oh okay." She swallowed hard.

He hesitated. "You all right?"

She felt sick, like the time her mom had found her journal and read it.

Not a typical teenager, Prue's journal didn't resemble a typical teenage girl's diary either. Rather than being filled with the identities of her secret crushes, or laments about the mean girls at school, Prue's journal had brimmed with scientific theories she'd researched at the library, inquiries of studies she'd wanted to pursue, and renderings of inventions she wished to one day, possibly, create.

She'd also loved to scribble her musings about the universe, the meaning and purpose of life, and what the concept of God, if such a thing existed, might look like.

That, of course, was the part her mom had zeroed in on. To her parents, Prue's words were a direct challenge to the teaching of their church and their faith. What's more, she'd disobeyed them. Again. Her dad had first flown into a rage before icing her out with deliberate cruelty while her mom had locked herself away in her bedroom for days, crying and praying for their wayward daughter.

To Prue, life was a wonder, and it'd filled her with joy to ponder its complexities and explore its mysteries. That journal had contained all her hopes and dreams for a future filled with science and truth-seeking. And her parents' reaction to it had made her feel ashamed. Ashamed of what she'd done to them, the family, and the church.

Ashamed of who she was.

Emotion clogged her throat, so she nodded.

Reaching into the hallway, Leo brushed her cheek with the tips of his fingers and she turned her head to soak up more of his touch. A slow, reassuring smile pulled at his lips, and then he slid the door closed.

Alone in the hallway of a stranger's home, Prue waited.

Minutes ticked by and she paced the hall, peeking into nearby rooms and studying a painting hanging on the wall.

Still the men remained in conference.

She was sitting on the floor, her knees drawn to her chest, when the figure of a woman appeared in the foyer.

"Prue?" The woman started toward her.

Prue climbed to her feet and tugged on the hem of her dress.

"They left you in the hallway?" Despite her expression

of disgust, the woman had a rather pretty face. Her auburn hair and deep blue eyes shone, and when she smiled, Prue relaxed for the first time since she'd entered the house.

"I'm Mina," she said. "Come, meet the others while you wait."

They returned to the grand foyer but then split off into another huge room with an oversized dining table. Passing by it, they pushed through a swinging door and entered a massive gourmet kitchen. Bright sunlight streamed in through large windows, washing the white cupboards and marbled gray-and-white countertops in radiant warmth.

Two women at the kitchen table, fat textbooks open in front of them, looked up when they appeared. Mina claimed a spot in front of the third textbook as she introduced Prue to Emily and Haven.

With all their attention focused on her, Prue's insecurities came rushing back. For a hundred different reasons, but mainly that she preferred schoolwork to friendships and her parents viewed socializing as the devil's doorway to temptation and moral corruption, she'd never had a lot of practice making friends. Or acquaintances. Or even small talk.

Luckily, she didn't have to.

"Did you guys figure out the answer to number eight yet?" Mina asked.

The two women's gazes dropped to their notebooks and they grumbled.

Haven tossed her pencil onto the table. "This sucks. Whose bright idea was it to go back to college anyway?"

"Yours," Mina and Emily said together.

"I was right to drop out the first time."

Prue sidled closer to peek at the content of their textbooks.

"M-maybe we could ask Noah?" Emily suggested.

Mina's frown deepened. "No way. It's so easy for him, and I never understand it when he tries to explain it to me."

"What do you expect?" Haven crunched on a pretzel. "He's a teacher."

While Prue stretched to read the problem numbered eight, Mina smiled.

"Honestly, it isn't him," she said. "He's patient and sweet and tries so hard to help me understand. But it only frustrates me more that he has to work so hard at it, and I either end up snapping at him or crying. It's humiliating." She snapped a pretzel stick between her teeth. "We're not asking him for help."

With a collective sigh, all three women frowned down at their textbooks.

"Actually," Prue said, pointing at Haven's textbook, "there's an easier way to solve that problem than they're showing."

She scribbled the shortcut calculation in the margin of Haven's notebook, and moments later three "ahas" were said in unison.

The kitchen door swung open and Luke, Noah, and a third man Prue didn't know filed into the room ahead of Leo.

The unknown man had the same striking features as the others, but instead of their dark hair, his was a warm silvery gray. Cut short, it stood in sexy disarray around his head and somehow enhanced the striking handsomeness of his face. Or maybe it was his tall, lean physique, or the smattering of tattoos on his arms, one of which circled a hard bicep, the other running along his forearm.

Leo went immediately to Prue's side. Around his shoulders hung the black straps of a gun holster, and two guns nestled under his arms, against his rib cage.

He peered down into her face and when she smiled up

at him, he relaxed. "You've met my sisters, then?"

Before Prue could answer, Noah interjected, "See, that right there." He leaned his narrow hips against the kitchen island and crossed his ankles. "That's why you're their favorite."

"That's not why he's our favorite," Mina said.

"You're not supposed to admit you have a favorite." The gray-haired man had a distinct accent, like Noah, and a deep, gravelly voice that thrilled the part of her recently awakened to the allure of the male species.

Mina shrugged. "Of course we admit it."

"The old man is Shea," Leo said near her ear.

"I thought I was your favorite," Luke complained. "I'm everyone's favorite. Why does he get to be?"

"He brought us Prue." Haven smiled at her. "And she knows math."

"W-we're keeping her." Emily pushed a lock of her bright hair behind one ear and her warm brown eyes landed on Prue. "At least until the semester is over."

Then Emily stretched, as if to work a kink out of her back, and her enormous pregnant belly wedged against the table. The action drew Luke to her. Sliding a hand over her stomach, he bent and pressed a kiss to the top of her head.

Beside her, Prue felt Leo stiffen and she turned in time to see the pained emotion that twisted his features before he dropped his head to stare down at the floorboards.

Her smile fell and she glanced back at Emily and Luke. Glimpsing no sign of unhappiness or worry in them, she frowned. Didn't Leo like his brother's wife? Did he like her too much, his negative reaction the evidence of his jealousy?

Her stomach knotted as Haven pushed to her feet and moved to stand next to Leo.

Reaching up, she rumpled his hair. "You need a

haircut."

His slow smile didn't banish the dark pain in his eyes. Seeing it, anguish seared Prue's heart.

Just then, the back door opened and yet another brother, this one carrying a hockey stick, entered the home. Prue deduced him to be Jack. He was taller and broader than the others, and Haven's face lit up when she saw him.

"Hey, baby," Haven said. "Did you get a gun, too? Can I touch it?"

One corner of Jack's mouth lifted. "You can touch my gun anytime, sweetheart."

Haven laughed. "Where is it?"

"It's tucked safely away."

"Will you teach me how to shoot it?"

A frown slashed across Jack's striking face. "Are we talking about firearms?" With a flick of his wrist, the hockey stick whirled, and then the butt of the blade smacked into his palm. "What the hell do I need a gun for? I've got my own weapon."

Noah twisted around and placed his cell phone in the center of the kitchen island. "All right, here's the layout of the property."

The men pulled into a tight circle around him. Standing broad shoulder to broad shoulder, the brothers made quite a sight. Darkly beautiful, fierce, and masculine.

Mina sighed dreamily. "Just... wow."

"I know, right?" Emily whispered.

Prue, studying the way Leo interacted with his brothers, was caught off guard when his eyes suddenly captured hers. One side of his mouth twitched with his smile, and her heart filled with soft fluttery surges of happiness.

"They're like an army of hotness," she said to the others.

Giggles floated around the table.

"We should provoke them." Haven's dark eyes shimmered. "I want to be conquered."

The howls of their laughter drew the men's attention.

"You girls want to settle down over there?" Jack called out. "We're very busy plotting our world domination."

"Sorry," Haven crooned.

"It's P-Prue's fault." Emily winked at her. "She makes math fun."

And just like that, Prue had friends.

Chapter Twenty

Four years earlier

Fresh from the shower, she dropped the towel from around her body.

A new fullness swelled her breasts, and the soft rounding of her belly struck a pang in the center of his chest.

He swallowed the painful lump in his throat. "I don't want you to go."

"I have to go. It's my job." She wrapped the bathrobe around her pregnant tummy. "Besides, you'll be with me, and I know you won't let anything happen to me. To us."

He wanted to argue, but he turned his head and gazed out their bedroom window.

"I need to go back." She spoke so quietly he almost missed her words. "Last time, it was so awful. If things are better, and they've worked out a ceasefire, I want to

be there. Then maybe I can forget...."

With a defeated sigh, he went to her and pulled her into his arms. "If they won't give us adequate staff–"

"They will. The network head talked to your supervisor directly. He's already agreed to it."

He squeezed her tight and buried his face in her hair. "I don't know if I can do it," he whispered, giving voice to The Fear. "I don't know if I can keep you safe."

"I trust you, Leo."

Leo woke in the black of night when she crawled beneath the sheets.

He rolled toward her. "Prue, you have to stop this. Stay in your own bed."

"Why?" She snuggled into his side. "We sleep better together."

His hand moved to her hip. "I don't want you here."

He was losing track of the lies he told her, as they became twisted and inverted. Unrecognizable. Was it that he didn't want her there, or that he didn't want to want her at all, let alone with a craving so deep that his bones ached with it?

She gazed up at him in the dark. Though unable to read her face, he could feel the hurt his words caused in the way she held her body.

Good, he thought, and dropped a kiss on the crest of her cheek. She should hate him. She should shrink from his tainted soul, not move toward it.

Then her hand slipped to the hem of her sleep shirt and she drew it slowly up her body to reveal the triangle of dark hair between her thighs.

"Then tell me to leave, Leo." Lifting one knee, she parted her legs for him.

Reckless, savage lust overcame him. With a fierce growl, he shoved her shirt to her shoulders and clamped his mouth around her taut nipple. Her gasp melted into a moan when he pressed two fingers into her silken curls and teased her lips apart.

She was tinder beneath his touch. Helpless to the sound of her sweet moans, he settled between her bent knees, in the cradle of her hips, and slid sure and hard inside her. She wrapped her arms and legs around him, capturing him even as the soft, mad love in her heart set him free.

He knew it was wrong to want her love, but feeling it unleashed a tidal wave of emotion and lust. Ferocious tenderness engulfed him as he used his body to please hers. His world dwindled to the spot where he invaded her. The rim of her sex clamped tightly around him, and a roar of need and triumph exploded from his chest.

But The Fear hovered, reminding him that he'd never be worthy of her love, and would never be able to give her the love she deserved in return. But he fucked her with everything he had, loving her with his body the way he couldn't with his heart.

"Dammit, Prue." He buried his face in her neck and pressed his cock into her moist opening. Into her heart. "What am I doing? What the fuck am I doing?"

Her flesh squeezed and pulsed around him, wringing agonizing pleasure from the darkest places inside him. She lifted her hips, and his name falling from her lips wrested ecstasy from him in great voluptuous rushes.

Lying in the dark afterward, emptied and aching, he couldn't find his voice to ask her to leave.

╍

As the first slivers of light filtered into the room, Leo left the bed. On his way out of the bedroom, he plucked Arlo from the bedsheets.

"C'mon, buddy, time for our walk." He scratched the cat behind the ears and tried to ignore the knotted ball of angst in the pit of his stomach.

Outside, the sound of the birds flitting through the trees caused Leo to flinch more than once. Arlo climbed to his shoulder and, with his one good eye, stalked the treacherous birds.

When a twig snapped in the distance, Leo jerked around. For a moment, the image of Prue in his bed, her throat slit and the life bleeding out of her, blocked his vision. He blinked rapidly until his sight cleared and nothing except a gentle deer walked through the woods.

He gave Arlo a sidelong look. "We're pathetic, you know that?"

The cat purred while they completed their check of the property. Just a couple of broken heroes trying to protect the woman who didn't accept their brokenness.

When he returned indoors, Prue sat on the couch, her legs curled under her, reading something on her phone. She looked up when he came through the door, and her eyes brimmed with unshed tears.

The air squeezed from his lungs. "What happened?"

"Paul Cook." One tear slipped down her cheek. "He's dead."

His world tipped on its axis and he gripped the back of the armchair as Arlo scrambled from his arms. Paul Cook, the journalist who, like Prue, was digging into Aron King's connections, was dead?

"When?" he rasped.

"Just this week. On Tuesday." She frowned at her phone. "He was only fifty-nine."

Tuesday. The day before Prue was attacked.

His limbs shaky, he sat heavily in the chair before his legs gave out. "How did he die?"

With a small head shake, she trained round, vulnerable eyes on him. "His obituary doesn't say anything about a cause of death. If he was sick, he never said anything."

Mercifully, she bent her head over her phone again.

"Here's a news article," she murmured.

As she read to herself, he fell slowly through the tunnel of fear and chaos. Had they killed him? Had they sent the same man who attacked Prue to do it? His heart raced and he swiped viciously at the sweat collecting on his forehead.

"They suspect it was a heart attack." She slid the phone onto the coffee table. "He was at home when it happened."

"Where is home?"

"Washington."

"State?" His voice croaked with the dryness in his throat.

"DC."

Gulping for air, he shot to his feet.

"Leo? Is everything all right?"

He clawed a hand through his hair and yanked at the ends.

Her face drained of color. "You think they killed him?"

"I don't know."

What should he do? He tried to think clearly, but the panic was closing in, pushing out everything else.

He should talk to Claymore, and Owen. And his brothers.

But none of that would stop them coming for her. Should he take her someplace else? How long could he keep her hidden there? Had they already stayed too long?

Maybe he could throw them off the scent. But how? He'd have to convince them that she wasn't a part of this, that it was all a mistake, and that Paul Cook alone acted alone. That she hadn't, in fact, helped to discover proof of their criminal network.

What if he failed? What if they hurt her? He couldn't bear it. He wasn't strong enough to live through it again.

"I don't think I ever thanked you," she said, a tremor in her voice.

He gaped at her. "What?"

"For finding me and bringing me here. If you hadn't, I might be de—"

"Don't say it." The words shot from like a cannon blast. "Jesus Christ, Prue, don't you dare fucking say it."

She blinked at him, her blue eyes huge in her pale face. "But it's okay. I'm okay."

Frantically he scoured the room, as though he might discover the way to save her from them, once and for all, sitting right there in front of him.

When his gaze landed on the wall covered in Post-its, he froze.

"We have to stop," he said quietly.

"What?"

"All this." His wild gesture took in the entire wall. "If we destroy the records and give up trying to expose them, maybe they'll quit." Slowly, he faced her. "Maybe they'll forget about you."

Her mouth fell open with her disbelief. "You want me to stop?"

"Yes."

"They're hurting people." She pushed up off the sofa. "They're hurting children. You want me to just pretend it isn't happening?"

"I want you to be safe," he rasped harshly.

"I am safe. I'm with you."

He recoiled as though she'd struck him. "I can't." Palms out, he backed away from her. "I won't do it again."

"Do what?" A plaintive wail crept into her voice.

"These people are not like us. If you're a threat, they'll take you out. Period. At this point, they don't even care who knows they're doing it. They won't stop until they know you're eliminated." He nearly bent over with the pain. "Prue, I need you—I need to know you're safe. We have to drop it. For real this time."

A slash of devastation crumpled her features. It shouldn't hurt so much to see her upset, wounded, but it nearly destroyed him.

When the hell had she snuck into his heart? And how had she entrenched so thoroughly there?

He shook his head. It didn't matter. All that mattered now was figuring out how he was going to keep her safe.

Her mouth turned down at the corners, she studied the wall.

Pain throbbed in his chest. He couldn't allow her to be harmed, or worse. He wouldn't survive it. If she wouldn't protect herself, he'd have to make the choice for her.

In two large strides, he stepped to the wall and, with a vicious sweep of his arm, ripped down the yellow slips of paper.

Her pained gasp shattered him. "What are you doing?"

"We're ending this now." He made another brutal slash across the wall.

She rushed forward and grabbed his arm. "Leo, no. Please, stop it."

His anguished heart cried out, but he ignored it and kept tearing stickies off the wall.

"Why?" She was crying now. "Why are you doing this?"

He whirled on her so hard and fast, she stumbled back. He wanted to pursue her, to get in her face and scream the truth.

Because I won't lose you, too.

Instead, he wrenched away from her and moved to the sofa where he hunched over her computer, waiting for it to power on.

"What are you doing?"

Unable to bring himself to look at her, he stared at the black screen. "I'm going to delete everything."

The outpouring of anger and pain that he expected, and deserved, never came. He lifted his gaze.

Drawing herself up, she wiped away her tears with the backs of her hands. "I know why you're doing this."

"I promised Owen—"

"No. You think you're protecting me. But you're not." Her hiccup-sob caused her chin to quiver. "You're trying to protect yourself. You're afraid of wh-whatever it is that's happening between us."

The Fear laughed. She knew nothing of what he feared. "Tell me, Prue. What is it you think is happening?"

"Forget it," she mumbled.

"I don't want to forget it." The Fear lashed out, adding a sharp bite to his tone.

Soft wounded eyes touched his face, and then she ducked her chin, shutting him out. "Nothing. Nothing is happening."

Then suddenly her head came up, her huge eyes filled with disappointment.

Disappointment in him.

"You told me this would happen." A single tear rolled down her cheek and she wiped it away even as she attempted a cheeky smile. "You said you wouldn't fall in love with me, and you didn't."

"It's not you. I won't fall in love with anyone." His voice sounded cool, clinical. "It isn't worth it to me."

"Because of her?"

Everything inside him went still.

"I'm not completely naïve, Leo. I can see you're hung up on someone else. What happened? Why aren't you with her now?"

The silence stretched out, and he knew the pounding of his heart must be audible to her.

"Did she hurt you? Break your heart? Did she di—"

He sucked in a sharp hiss of air. "Stop. Do not say another word."

"Why? Why won't you talk about her?"

"So now you want to talk about our hang-ups?" He

pinned her beneath his gaze. "Fine, let's talk about yours."

"What do you mean?"

"You have a PhD. From freaking MIT."

She lifted her chin defiantly, but her eyes filled with panic. "So?"

The spot in the center of his chest softened, but he hardened himself against it. "So why the hell are you making coffee and answering phones?"

Her cheeks flushed a bright shade of pink while hurt and anger battled for control of her features. Hurt won out.

"When I saw those pictures–" Her voice broke and she swallowed the painful words. "I don't want to do anything that could be used to hurt someone like that ever again." One shoulder hitched higher. "So I make coffee instead."

He dragged a trembling hand over his mouth. His insides shredding, he lurched to his feet to pace.

An awful, angry silence smothered them. Until her quietly spoken words forever shattered whatever pitiful peace remained in him.

"I know what he's capable of, Leo. I've seen it." Her throat spasmed. "If I have to die in order to stop him, then so be it. I'm not afraid."

Stumbling to an abrupt stop, he stared at her. She was bathed in the warm glow of the summer sun, and her beautiful heart called out to his. The organ in the center of his chest throbbed and bled, and in its half-dead state, it whispered a simple, elemental truth.

"I'm sorry, Prue. I can't let that happen." With a vicious yank on the computer cord, he ripped the plug from the socket, and then he tucked the laptop under his arm.

When he escaped to his bedroom, he couldn't bring himself to shut her out behind the door.

She didn't pursue him.

CB

As daylight melted into dusk and then total darkness, Prue lay on her bed, too depressed to do anything other than shed tears for Paul Cook and for the corner of her heart left bruised by Leo's pointed questions and his demand that she stop investigating Aron King.

She didn't know why, exactly, it hurt so badly. He wasn't wrong in his belief that she was too cowardly to do the work she'd once loved, or to be worried that their situation had become even more dangerous. He was right about all of it.

So why did she feel so raw and aching?

Maybe because it felt like all those times her parents commanded her to stop being who she was, and rebuked her when she inevitably failed to do so? Or maybe because she'd let herself believe, let herself hope, that Leo was on her side? That he cared for her as more than a mere fuck buddy?

It neared midnight when she started to doze, but then she became aware of him at her bedroom door. Standing just outside the doorway, he silently contemplated her, a strange expression on his face, of undeniable emotion mixed with heat and vulnerability.

She lifted her head off the pillow and pushed upright.

"You should eat," he said.

"I'm not hungry."

Slowly, painfully, he took one step inside the room. "I'm not trying to hurt you. I'm afraid for you."

Her heart convulsed. "Did you... delete everything?"

"No."

With the bloom of hope in her chest, a small gasp slipped from her. "Why not?"

He folded his arms over his chest, but his veneer of calm was betrayed by the ticking along his jawline and the frantic, cornered look in his eyes. "I don't know."

In the way he hung his head, she sensed shame and regret. She slid off the bed and went to him. For many long moments, they stood next to each other, only just touching, feeling the other's nearness and the lick of fire that enfolded them.

He whispered her name.

She closed her eyes and his lips brushed her eyebrow, her temple, the corner of her mouth. Her hands trembled when she placed them on his shoulders.

A shudder passed through him, and with gentle hands, he removed her clothing and eased her onto the bed. His mouth explored her body, visiting all the nooks and hidden recesses, because no part of her would remain unknown to him.

With his wicked fingers, he coaxed her until she could no longer hold back the pleading noises in her throat. He drove her close. She buried her face in the pillows and rode his hand. Reason tumbled into oblivion. Hurt into pleasure. Anger into love.

Just before she crashed to completion, he pulled back.

He repeated the torturous dance, taking her to the precipice and holding her there. She begged him with naughty words born of frustration and painful arousal until he rose over her, his eyes glittering in the shadow of his face.

The desperation with which she wanted him terrified her.

His erection reared hot and hard, and she surrendered to him easily when he nudged fully inside her aching flesh. Her arms raised above her head, she arched her back to take more of him. His arms wrapped around her rib cage and he clutched her tightly to him as he took his pleasure in her body.

For every plunge of his hips, she met him with eagerness. Her breath came in quick, sharp pants. His mouth moved near her ear, but she could hardly hear his whispers over the thrumming of her heart.

"I need you, Prue." He dropped kisses on her face and shoulders, her collarbone, and the tips of her breasts. "I need you to let it go."

When his words penetrated the luscious haze of her desire, her heart fractured.

"Promise me," be pleaded.

There was a time she would have promised him anything. Everything.

Please don't ask this of me, Leo. Not this.

With a delicious slide, he withdrew. Then he teased her with the head of his shaft, barely penetrating her before withdrawing again.

She whimpered.

"Prue." The warning in his voice held a hitch of heartbreak and desperation.

In the absence of his prodding thickness, his fingers stroked her, and her arousal built to an unbearable agony. Just as she reached the edge, he retreated. He hovered at her entrance, withholding his hard fullness. Waiting.

On a sob, she wrapped her arms around his neck. "I want to make you happy, Leo."

He gave it to her.

With deep plunges and slow, languid slides, he drove her higher and higher until she shattered with her climax. Then he buried his face in her neck and shuddered with his release.

The aftershocks still rippling through her, she wondered if she would ever forgive him.

Chapter Twenty-One

Prue woke in her own bed.

She listened for sounds of Leo moving through the house, but all was quiet. Her stomach wrenched at the thought of seeing him. What would she say? What would he say?

Loath to argue with him again, and unable to bear the massacre of yellow stickies littering the living room floor, she retreated to the patio. He seemed as reluctant to face her, and all morning left her alone to swing in the hammock.

Despite the bright sunlight, the dark haunts from her past taunted. Hopelessness whispered doubts in her ear. Insecurity reminded her that the very fact of who she was made her too difficult to love.

Her chest spasmed with a short, painful hiccup. Afraid she would start crying again, she bit down hard on her lip and tried to come up with a rational explanation to explain the misery she felt.

She was a scientist. Or she used to be. She followed the facts wherever they might lead. But the particular set of facts laid out before her kept adding up to one simple, devastating conclusion.

She was in love with Leo Nolan.

She was in love with him, and it was hopeless. Prue would never have his heart, because she still had it. She'd never be a part of his life, because he refused to share it with anyone who wasn't her.

Her stomach tangled in knots, she had no appetite and skipped breakfast and lunch. She preferred to stay outdoors, letting the lake and the breeze cleanse the ache from her soul. Sometime in the early afternoon, while she tended to the heartening rose bush, she heard voices inside the house.

Climbing to her feet, she moved to the patio door. In the living room, Leo and Shea stood talking amidst the carnage of Post-it Notes.

"Luke talked to his old boss," Shea was saying. "And they're going to send a patrol out a few times a day when they can, to help keep an eye on things."

When she slid open the screen door and stepped indoors, Shea made a half turn and greeted her with a warm smile.

"Why didn't Luke tell me himself?" Leo asked with a frown.

"He's at the hospital with Emily," Shea said, turning back. "She had the baby yesterday."

Prue's delighted smile faded when she saw the expression that darkened Leo's face. His tawny skin drained of color, and for a moment, she feared he might be ill.

Without giving a thought to their earlier disagreement, she went to him.

He didn't seem to notice her until she touched his

arm, and then he flinched. His gaze swung to her face, and when she pushed back a strand of her hair, his eyes clamped onto her hand.

Pulling it away from her face, she looked down at the rose clippings clutched in her palm.

Confused, she whispered his name.

He blinked several times and the frantic anguish cleared from his eyes, but the blank emptiness that replaced it caused her heart to seize.

She knew what would come next, and even knowing it, it tore at her insides to watch him retreat into his bedroom, shutting her out behind a closed door.

"What's wrong with him?" Shea wanted to know.

"I wish I knew," she murmured.

ଓଃ

Four years earlier

When they arrived in Damascus, airport security met them on the runway. A "tip" from an unnamed source had convinced local authorities that the TV crew were in fact a gang of drug smugglers. They were held for questioning for eighteen hours before being released with no charges, or apologies.

While they were detained, the warring factions negotiated an end to hostilities.

As their convoy of vehicles traveled through the city to their hotel, their progress was slowed by revelers crowding the streets to celebrate the ceasefire.

Through her exhaustion, her smile appeared as a band of cheering men passed by the car windows.

The next day, she wanted to film live from the city center, but he convinced her she needed another day to rest, and so she filed her report from the hotel grounds.

On the third day, he couldn't keep her from the city.

"We won't stay long," she promised him. "I just want to talk to a couple of locals, and then we'll come right back here."

But the moment they arrived downtown, Leo regretted not putting up a bigger fight. Bodies packed the city, and the revelry of the two preceding days now carried a much darker vibe. He couldn't point to any one thing to prove the change, but it was there in the thick, cloying tension that seemed to build as they walked toward the crowded city center.

His skin crawled. Whether from intuition or years of experience in combat zones, everything in him screamed to get them the fuck out of there.

He signaled to Owen, who nodded and turned to deliver the instruction to the others.

With the crack of gunfire, chaos erupted around them.

The crowd surged, bodies pushing and shoving and trampling in their desperate struggle to escape the barrage of bullets.

In the madness, she was torn from him.

He dove for her, but he was knocked off his course by another wave of crushing bodies. Clawing and scrabbling, he fought to reach her. Her name tearing from him abraded his vocal cords. If he could get ahold of some part of her, any part, he'd never let go. If he could just get a little closer.

His fingers brushed hers—then a slash of pain ripped through his hip.

He cried out with the searing agony and stumbled. His hip on fire, he lunged, and his excruciating screams had nothing to do with the stabbing pain in his hip. With one last, desperate plunge, he hurled himself at her.

And caught only air.

Gasping for breath, he jolted awake.

Sweat coated his skin and drenched the hair at his temples. Around him, the black hole of his grief sucked in everything. There was no light. No hope. Only darkness and the crushing weight of the universe pressing in on him.

He wasn't alone in the bed. Arlo, curled into a tight ball and wedged against his hip, slept on. Leo's arm stretched out, searching for her. Seeking her sweet comfort.

But she wasn't there.

Chapter Twenty-Two

Morning had dawned on another bright summer day when he woke with a pounding heart. It ached inside his chest, raw and throbbing, as though it'd done battle with a meat tenderizer. Alone in the bed, he sat and, swinging his feet off the edge, scrubbed a hand over his face.

In the living room, he scooped up Arlo. A quick glance through the patio doors turned up no sign of Prue and when he passed by her bedroom door, the room was empty. He stumbled to a stop with the surge of fear that knocked into him.

The throbbing in his chest grew stronger, more painful.

But his frantic search for her ended before it really began when he spotted her knee-deep in the lake, her face turned toward the sun.

In the moment of relief from the pain, a calming breath rattled through him.

Then abruptly, he stilled.

His senses tingled. Something wasn't right.

The thought materialized just as a jarring bang ripped apart the quiet inside the house. Leo jerked, then soothed the cat in his arms.

"It's okay," he told Arlo as he moved toward the front door. "The bad guys don't knock."

But when Leo unlocked and pulled open the heavy door, he recoiled to find Owen standing beneath the archway.

Grief and longing battered him. "Owen. What are you doing here?"

Bags sat under his eyes, and the black slacks and white undershirt he wore were wrinkled, as if he'd been dressed in them far too long in a confined space.

"We managed to wrap things up a few days early." He moved inside and gave the home's interior a quick scan. "Nice place," he said before facing Leo. "Where's Prue?"

Damn, his chest hurt.

"She's safe."

Owen's sharp gaze homed in on him. "I had no doubt she would be. As long as she was with you."

Leo looked away.

"You mind if I use your bathroom?" Owen said suddenly. "This place is damn hard to find."

Leo pointed to his bedroom door. "In there."

When Owen disappeared into the other room, Leo set Arlo on the chair back and turned toward the patio.

But just then, Prue moved across the deck and came through the screen door. Her hair wet and windblown, her skin glowing with the sun's warm kiss, she glanced at him warily.

The ground opened beneath his feet to swallow him. He was falling. When she was gone, how would he breathe? What purpose would he have for doing so?

Her expression softened and she closed the distance

between them. Lifting onto her tiptoes, she dropped a soft kiss on his mouth. Her fingers touched the side of his face with tiny, feathery strokes that set off a series of tremors in his body.

His heart wedged in his throat. "Prue—"

"Don't say anything," she whispered against his mouth. "Please, Leo, don't speak."

Her lips parted and she took the sweetest, sexiest little nibble of his mouth.

At the movement over her shoulder, Leo stiffened. He moved his head an infinitesimal amount, just enough to break the kiss and shatter his crumbling heart into a thousand pieces.

She turned her head, and when she saw what he'd seen, she gasped and whirled to face her brother.

"Owen. Wh-what are you doing here?"

Owen's gaze swung from Prue to Leo. "You two are...?" He seemed to gulp down whatever word he'd been about to say. His expression darkened.

"Let me explain," Prue began.

But Owen's gaze remained locked on Leo. "Tell me it's only the jet lag and that I'm reading this all wrong."

Unwilling to lie, Leo bent his head, and the movement unleashed a fury in his friend.

"I trusted you."

"Owen, he didn't do anything—"

Owen's dark eyes blazed in his lean face. "Do you love her?"

Prue gasped. "Leo, don't answer that. Owen, that's none of your business."

"I asked for your help." His words lashed. "That did not include fucking my sister."

"Stop it." A hitch of heartbreak weakened Prue's command. "Owen, it's not like that."

"Get your things."

"No." Two huge blue eyes, filled with hope and

anguish, swung to Leo. "I don't want to go. I want to stay."

"Goddammit, Prue, get your goddamned things. Now!"

"That's enough," Leo said, his voice even and unyielding.

Chest heaving, Owen stared him down.

Leo held his friend's gaze. "Prue, can you please give us a minute alone?"

She hesitated, but she did as he asked, slipping into her bedroom.

"Do you have any idea what you've done?" Owen dropped his voice to a low, seething growl.

"Yes."

"How could you?"

How could he not? When Leo had nothing, she offered him everything, and he realized now he never really had a choice in refusing her. His need for her was beyond reason or self-control. That was the thing about madness and love.

Leo matched Owen's low register. "What can I say to make you okay with this?"

"Nothing. There's not a goddamn thing you can say." He dragged a trembling hand across his mouth.

"Owen, you're my friend, but I think you might be overreacting."

"Am I?" Owen bit out. "After the last guy fucked her over, she tried to kill herself." His voice wrenched with pain.

"I know," Leo said. "She told me."

Surprise penetrated Owen's anger. "Did she tell you they locked her away?" His mouth twisted. "I didn't think so."

"What are you talking about? What does that mean, locked her away?"

"It means they committed her."

Leo's heart burst, and he closed his eyes against the eruption of pain.

"They kept her for five days," Owen said. "Five days of hell for us. I can only imagine what it was like for her."

"She's stronger than you think."

"You have no idea what I think. When you watch them put your sister in the psych ward, then you get to have an opinion." Owen twisted away, only to wrench back around. "Damn you, Leo, if she goes through that again because of you, so help me God, I will—" He bit off the threat and paced away again.

"I'm sorry," Leo heard himself say. "I never wanted to hurt her. Or you."

Silence dropped between them. In the heavy stillness, Prue appeared in her bedroom doorway.

As he looked at her, Owen's hot fury cooled to a cold rage. "I lied. I am going to ask you for one more favor." He faced Leo. "Never come near my sister again."

"That isn't your decision to make," Prue said.

Owen strode to the front door and yanked it open. "Let's go." He waited. "Prue, I mean it."

"Just give me a minute," she said quietly. "Please."

With a look that'd unleashed terror in hundreds of men but had no visible effect on Prue, Owen slammed through the door.

For several heartbeats, neither of them spoke. She hovered in the doorway to her bedroom, appearing young and vulnerable. The urge to pull her into his chest nearly overcame his wish to abide by Owen's request, at least for the moment.

She watched him closely, her blue eyes big and guileless. "I mean it, Leo. I want to stay. If you want me to."

"Why didn't you tell me about the hospital?"

Her face crumpled. "Probably the same reason you won't tell me what happened between you and Rose."

At that name on her lips, he stumbled back until he came up hard against the coffee table. "How do you know that name?"

She started toward him, then stopped. "Sometimes, while you're sleeping, you talk to her."

His legs gave out and he dropped onto the table. "I don't want to talk to you about her."

"Why not?" He heard the anguish in her voice and regretted it. "Was she so special that you'll throw the rest of your life away if you can't be with her?"

Leo made a sound in the back of his throat like a moan, but emanating from someplace darker, more primal.

"Leo–"

He surged to his feet. "She died, okay? Is that what you want to hear?"

"Leo, no. Never."

"She's dead and I killed her." The truth seared him, the fire flaring to consume them both. "I fucking killed her."

"That's not true." She was shaking her head and tears were streaming down her pale cheeks. "Whatever happened, whatever you think happened, it wasn't your fault. You loved her. I can see how much you loved her. You'd never hurt her."

A sob choked him. "Stop it. Please."

She fell quiet. Dropping onto the coffee table, he propped his elbows on his knees and shoved his hands through his hair. He stared down at the floor while a lifetime's worth of self-loathing and regret crashed over him.

Prue crept closer. "Leo, I want to help you. Please let me."

He stilled her with a look. "Can you bring her back?" The wound reopened, his heart gushed with agony. "Then you can't help me."

"I can love you."

He wanted it so badly, his body shook with the need. But he also knew what he'd do to her if he let her stay.

Far beyond the hurt he'd already caused, he'd ruin her. Like he did them. It didn't matter if he loved her. It was what he did to the people he cared about.

Arlo bounded onto the coffee table and pushed his pink nose into Leo's thigh. Leo stared down at the kitten while his heart was dying and suddenly he realized that it did in fact matter that he loved Prue.

He loved her enough to let her go.

Standing, Leo swooped up Arlo and dumped him into her arms.

"Go with your brother, Prue. There's nothing for you here."

☙

The Fear thrived in darkness.

Shadows danced along the walls while Leo lay in his bed. He didn't bother to crawl under the covers, or sleep.

Or bathe or eat.

A week, a month, a year might've passed, and he'd still be lying in his bed, unclean and unfed, exhausted, if not for the torment of Prue's memory.

Her scent lingered in his bedclothes, and the house made weird noises, as if it moaned with pain, empty and ill without her in it. Like him. Even the lake lamented her absence, its waters churning and wailing for her to come back.

He never wanted to see her hurt. Or to be the one to hurt her. But he was. As he knew he would be.

Her bedroom called to him, and he approached slowly, his legs heavy with dread. Standing in the doorway, he leaned with his back against the doorframe, needing the support to stay upright. To keep him from doubling over with agony.

The first time he'd gazed upon this room, when the

realtor had shown him the property, he'd been filled with such hope. So much love. A little fear, too, because he wasn't a complete idiot and knew life had a way of keeping him grounded, but even in the face of the fear, he felt secure, certain they'd be okay.

This should've been their home.

When he'd impulsively bought the house, it'd needed a ton of work to make it inhabitable through a Michigan winter, but its ramshackle condition was the only way he could afford so much land with waterfront access. It was the only way to get the yard for their little ones and give Lauren her view. He was a hard worker, and he knew she would've had the vision to revive the tired old house.

He'd imagined they'd start here, in this bedroom.

The nursery.

His legs wobbly, Leo sank to the floor in the doorway of what should've been his daughter's bedroom.

He would've positioned the crib on the far wall, between the two north-facing windows. When she was older, he'd wanted to teach her how to swim, and sail, and build sandcastles, and execute a leg-sweep on any boy who dared to touch her.

After the attack, Lauren went into premature labor, and in the hospital, Leo got to hold his little girl. She was small. Too small. Beautiful, but fragile.

Precious as a Rose.

That's what he named her, after she died.

Lauren had been inconsolable. The first horrible day, she refused to let him into her hospital room. On the second day, he refused to be kept out.

"Lauren, honey, we need to give her a name. For her tombstone."

Silent tears streaming down her cheeks, she turned to her side in the hospital bed, giving him her back.

"Go away," she'd said, her voice devoid of emotion. "I can't even look at you. It hurts too much."

MAD LOVE

The memories gashed him. Curling into a ball on the hardwood floor in Prue's bedroom, Leo tumbled down the long tunnel of despair.

Chapter Twenty-Three

Two weeks after he'd come to the island to get her, Owen allowed Prue to return to work. In those weeks, he'd been in constant communication with Claymore, and after determining Paul Cook had in fact died of natural causes, and Aron King had once again left the country, they deemed things safe enough for her to begin to resume her normal life.

But nothing felt normal to Prue. Everything seemed different from when she left it. The packed streets and sidewalks made her long for soft, swaying beach grass and movable sand beneath her feet. She missed the steady, soothing drone of the lake, and tried to convince herself the sounds of city traffic, with its intermittent horns, sirens, and alarms, rendered a comparably pleasant effect.

Adding to the new strangeness of her old life, Owen insisted on delivering her to and from her office, and monitoring her every move, all day, every day, including while she toiled away inside the Institute.

Oh, who was she kidding? Though she'd missed nearly a month of work, by the end of the second day back she'd caught up on her tasks. With little else to do, she sat at her desk and tried to act as though everything were fine. That her life hadn't been threatened and that she hadn't had her heart shattered by a beautiful, broken, infuriating man.

She missed him. That morning when she'd awakened, her first thought had been of something outrageous she would say to coax a shocked smile or a laugh out of him. Anything to get him to react. To jolt him out from behind that deadened stare, or the lifeless wall that struggled to confine him.

Her heart ached for him. For what he'd told her about Rose. She'd once thought him too cold, his heart too hardened to love her. But his heart wasn't hard. It was big and gentle, and completely lost without *her*. Prue couldn't bring herself to be angry at him now that she understood a little of the heartache that had convinced him it was safer to withdraw from the world than risk suffering such anguish ever again.

By the end of her second week back at work, Prue had begun to loathe the new normal of her life. Leo was everywhere, all the time. She kept waiting for his memory to fade, or to be replaced with the newest details from her life, but so far, nothing could compete with him. Impulsively, she'd applied to a job opening for a science journalist with a national magazine, hoping a new challenge would leave little room for him in her mind at least.

He'd always occupy a corner of her heart.

Friday afternoon, she climbed into Owen's car and gave him a stiff smile.

As he did every day, he raked his gaze over her face,

giving her a thorough, somber assessment. Seemingly satisfied, he put the car in gear and eased out into traffic.

She puzzled over that look. Why did he do that? It was strange.

"Do you think there's still some danger?" she asked.

He turned his head and peered into the side mirror. "The thing is, we just don't know."

Prue scrunched up her face at his uncharacteristically wishy-washy reply. "Well, when will we know?"

"Soon enough, I imagine."

She narrowed her eyes at him. "Are you okay? You're acting weird."

"I'm fine." But a scowl tipped down the corners of his mouth when he shifted in his seat, as though he were uncomfortable.

They drove in silence the rest of the way to her apartment, where he steered his car up close to the curb and put it in Park.

He didn't turn off the engine.

"Aren't you going to walk me up?"

Frowning, he gave her another eerie once-over, and then his expression cleared. "I don't see any parking spots. Do you mind if I just drop you off here?"

That's when it hit her. A month after taking over her safekeeping, the threat he feared wasn't external but internal. He wasn't worried someone might attack her again. He was worried about what she might do to hurt herself.

Her cheeks heated with her mortification.

When he snuck a glance at her, she saw the same gravity that had been there since he'd collected her from Leo's home, but for the first time she noticed the touch of pity in his eyes.

He felt sorry for her, and she had a sickening suspicion it wasn't due to the ordeal of the last few weeks. More likely, he believed she'd fallen for a guy that would never want her. Again.

She scrambled from his car and darted up the brick path to her apartment building, her feet pounding in time to her racing heart. At the top of the stairs, she flung open the door to her apartment and slammed it shut behind her, barricading herself inside.

She didn't want Owen to feel sorry for her, and she certainly didn't need him to tell her she'd been an idiot to fall in love with Leo.

Why had she done it? Why had she given anyone the power to hurt her again? Of all people, why him, her brother's best friend?

She would've cried except she'd shed all her tears. Her heart was empty and she had nothing left to give.

Not to anyone else, ever again.

ᘓ

The bullet had shattered Leo's hip bone. After two surgeries, it'd taken months of recovery and grueling rehab before he was well again. Physically, at least.

In all that time, Lauren's tears never stopped. All she did was cry, and the rare times they talked, she would look at him with accusation in her eyes. He wanted to keep trying to rebuild their lives, believing they could find their way back to each other, and he told her that as often as he could, every time they spoke about anything of substance.

Until one day she asked him to stop.

"I won't stop saying it, Lauren. I love you."

"No, I don't mean stop saying it. I mean stop trying." She spoke in a flat monotone. "I don't want to try anymore, Leo."

Blinking away the memory, Leo turned his head.

Above him, a form appeared in the shape of a man.

Jack scowled down at him. "What happened to you?"

With effort, Leo sat. Light-headed, he rubbed a hand across his eyes. He had no idea how long he'd lain there, in the doorway of her bedroom.

"Where's Prue?" Jack wanted to know.

"She's gone."

Jack put a hand under Leo's arm and dragged him to his feet. "You been drinking?"

"No. You got anything?"

A wide smile split Jack's face. "I got something better than alcohol."

Moments later, Leo glared at Jack from his spot at the opposite end of the garage. "In what world is this better than alcohol?"

Jack drew back his hockey stick and with a sharp slice sent the tennis ball rocketing at Leo's head.

Reflexively, Leo knocked the ball down with his stick before it took out his teeth. The surge of adrenaline winged through his veins, and Jack's low, taunting chuckle was the dog whistle of his youth. The youngest of five boys, he'd had to fight to get anything he wanted. A turn on the bike, the last cookie, a chance to steer the boat. Everything came down to who wanted it more, and for Leo, who for years had been smaller and slower than the others, that fight was never easy.

He turned the stick over slowly in his hands, getting the feel for it again after so long. Then he wound up and struck, trying to hit his brother in the face because admittedly, that would be better than alcohol.

The nastiest game of one-on-one hockey they'd ever played ensued. In their epic struggle, the ball pinged off walls and ricocheted off their cars parked in the driveway. When they took out one of the overhead lightbulbs and stopped to clean up the broken glass, Jack checked the time on his cell phone.

"We better get going or we're gonna be late," he said,

sliding the phone into his hip pocket.

"I didn't know we were going somewhere."

"Haven wants to see you." His teeth flashed white in his tanned face. "She wants to do your hair and dress you up like you're her little dolly."

Leo's mouth twisted with his dry smirk. "I'd bet my left nut that Haven never played with dolls."

The smile on Jack's face turned to pure adoration. "No way am I taking that bet." He lifted the tennis ball on the end of his hockey stick and flipped it to Leo. "Keep your balls. Something tells me you're going to need them."

Leo made Jack wait while he took a quick shower, his first in days, then together they climbed into Jack's car. But fifteen minutes later, when they pulled up at Luke and Emily's home, Leo balked.

"I thought we were going to your place," he said.

"The builders are putting down the floors today. Haven's here to study and get away from the noise for a while."

Inside, Jack went in search of his soon-to-be wife while Leo hung back, his stomach knotting with The Fear. Where the hell was Haven? She needed to give him this damned haircut so he could get out of this house.

He moved into the living room and sank down on the overstuffed sofa. Closing his eyes, he dropped his head onto the sofa back and concentrated on taking slow, even breaths.

At the sound of rustling nearby, Leo cracked open one eye to find Emily collapsed in an armchair. Like him, she laid her head on the chair back and closed her eyes.

He lifted his head and shot a few quick glances around, not sure what to do. Just as he started to get up, Luke staggered into the room and flopped onto the sofa beside him. His brother burrowed down into the cushions, and the sounds of his deep, even breathing soon joined Emily's.

Leo gaped at them. He noted the heavy bags under both their eyes and their rumpled appearances.

A shriek punctured the quiet in the room.

Luke and Emily awoke with panicked jolts while Leo surged to his feet, the sound of the crying baby grating across his heart like broken glass. His chest ached and he rubbed a hand over his pec, trying to massage away the pain.

"Luke, sweetie, it's your turn."

Luke had already started to doze again.

"Luke." Emily's voice snapped in a way Leo had never heard before.

His brother thrashed to an upright position in the cushions.

"The baby," Emily said. "It's your turn."

With a groan of frustration, Luke sagged. "Okay, I got him."

But Luke didn't move. The baby's howls intensified and, with frantic head jerks, Leo looked from one exhausted parent to the other and back.

"Luke," Emily whined.

Leo swallowed with difficulty. "I'll get him." Instinct to tend to the cries overrode his fear. "If you want...."

Luke's emphatic "Yes" shot out over Emily's quiet plea of "Oh, please, go."

His legs filled with lead, Leo walked down the hall, every painful step taking him closer to the heartrending sound. The door to the family suite stood open, and he passed through it to arrive at the baby's room.

With a bracing breath, he pushed the door open wide.

The crib stood in the corner beneath a mobile of flying elephants and he crept toward it. Fear and anger and despair choked a sob from him as he peeked over the crib rail.

The little guy kicked his tiny arms and legs in frustration. His eyes were squeezed shut, and his small mouth contorted with his wails.

Wetness streamed down both his and the baby's cheeks when he reached into the crib and lifted the squirming bundle into his arms. A moment later, the baby realized someone held him and his shrieks quieted to weak protests. Leo gently jostled him, and with a few furious blinks, the baby's cloudy blue eyes latched on to his face.

Emotion piled in Leo's throat and he made a strangled sound, like a sob or a laugh.

The severe scowl in place, the baby gurgled and cooed, registering his list of complaints with his uncle.

"I know." Leo stuck out his finger and a teeny fist clamped around it. "Wow, you're a strong little guy, aren't you?"

Leo kept up the rhythmic jostling until a yawn caused his nephew's miniature chin to quiver, and then, finally, his eyes drooped shut. The moment Leo thought it safe to do so, he returned the infant to the crib.

Then he bolted, bursting out into the hallway as his sobs broke loose. He pulled the door closed and, pressing his back against it, sank to the floor.

Goddammit, would the hurting never let up? His chest ached, and he dragged painful breaths into his lungs.

Footsteps sounded in the hall and he wiped the wet from his cheeks a moment before Haven appeared.

"Wait. What is that sound?" After a beat, her hands dropped to her sides. "Oh my God. It's silence. How did you do that?"

As she collapsed on the floor beside him, Leo scrubbed a hand through his hair.

Jack appeared in the doorway and stumbled to a stop to find them on the floor at his feet. "Oh no. He defeated you, too? A fucking Marine? His mom and dad don't stand a chance."

Haven nudged Leo with her shoulder. "You okay?"

Leo stared at the wall across from them. He hadn't been okay in years. Not since he lost her. He was sick, and he was tired, and he had no idea what to do about any of it. He was tired of the pain that never ended. Tired of turning that pain on others who didn't deserve it. Tired of holding it all inside him. Holding her inside him instead of letting her memory live in the world.

His mouth moved before he finally forced out the awful words. "I had a daughter."

"Fuck, Leo...." Jack stepped over Leo's legs and dropped to the ground beside him. "What happened?"

Leo met his brother's troubled gaze. He swallowed hard. "She died."

Jack's eyes glittered with pain. "I'm sorry. I had no idea."

Haven had hooked her arm under Leo's, and she laid her head on his shoulder.

"She was born too early." Leo spoke softly while his heart screamed. "She was a fighter and fought hard the whole first week but... she... didn't make it through her second week."

"How long ago did she die?" Haven asked, her voice a suffocated whisper.

"She would've turned four next month."

Jack dragged a hand over his mouth as if to hold back the storm of emotion visible on his face and Haven's silent tears fell onto the sleeve of Leo's T-shirt. They sat together in silence for a long time, guarding the baby's bedroom door and tending to their broken hearts.

"I think she's with your mom," Haven said softly. "And your mom is so happy because she finally has a baby girl. Her baby's baby."

Beside him, a light sound escaped Jack.

"Oh c'mon, you know I'm right," Haven said. "I mean, the poor woman had five boys."

"Maybe she's taking care of Noah's baby, too," Jack

said.

Leo's breath caught. "Noah?"

"Mina miscarried last year."

Leo dropped his head against the wall with a soft thud, a fresh wound tearing across his heart.

"What was your mom's name?" Haven asked.

"Fiona," Jack said.

"Fiona." The name held Haven's smile. "I think my brother is with them, or he visits, or lives nearby, or something—I don't really know how it works."

Unbelievably, a laugh rumbled in Leo's chest.

"But they're together," she continued. "And one day we'll all get to be there with them."

Leo laid his head on top of hers. "I like the sound of that."

"But not yet," Jack clarified.

"No, not yet," Haven agreed. "Let them have their fun. Five boys, for crying out loud. Can you imagine how ecstatic she is to have a little girl?" She pinched Leo's arm. "You know I'm right."

"I will never admit that," Leo said.

"Smart man," Jack muttered under his breath.

Chapter Twenty-Four

As the sun neared the horizon, Jack dropped Leo off back at the cottage.

Inside, the home was quiet. Empty.

Drawn like a moth to the fatal flame, Leo returned to her bedroom doorway. The fading light cast the room in a warm orange glow, and for the first time since he'd returned to this place, he found the courage to truly look, to see the space that would have been his daughter's.

His gaze touched the flooring and the walls, noting the work he had wanted to do. He considered the bookcases, which he'd wanted to fill with the toys and books and stuffed animals of a child spoiled by her parents' love.

Then his eyes landed on the bed.

More precisely, on her computer, lying alone atop the bedspread.

The punch of love knocked him square in the chest.

He moved to the device and, opening it, flipped it on. Quickly, he searched and found all her files there, plus a few he hadn't seen before, and all of Claymore's files as well.

Emotions rushed in to fill his heart, but they were coming too quickly for him to pick apart and analyze.

She'd given up her work. All of it. Everything.

For him.

Too full, his heart exploded.

Of course, she could've made copies, or moved everything to an external storage space that she could access later, but her gesture was as clear and true as the blue of her eyes.

She gave it all up, everything that mattered to her, at the off chance it might make him happy. And she did. Damn, she really did. Unfortunately, he hadn't recognized that truth until he saw her laptop.

Regret and longing snarled through him. He wished he could've made her happy, too. Instead, he'd been the source of her pain.

If he knew a way to make it up to her, he would. If there was anything at all—

The thought struck him like a thunderbolt. He knew exactly what to do with her research.

Well, not all the steps, but he'd figure them out as he went along. It's what he should've done the minute he'd realized the magnitude of her discoveries about Aron King, except he'd been too much of a chickenshit to see the thing through for her.

Suddenly his feet were moving under him, and for the next several days, he plotted it all out, then set the plan in motion. He placed phone calls and scheduled meetings, talked to Claymore and Owen and Gideon, and to several of their contacts, too.

When he'd guaranteed everything was in place, he booked his flight and packed his bag.

And that's when he received the text from Claymore.
Our man is on the move.

❧

Hours later, Leo's plane touched down in Boston. He didn't get a hotel room because he didn't plan to stay that long, but Owen hadn't called with their meeting location yet. With time to kill, he picked up his car at the airport rental counter and headed to Prue's work.

A few hours remained to her workday, and he didn't wish to drop in on her while she was at her day job, so he contented himself with driving through her parking lot and peering through the windows of her car.

Except her car wasn't in the lot.

Leo didn't panic, however. Knowing Claymore and Owen checked in with each other daily, Leo had kept informed of Prue's protection by badgering Claymore for constant updates. Hence he knew Owen dropped Prue off and picked her up from work every day. He did a recon of the neighborhood, which turned up nothing suspicious or worrisome.

When he returned to his car, the late-summer sun warmed his head and back, and he dropped his suit coat on the passenger seat and rolled the sleeves of his dress shirt up to his elbows before slipping behind the wheel.

He exited Prue's work lot and headed east. There was one more stop he wanted to make while he waited for the call from Owen.

The cemetery was one of the oldest in Boston, the town where Lauren had grown up. After the attack, they'd flown her and the baby to the hospital there, and so that's where Leo had buried his daughter.

He steered his vehicle through the sprawling grounds, toward the far end of the cemetery's property where the newer plots were, and pulled off the lane to park beneath the umbrella of a tree.

He'd picked out a small headstone and chosen a simple engraving to honor her too-brief life. The last time he'd visited her resting place, all he could do was tell her how much he missed her, and wanted her back, and how sorry he was that he'd failed to protect her.

He told her all those things again now, but the truth didn't empty his soul the same way it had only weeks ago. This time, he told her what he remembered of his mom, her grandma, and asked her to help Grandma watch over the others. He told her how he was going to try to be a better man, one who deserved her for a daughter, and was worthy of a woman like Prue. A smile even touched his heart when he told his baby girl about Prue.

Then he said goodbye.

Sliding the smooth, round stone from his pocket, he placed it on Rose's headstone as Mina had asked him to do. Then he turned and walked back to the car.

He wanted a drink, but knew he wouldn't have one.

As he reached for the door handle, a black sedan pulled up behind him, and when he glanced through the windshield, the hairs lifted on his neck. The man behind the wheel and the woman in the passenger seat both watched him, but they didn't get out of their car, so he pulled open his door.

When he had one foot inside his vehicle, the sedan's passenger door opened, and Lauren emerged.

He grasped the car door for balance. She approached him cautiously, and his grip on the door tightened as memories of the last time they'd spoken flooded his mind. He wanted to flee, or be sick.

Instead, he thought of Prue.

Then he drew in a deep, fortifying breath and closed the car door. Maybe if he forced himself to look her in the eye, and finally confronted the righteous anger and betrayal, The Fear might lose some of its power over him. He wanted to try, at least, for Prue's sake.

Or maybe he was just a masochist.

Either way, he turned toward Lauren.

"Hi," she said softly.

Though still pretty, she wasn't as sparkly as he remembered. She wore little makeup, and no artificial color lightened her hair. She was older, sadder, and, in every way that mattered, still the woman he'd loved once.

"Hi." He cleared his throat. "How are you?"

"I'm okay." She rubbed a hand on the thigh of her blue jeans, then snuck a glance over her shoulder to the driver of the car. "Good. I'm good." She pushed her thumb at the car. "That's Brian. My husband. We married this summer."

"Congratulations," Leo said, and meant it.

Her eyes skipped around, jumping from the car to the tree to the ground, and finally to his face. "Leo, I...."

Inwardly, he braced for her anger.

Her gaze fixed on his face. "I'm sorry," she whispered.

The air leaked out of him and he dropped his head. "Me, too."

"I should've listened to you." Her voice started to tremble. "When you asked me not to go back there."

"Lauren, don't. Please. You didn't do anything wrong." The shaking in her voice moved to his hands. "It was my fault. I didn't do my job. I didn't protect you."

"You did." Her forehead crinkled. "Don't you remember?"

He frowned at the ground. In all honesty, he didn't want to remember.

"That day, you told me it wasn't safe to go into the city. You told me, but I didn't listen—" Her voice broke.

He dragged her into his arms. "Please, don't blame yourself." He propped his chin on top of her head. "I can't take any more misery."

Shudders trembled through her, but then he felt her

muscles relax. "I won't if you won't."

Releasing her, he returned his hands to his pockets.

She twisted her hands in front of her. "I know I said awful things to you."

"Lauren—"

"I didn't mean them, even then. I was just so mad and sad." She squeezed her eyes shut and covered her face with her hands. "I should've told you that I didn't really believe it was your fault, but I couldn't bring myself to say the words."

The hammering of his heart echoed in his ears.

"I think I thought if I could convince myself everything was your fault, then it couldn't be mine, you know?"

"It wasn't your fault." He couldn't bear the anguish. "It was war, and war is always unpredictable. And it always sucks."

Her eyes were huge in her pale face, and tears streamed down her cheeks. "Please forgive me."

"Done."

A soft laugh trickled from her. "Leo, I'm serious."

"So am I. Jesus, Lauren, we'd just lost Rose, and I know as much as anyone what you were going through. So maybe you acted less than perfect." He lifted his shoulders and dropped them heavily. "You were mad, and you wanted someone to blame. I get that. I do."

"You didn't deserve it."

With her words, something released inside him and soared.

The sensation brought a wry smile to his lips. "Whether you blamed me or not, I'm not sure I would've believed any differently."

Between them, a comfortable silence arose, and when she lifted her hand to tuck a lock of hair behind her ear, the diamond on her left ring finger glinted in the sunlight.

"Where did you meet Brian?" he asked.

"At work." She smiled. "He's the weatherman. What

about you? Is there anyone?"

"Yes." The word emerged of its own accord.

"I'm glad." Her smile turned a little sad, but it remained genuine. "I didn't think I'd be able to love anyone ever again, not after losing her, and you."

Suddenly, his lungs seized.

His throat worked with his dry swallow. "How did you do it?"

He held his breath while he waited for her answer, because quite literally, his life depended on what she would say. Either he had a future or he didn't, and it surprised him to realize how much he cared which one it was.

She appeared to chew on his words. "I don't know. I used to cry all the time. Every day. But then I met him and... I cried a little less. Then, when I was with him, I could think about something other than her."

"And now?"

"Now I want to try to be happy. For him. With him. Some days it's hard, but..." Her shoulders rose and fell. "He makes me happy."

Her words momentarily stunned him. Was it that simple?

A part of him grasped the truth in what Lauren had said. Prue made him happy, and every time Leo thought about her, the happiness grew. Like a snowball rolling downhill, it steadily increased in size and momentum.

After telling himself a million lies, did it all come back to that one simple truth?

She'd come to him in his darkest hour, and maybe it needed to be so dark so that her star might shine bright enough for him to recognize it. So that her light might help him navigate his way out of the darkness. She was more than a bright star, or even the brightest. She was his whole damned sky.

When he'd finished with Claymore and the others, he

would go to her, and maybe she could find a way to forgive him one last time.

Before he left, he shook Brian's hand and hugged Lauren. He returned to Rose's grave to tell her again how much he missed her and that he loved her, and then he climbed into his vehicle.

Owen had texted him an address, and Leo headed in that direction. He arrived at an office building and went to the front door, only to find it was locked.

Working through Claymore's contacts within US intelligence, they'd filed a complaint about Aron King, which had rocketed up the chain of command. Today they were meeting with a senior official within the FBI to turn over the evidence that Prue had uncovered about King and his co-conspirators.

After the meeting, he hoped to be able to tell Prue that all her hard work had paid off, and that King's downfall was all but assured. He hoped it might make her happy.

That *he* might make *her* happy.

His phone rang and he accepted Claymore's call.

"Change of plans," Claymore barked. "King slipped by me."

Alarm stole through Leo as a vehicle pulled into the parking lot and eased up to the building. "You have no idea where he is?"

"We're on it," Claymore said, his voice strained. "Can you take the meeting with the Feds and fill us in later?"

Owen climbed from the car and approached Leo, who was too busy quietly panicking to give a fuck about the angry scowl on his friend's face.

"No, I'm going to help." Leo's tone left no room for debate. "Tell me what to do."

"Owen's checking on his sister while I deal with King," Claymore said.

The Fear snaking through Leo's gut constricted. "Owen's standing right in front of me."

"Where's his sister?"

Leo angled the phone away from his mouth. "Is Prue with you?"

"No." Owen frowned. "She's at work. Why?"

In Leo's ear, Claymore interjected, "Tell him to check his fucking messages."

"Call her," Leo said. "Make sure she's okay."

His head bent over his phone, Owen growled, "Tell me what's going on."

"King shook them," Leo said, his mouth filling with sand.

"When?" Owen pressed the phone to his ear.

"How long have you been looking for him?" Leo asked Claymore.

"Not long. Fifteen, twenty minutes."

Owen grimaced. "She's not answering her cell. Hold on, let me call her work number."

It took everything Leo had to hold his panic in check.

"Hey, Amanda. It's Owen. Can I talk to Prue for a minute?" Owen's gaze snapped to Leo's face. "When did she leave?"

Claymore cursed.

"Did she say where she was going? That's okay. Thanks anyway." Owen yanked the phone from his ear. "We gotta find her. Now."

Leo was already moving.

Chapter Twenty-Five

Her heartbeat thundering in her ears, Prue reread Owen's email.

Hey sis,
It isn't safe for you to stay at work. Get out as soon as you can and head home. I'll meet you there to explain what's going on.

With clumsy hands, she called a cab service and typed an email to Amanda, who wasn't at her desk, to let her know she had to leave work early. Then she lurched to her feet and fled the building.

On the cab ride into Boston, Prue wondered why Owen hadn't called her cell phone to deliver such an urgent message, until she remembered her service was often spotty inside the Institute's steel and concrete structure. He'd probably wanted to make sure she received his warning. Not to mention, wherever he was, he likely couldn't talk openly.

Whatever his reason, she was just relieved she'd received his message and got out before anything bad happened.

Through the cab's window, she watched the cityscape pass by and tried to calm herself. Her entire body trembled with the adrenaline coursing through her veins, and the heavy weight of despair pressed down on her. In the past month, she hadn't so much as contemplated Aron King and his shady dealings. She'd hoped in surrendering her mission, the danger had passed, and the fact that it hadn't sent a wave of dismay rushing forward to drown her.

She wished Leo were there, because she'd never felt so scared and hopeless when she was with him. Would she live the rest of her life in fear? Did Leo ever wonder if she were safe?

Had he found her laptop? What had he thought about her leaving it behind? Did he even notice?

Had Owen ever called her "sis" before?

The cab eased up to the curb and she climbed from the car. Fear nipping at her heels, she scrambled up the front steps to her apartment and ducked inside the building. She pounded up the stairs, but when she hit the landing, her feet skidded to a stop—along with her heart.

Aron King stood at her apartment door.

"Now that's a good girl." A cruel smile curled his mouth. "You obey better than my dog."

Shock held her immobile while her mind reeled. It was a setup. Aron had sent that email, not Owen, her brother who never called her "sis."

She choked back a cry and twisted away to flee back down the stairs, but a hand came down around her face. Large and gloved, it clamped tight over her mouth to muffle her scream, which died in her throat completely when fingers pinched her nose closed.

Her captor's hot breath slithered over her skin as he hauled her down the hallway to Aron.

Panic gripping her, she shook her head, desperate for air.

"Shhhh. Calm down," Aron soothed. "I'm not going to hurt you. I only want to talk."

With a punishing jolt, the man shoved her face-first into the door. "Open it."

She gasped, sucking in a lungful of oxygen. Through her terror, her mind scrambled, searching for a way to escape. In her hesitation, the hand clenching her neck compressed.

Shaking with icy fear, she fumbled to fit the key in the lock. When the door finally gave, he thrust her ahead of him into the apartment and she jerked around as they closed her in.

The other man stood at least a foot taller than Aron, with cropped hair and cold, dead eyes. Immediately, she recognized them as the same emotionless eyes as her attacker.

Her gaze swung to Aron, who stalked slowly toward her. "You've caused me a lot of trouble, you know that?"

Fear stole her voice and she backed away, her gaze darting between the two men.

"I thought I made myself clear, but you couldn't leave it alone, could you?" Aron hunted her deeper into the room, and she focused solely on him. "You had to keep provoking me."

"Watch your nuts, man," her attacker warned as he moved around the room, searching for something. "She sure likes 'em. Crazy bitch."

Prue came up hard against the door leading onto the balcony. Anger churned in Aron's eyes, belying his cool pretense, as he pursued her until his body nearly pressed against hers. Then he reached up, and she strained her head to one side to evade his touch.

"Is this what you wanted?" His cold fingers caressed her cheek and her stomach pitched. "A little attention from me?"

She shook her head.

He grasped her face and the bite of his fingers stung her flesh. "I might've been able to forgive you, but then you had to go and try selling your crazy lies to the Feds."

"I didn't."

The back of his hand cracked into her cheek and her head snapped around with the force of the blow. She crumpled over but made no noise because the hit had robbed her of breath.

Her attacker was speaking again, and Aron turned his head to say something. His voice sounded far away.

Dazedly, she twisted around, and her fingers moved clumsily over the balcony door latch. The glass door pulled open and hope took flight when she stepped a foot outdoors.

Aron's cruel laughter rang in her ears when he clamped his arm around her waist and hauled her back inside the apartment. Her head foggy, she couldn't recall a single defensive tactic Leo had showed her, so she thrashed her arms and legs wildly. He cursed, and when his hold on her weakened, she lunged for the balcony door.

With a series of short, hammering footsteps, he chased her down. He clutched a fistful of her hair and wrenched. She cried out when she fell back against him.

"Did you find it?" His yell boomed in her ear.

From the other room, her attacker roared back. "Fuck. No!"

Just then, through the balcony door, a sudden burst of movement erupted. Her brain grappling to make sense of what her eyes saw, Prue blinked.

Leo crouched on the balcony railing, a hockey stick braced across his knees. With the light-footed stealth of a cat, he landed both feet on the balcony floor and slipped inside the apartment.

Aron stilled, though his chest heaved with his laborious breathing from their struggle.

Was it really him, or was she imagining him there? Clean-shaven, and with his hair cut close to his head?

Wearing dark gray suit pants and a crisp white dress shirt unbuttoned at the neck?

What the...?

"Take your hands off her," Leo said, a lethal edge to his voice. "Now."

"This doesn't concern you, Nolan."

It made no sense that he was there, and yet, he was. She didn't know how, but once again he came when she needed him. He came even though she never called him. Tears prickled behind her eyes.

Leo's gaze remained fastened on Aron's face. "Let her go. I'm not going to say it again."

With Aron's sharp movement, something cold and hard bit into the side of her neck.

Leo, who had been creeping toward them, froze. His gaze sliced quickly behind them, then back to Aron.

"You're outnumbered," Aron said smugly.

A muscle along Leo's jawline twitched. "You're a dead man."

Aron tugged on her hair to expose her throat.

Fear speared her, and Leo's name fell from her lips as a terrified whisper. For the first time since appearing, his eyes met hers. Amidst the glittering green and gold, an inner light that she didn't recall ever seeing before gleamed. She tipped her head, wondering at the look.

There was no panic or fear, only a steady calmness when the corner of his mouth lifted in a faint smile. "No more fear, Prue."

Her pounding heart tripped as understanding slammed into her, and at the calm strength in his eyes, she almost wasn't afraid when she struck.

In one motion, she captured Aron's wrist while she wrenched back his thumb and twisted away from him. Leo bellowed, and then everything seemed to happen at once.

She took Aron's feet out from under him with a messy rendering of the leg-sweep Leo had tried to teach her, except she ended up on her backside on the floor along with him. From her horizontal vantage point, she watched the blade of Leo's hockey stick catch her attacker's face on the upswing even as more men burst into the room through the front door and balcony. In the chaos that followed, Leo pounced on Aron and then another man landed flat atop Leo. That man, who Prue didn't recognize, threw a savage, well-placed punch and Aron's body went limp.

Leo squirted out from between the men and clambered across the floor on his knees to reach her side.

"Where are you hurt?" His hands rushed over her body, searching for injuries.

"I'm okay." She caught one of his wrists. "I'm not hurt."

His chest heaving, a sob wrenched from him and his gaze latched onto her face. Lightly, his fingers touched the sore spot on her cheek and for a moment, there was no wall or invisible barrier shutting her out.

Hence she experienced the full force of the black storm cloud that swept across his features. "Why in the hell did you do that?"

With a groan, she sat. "You told me to."

"No, I absolutely did not."

"Uh-huh. You said, 'No more fear, Prue.' I thought that was my cue."

"Your cue to do what? Get yourself killed?"

"To use my training."

On a curse, he dragged her to his chest. "No. Jesus, no."

He held her so tightly she might've protested if she didn't love the feel of his arms around her so much.

Then the most unexpected thing happened.

He laughed. It started in his chest as a soft rumbling, but then it built and finally burst from him. A real, out loud, heartfelt laugh.

She laid her head against his chest and let the sound of his laughter melt away the fear that wanted to crush her.

He pushed his hands into her hair and pulled her face close to his. "No, Prue, I was not asking you to put your life at the greatest possible risk." With a gravity that shredded her heart, he peered into her eyes. "I was trying to tell you what I should've said that day I let you leave with your brother, but was too much of a coward."

"Get your filthy hands off my sister, Irish."

"Never," Leo said.

At the fierce snarl that was his refusal, she gasped. Her mind slow and fuzzy, she struggled to grasp the meaning of his words and touches. Even the fact of his presence in her apartment befuddled.

The man sitting on Aron's chest shot Leo a sidelong look. "You know, I think I'm starting to see the appeal of opening our own business." A lopsided grin pulled up one corner of his mouth. "Chicks dig bodyguards, am I right, fellas?"

"That's my sister, jackass." Owen's growl held no bite.

While Owen stood over the prone body of her attacker, one of the other two men who had burst into her home leaned over the unconscious victim.

As he peered down at the prostrate form, a lock of his black hair fell across his forehead. "What happened to him?"

A wicked smirk split Owen's face. "Hockey stick."

The man returned Owen's smile and one eyebrow lifted when he looked at Leo. "I think you broke his jaw."

Absent remorse, Leo shrugged. "Whoops."

The last unknown man in the room snickered.

With Leo's steady help, Prue climbed awkwardly to her feet. His hand under her elbow, he walked with her to the dining table where she dropped heavily into a chair.

She frowned at the gaggle of men filling her living room. "Who are you people?"

Owen pointed to the man sitting on Aron's chest. "Claymore and Gideon." He gestured to the black-haired man before singling out the last stranger. "And Special Agent Watts."

She had no idea how they all came to be here and was

about to ask them when, beneath Claymore, Aron moaned.

Leo swung toward the sound. A nasty scowl on his pleasant features, he scooped his hockey stick off floor and crossed to him in two ground-eating strides. Pressing his foot to Aron's chest, Leo wedged the blade of the hockey stick under his chin.

Suddenly alert, Aron stared up at him with wide eyes. "Whatever she told you, it's a lie." His voice rasped with the pressure Leo applied to his throat. "I swear. She's insane. She needs help."

A slash of painful mortification sliced through Prue.

"I admit the whole thing sounds outrageous," Leo admitted. "Especially to those of us who know you. I mean, it's hard to believe you, of all people, are capable of organizing an elaborate criminal enterprise."

Aron balked. "Fuck you. I founded a billion-dollar company."

"That you almost ran into the ground," Owen muttered.

Fury seethed in Aron's cold eyes. "You don't know what you're talking about."

"Those days are over, King," Leo goaded. "Now you're nothing but a Mafia pawn."

Gideon snorted. "Shh. Don't tell him. I think he thinks he's one of them."

"I'm not one of them, I'm the boss of them, you fucking piece of shit." Aron lifted his head, straining against his confines. "They don't whip their ass without my permission."

"Nah, I don't buy it," Claymore chimed in. "If that were true, you would've sent someone else here to clean up this little loose end." He wiggled his fingers in a gesture that indicated Prue. "But here we all are."

"I did send someone else," Aron fumed. "But he couldn't get the job done, so I had to do it myself."

"I don't know about anyone else, but I would love to hear more about that." Agent Watts removed his suit coat to reveal his Kevlar vest marked with the bright yellow letters FBI.

Alarm flashed across Aron's face, then the reality of what he'd just admitted to sank in. He dropped his head onto the hardwood floor with a thud.

"Damn, we're good." Claymore smiled. "What should we call ourselves?"

Ɔʒ

When the police had gone, and they'd briefed Special Agent Watts on everything they knew about Aron King's activities, Leo turned to Prue.

He held out a thumb drive to her.

Her expression questioning, she took the device from him.

He tipped his head toward the FBI investigator. "It's your work on there. All of it."

She frowned down at the stick a moment, but when she lifted her head in the next, a smile touched her lips. Biting it back, she handed the flash drive off to the federal law enforcement agent.

Claymore and Gideon walked out with Watts, but Owen paused at her apartment door.

He fixed Leo with a hard stare. "After you."

Leo remained where he belonged—at Prue's side. "I'm staying."

A dark scowl rumpled Owen's face. He opened his mouth to speak, then clamped it shut tight without uttering a word.

Leo held his friend's gaze. "You're a good brother, and you've been a better friend to me than I deserve. Say or ask me anything you want."

"Thanks, but I only want to hear from my sister."

Both men pivoted to Prue.

Wariness filled her blue eyes when she searched Leo's face. Though he understood it, he hated that she doubted him. Hated that he'd given her every reason to distrust him.

It wasn't easy, but he allowed her assessment of him, without the barricades and the pretenses. With nothing but truth between them.

Another odd look flitted across her features, but she offered her brother a reassuring smile. "It's okay."

Owen hesitated but eventually stepped through the door, pulling it softly closed behind him.

In the quiet apartment, she had difficulty meeting his eyes. The red mark on her cheek hadn't begun to swell, allowing him reason to hope that it wouldn't.

"How does your head feel?"

"It hurts a little."

The urge to haul her into his arms was overwhelming, but her peculiar expression stopped him. "This time I'm going to insist we get you checked out at the hospital."

She didn't argue. "First, will you tell me how... why are you here?"

"I miss you." At the soft hitch in her breathing, he frowned. "Why does that surprise you?"

"It's not what I expected you to say." Her voice softened.

"What did you expect?"

"I don't know." Pink touched her cheeks. "That you'd been tracking Aron and wound up here when he did, or that you needed me to talk to Agent Watts."

"All that's true, I suppose, but I came for you, Prue." He took a small step closer to her. "I'm staying for you. Only you."

She studied him with that quizzical, confused expression on her face, almost as though she didn't recognize him.

It struck him then that, in fact, she didn't know him. He wasn't the same person she'd left on that island. Since the last time they saw each other, he'd changed. He'd changed because of her. She'd given him a reason to change, a second chance, and by God, he was going to make the most of it.

To start, if he was going to convince her to spend the

rest of her life with him, he'd better introduce himself.

He faced her squarely. "My name is Leo Aidan Nolan, and I have four older brothers."

Confusion puckered her brow.

"We were born in Ireland, but after our mom died, we came here to live with our uncle. On the island. I was five years old at the time. Our dad was pretty much a piece of shit. A convicted felon, and a drunk. Most of the time, he was not a very nice person. He died a couple of years ago."

Softness rippled across the pools of her blue eyes.

"I've never been bitten by a shark."

The corners of her mouth pinched.

He pushed out a sharp breath from deep in his lungs. "Six years ago, I was assigned to security detail for a TV news network. I met a woman, Lauren, and I bought the house for her."

Words abandoned him then. He dragged a hand through his hair, trying to gather his thoughts after losing the thread of what he was trying to say to her. He stared at the floor in her apartment so long he feared she'd grown impatient waiting for him to speak and wandered away.

"We had a little girl," he whispered. "A daughter."

On the floor, her feet came into his view, and he lifted his head.

"Rose," he croaked. "Her name was Rose. But she died."

"Leo, I'm so sorry. I didn't know...." She eased closer and laid her palm on his chest, over his heart. "I didn't know."

"Last winter, I slammed my car into a tree." He smoothed his hand over hers, and squeezed. "When I came to and realized what I'd done and that I wasn't dead, all I felt was... disappointment. I'll never forget it. The disappointment was so consuming, there wasn't room for all the other things I should've felt, like relief or fear. Shame that I got behind the wheel of a car in the condition I was in. That I ruined my brother's wedding."

She pulled his hand to her mouth and dropped kisses on his knuckles.

"Rose died because I couldn't protect her, and nothing's been the same since. Nothing's been good since." Turning over his hand, he trailed his fingers across her cheek. "Until you."

She tilted her head toward his touch.

"I hated every moment I spent with you. Don't frown at me, let me finish." He inhaled a bracing breath. "When we were together... it hurt. It hurt so bad to be near you and to want you, to want to love you but knowing I couldn't. I couldn't let the love in because it hurt too much.

"At first, it seemed wrong, what we were doing. I felt like I was betraying them. Her." He dragged a hand over his face, fighting the despair. "It isn't fair that I get to experience it again, but Rose will never know what it feels like to fall in love."

"Oh, Leo...."

Her tears spilled over and he wiped them away with the pad of his thumb.

"I thought I didn't deserve you. That I don't deserve to be happy. For four years, I've either been drunk or too depressed to feel anything, and then all of a sudden, I felt everything, all at once, and it fucking hurt." He shuddered with the vivid recollection. "But that didn't hurt half as bad as it did when you left."

"I didn't want to go."

"I know. I made you, because I was afraid. I am afraid. I'm afraid to love you, Prue. Terrified, in fact." His throat tightened with The Fear and he swallowed hard. "But I'm more afraid to lose you."

"Well, lucky for you, you can't lose me." Through her tears, a shy smile worked its way to her mouth. "I'm yours, Leo. I've always been yours and I always will be, whether you want me or not."

He wrapped his arms around her waist and buried his face in her hair. "Thank you, Prue. Thank you for seeing something in me worth saving. If you think you can ever forgive me–"

"I forgive you." Her arms circled his neck. "I forgive you for everything, and for all the things you're going to do in the future that need forgiving, too."

His laughter erupted, like the love in his heart.

He cradled her face in his hands and nibbled her plump mouth. She tasted like whiskey and sunshine. And love. She tasted like love. Sweet and heartbreaking, a little dangerous, and completely, deliciously foolish.

At their feet, Arlo weaved between their legs.

A smile in his heart, the tips of his fingers danced across her cheek. "One of these days, I want to see what you look like without a black eye."

She winced. "Is it bad?"

"Bad?" He shook his head. "No. It's hot."

Color rushed into her cheeks with her obvious pleasure. "Leo?"

"Hmm?" He murmured against her temple.

"I'm having impure thoughts again," she whispered.

"There's only one thing to do about that."

Passion flared in her eyes, and his body's eager response left him light-headed.

"Not that. At least not right now." He plucked another kiss from her sweet mouth. "Your thoughts won't be impure when you're my wife."

<h1>Epilogue</h1>

A blazing orange sun hovered above the horizon. Still dressed in their wedding attire, Leo and his brothers reclined in a row of beach chairs.

Luke gaped at him. "You can't be serious."

Relaxed in his chair, Leo smiled. "I am."

After the long day, his four-year-old nephew, Connor, slept in his arms. His head lolled on Leo's shoulder, and his little body sprawled across Leo's torso.

"You're going to marry her?" Jack said.

"How long have you known her?" Shea wanted to know. "A couple of weeks? A month?"

"Long enough," Leo said. He would've married her that first week if he hadn't been letting The Fear make his decisions for him.

"Seems kind of sudden," Luke observed. "Any particular reason?"

Leo's gaze swiveled to his brother. "None."

"He isn't you," Noah muttered from behind his drink.

"Then you should take some time." Concern filled Shea's gravelly voice. "Get to know each other better."

"Have some fun," Jack added. "You deserve a little fun."

Leo gaped at him. "Dude, it's your wedding day."

"Yeah, so?"

"Are you really advocating sowing your oats over marital bliss, on your wedding day?"

Jack recoiled. "Not for me, no. Hell no. But we're not talking about me and Haven. We're talking about you and Prue. The woman you've known two weeks?"

"Two months."

"Why don't you give it another two months, then decide?"

"Jesus Christ." Noah lurched to his feet and spun to face the four men. He jabbed a finger at Shea. "You married your high school sweetheart, for God's sake."

"Yeah, and see how that turned out?" Luke said. "She's not his wife anymore."

"She's still my fucking wife," Shea snarled.

In the awkward silence that descended, a smirk tugged at Luke's mouth. "So what are you going to do about that?"

Shea dragged a hand through his hair. "This isn't my therapy session, it's his."

"And you two." Noah pinned Luke and Jack under his gaze. "You married your wives after knowing them, what, three, four months?"

"Yeah."

"Yep."

Noah faced Leo. "From the time I met Mina, it took me fifteen years to ask her to marry me. Don't be a dumbass like me. If you want Prue, marry her, and do it now before fate or pride or stupidity comes between you." Noah shot a look down the row of beach chairs. "Anyone disagree with that?"

Amidst a chorus of consensus, Noah returned his focus to Leo. "Go then. Get yourself a wife."

Leo's smile matched Noah's when he stood and handed Connor off to Shea. He climbed the steep wooden stairway up the side of the bluff and instantly spotted Prue on Jack's patio, chatting with Shea's wife-for-now, Isobel.

As if she felt his warm gaze, she looked up and right at him. She smiled.

He loved her smiles. The soft, almost shy smile, and the full-wattage one. The self-satisfied grin that curved her lush mouth after a particularly feverish bout of scribbling in her notebook, and the gentle smile she wore when she was with his family.

Then there was his favorite smile. The one that whipped color into her cheeks when she caught him watching her. When she came to him, and came for him.

With her smiles, the shadows receded. The storm winds calmed. They still blustered from time to time, but he knew all he had to do was wait it out and the sun would rise again. Her smile would reappear to banish the shadows. It always did.

He waited at the edge of the patio, and soon she disengaged from her conversation to move toward him. As he watched her cross the patio, her pace increasing the closer she drew to him, his heart ached with the best kind of pain.

She stopped before him.

"Hi." She sounded breathless. "You okay?"

"I'm better than okay," he said, and it was the truth.

She'd tucked a rose behind her ear, and he reached up to finger the pale pink petals nestled in the soft waves of her dark hair. After Rose's funeral, Lauren's mom had insisted he take home the plant, but he hadn't been able to so much as look at it for the devastating reminder of what he'd lost.

Over the past several weeks, the plant had heartened, and when its first buds peeked open, he smiled while tears burned in his eyes to glimpse the miracle.

Somehow, Prue had saved that pitiful, scraggy rose bush.

Just as she'd saved him.

THE END

ABOUT THE AUTHOR

Amy Olle is a USA Today bestselling author of sexy contemporary romances filled with charmingly flawed characters and cozy settings. Her debut novel, *Beautiful Ruin*, is the first book in the series about the five Irish-born Nolan brothers sent as children to live with family on a remote island in northern Michigan. She is delighted to put her Psychology degrees to good use writing romance.

Amy lives in Michigan with her longsuffering husband, brilliant son, and (female) turtle named George.

Amy loves connecting with readers! Find her on the web at www.amyolle.com.